# A MORNING INQUIRY

Chief Inspector Quantrill leaned forward, his elbows on his desk, frowning at the tip of his cigar.

"Now in this division," he said to the young Sergeant Tait standing in front of him, "We get very little large-scale crime. We don't attract the big-time crooks. We've got crime, all right, thefts and burglaries and assaults and vandalism, but very little organized crime. From an individual detective's point of view, it's not what you might call an intellectual challenge."

Tait's jaw tightened.

The internal telephone rang. Quantrill answered it, sat up abruptly, then relaxed. He put down the receiver, and began to scratch the side of his jaw with his forefinger.

"Radio message from Charlie Godbold at Ashthorpe," he said conversationally. "When you were out with him this morning, did you happen to go over Ashthorpe bridge—narrow stone hump-backed affair?"

"Yes we did."

"Ah," Quantrill acknowledged. "Didn't happen to see a dead body in the river there, I suppose?" he asked casually . . .

Bantam Books offers the finest in classic and modern English murder mysteries.
Ask your bookseller for the books you have missed.

**Agatha Christie**

DEATH ON THE NILE
A HOLIDAY FOR MURDER
THE MOUSETRAP AND
 OTHER PLAYS
THE MYSTERIOUS AFFAIR
 AT STYLES
POIROT INVESTIGATES
POSTERN OF FATE
THE SECRET ADVERSARY
THE SEVEN DIALS
 MYSTERY
SLEEPING MURDER

**Patricia Wentworth**

THE IVORY DAGGER
MISS SILVER COMES TO
 STAY
POISON IN THE PEN

**Margery Allingham**

BLACK PLUMES
DEADLY DUO
DEATH OF A GHOST
THE FASHION IN
 SHROUDS
PEARLS BEFORE SWINE

**Aaron J. Elkins**

MURDER IN THE
 QUEEN'S ARMES

**Dorothy Simpson**

LAST SEEN ALIVE
THE NIGHT SHE DIED
PUPPET FOR A CORPSE
SIX FEET UNDER

**P. C. Doherty**

THE DEATH OF A KING

**Sheila Radley**

FATE WORSE THAN
 DEATH
DEATH IN THE MORNING

**John Greenwood**

THE MISSING MR.
 MOSLEY
MOSLEY BY MOONLIGHT
MURDER, MR. MOSLEY

**Catherine Aird**

HARM'S WAY
LAST RESPECTS
PARTING BREATH
SLIGHT MOURNING

**Elizabeth Daly**

THE BOOK OF THE LION

**Ruth Rendell**

THE FACE OF TRESPASS
THE LAKE OF DARKNESS
NO MORE DYING THEN
ONE ACROSS, TWO DOWN
SHAKE HANDS FOREVER
A SLEEPING LIFE
A DARK-ADAPTED EYE
 (writing as Barbara Vine)
A FATAL INVERSION
 (writing as Barbara Vine)

# DEATH
## IN THE
# MORNING
### *Sheila Radley*

BANTAM BOOKS
TORONTO · NEW YORK · LONDON · SYDNEY · AUCKLAND

DEATH IN THE MORNING
*A Bantam Book / published by arrangement with
Charles Scribner's Sons*

*PRINTING HISTORY*
*Scribner's edition first published June 1979*
*Bantam edition / September 1987*

*Bantam Books are published by Bantam Books, Inc. Its trade-
mark, consisting of the words "Bantam Books" and the por-
trayal of a rooster, is registered in U.S. Patent and Trademark
Office and in other countries. Marca Registrada. Bantam
Books, Inc., 666 Fifth Avenue, New York, New York 10103.*

PRINTED IN THE UNITED STATES OF AMERICA

O     0 9 8 7 6 5 4 3 2 1     .

# ONE

The river Dunnock rises without much enthusiasm in the northern uplands of Suffolk and sets out in the direction of the Wash, taking its time over the journey. A narrow, shallow brook of a river: not navigable at any point in its meanderings, nor deep enough to swim in; and nowhere deep enough for an eighteen-year-old girl to drown, unless she chose to end her life, or unless someone intended that she should die.

The body lay—barely afloat in the shallows, long hair waving indistinguishably among the river weed—some yards downstream from Ashthorpe bridge.

Ashthorpe is a village six miles south of Breckham Market, the small town where the Dunnock finally gives up all pretension to independence and joins a tributary of the Ouse. The narrow, humpbacked stone bridge about one mile out of Ashthorpe has always been regarded as a local beauty spot. A gap in the roadside hedge near the bridge leads down to a meadow, and older inhabitants of the village can remember walking here in couples on warm summer evenings in search of privacy under the willow trees on the bank of the river.

The meadow must be much the same, though the pollarded willows have grown arthritic. The hawthorn hedge still screens the meadow from passers-by on the road. Buttercups and cowslips and lady's smock and daisies embroider the grass in season, wild yellow iris flaunt among the reeds, birds sing, cuckoos call, the river noises are as agreeable as ever they must have been; but the lovers have gone, because there is nowhere for them to park their cars. The river bank below Ashthorpe bridge has been given over to children who paddle and make dams and hunt for birds' nests and water rats, and to an occasional small boy fishing in earnest for tench and gudgeon.

The fish flourish because the Dunnock is remarkably unpolluted. It runs through no town, and receives little sewage

1

and no industrial effluent. Naturally, it collects its share of unnatural and nondegradable rubbish: old car tires and cooking
stoves, non-returnable bottles, empty aerosols and beer cans,
plastic margarine tubs, squeezy detergent containers. But as
rivers go, it is remarkably free from pollution. A clean place to
die.

The girl lay facedown, arms outstretched, rushes woven
among her fingers. She wore a long dress of cotton, sprigged
with tiny flowers, and the hem of the dress swung and rippled
round her legs with the motion of the water. Gathered
flowers—enamelled buttercups, mauve lady's smock—floated
about her body and clung to her hair and her dress wherever
they touched. It looked a quiet way to die.

There had been heavy rain overnight and the morning was
washed dazzlingly clean, but the two policemen were too busy
watching where they put their feet to notice the blue and the
green and the gold of the first day of May. One was a solidly
middle-aged constable in uniform and flat cap; the other, elegant in plain clothes, was shorter, slimmer, much younger.
They were retreating from a ramshackle stud and plaster farm-
house to their police van, seen off by a sardonic farmer whose
Jack Russell terrier had yipped itself to the edge of hysteria.

'Well then?' demanded Detective Sergeant Tait when he
could make himself heard. 'You're the local man. Do you believe what he said?'

The constable considered the question as he sploshed on
down the muddy track that led from the house to the road.
'About pigs,' he said eventually, 'yes. I wouldn't trust anything
he said about his neighbour, but he likes pigs.'

Tait laughed without amusement, side-stepping the last foul
puddle and taking a leap onto the roadside grass, where he
tried to wipe the mud off his fashionable, expensive shoes. Pc
Godbold was watching him with a hardly concealed grin, a look
not unlike the one the farmer had just given him. It was a look
that Tait had come to recognise and identify in the last two
days, a countryman's way of looking at a townee, half derisive,
half defensive.

'What you want to do,' Godbold volunteered, pleasantly
enough, 'is to carry a pair of wellies in your car. Inspector

Quantrill always does—*Chief* Inspector Quantrill, I should say.'

'Does he?' said Tait coldly. He was growing a little tired of hearing his new chief's name.

'That's right,' said the constable, lowering himself into the driver's seat of the van. 'But then, of course, he's a countryman. Makes a difference.'

'So I imagine.'

The road was narrow, and Godbold had pulled the van on the verge after Tait had got out. He made no offer to move the van back to the road, and the long grass soaked the bottom of Tait's trouser legs as he pushed his way to the passenger door. Hedgerow sprays, curdled over with hawthorn blossom, slapped against him; the flower clusters were wet, almond-scented, sickly sweet. Tait wiped his splattered face and neck irritably.

'Where to now?' asked Godbold.

Tait checked his watch and decided with relief that he could justify a return to civilisation. 'Back to your place to pick up my own car. I'd better see what's happening at division.'

'Right you are.' Godbold turned the van towards Ashthorpe, where he lived in the police house. He drove silently for a few minutes and then, since he was old enough to be the new detective's father and felt slightly guilty about Tait's sodden trousers, he said conversationally, 'Daresay you were riled about being sent to this division, Sergeant Tait?'

He chose the formal address deliberately; you couldn't call a green youngster 'Sarge'. 'I mean,' he elaborated, 'it's very quiet here. Oh, we've got more than enough to do, but mostly we're dealing with petty crime. A bit of a comedown after that high-powered stuff you must have learned at police college.'

Tait shrugged. 'All good experience,' he said.

The sardonic grin again: 'Looking for missing pigs?'

'It's not just pigs that go missing.'

There was a silence. Both men, temporarily forgetting each other, were contemplating an impossibility. A quiet, home-loving fifteen-year-old girl simply does not vanish without trace from the mile-long stretch of road between her home and the village shop, not in broad daylight, not in the middle of the placid English countryside.

'Hoping to find her?' asked Godbold. No derision now, but bitter hopelessness. 'Mr. Quantrill's been working on the case for three months, and if *he* can't find her . . .'

'Don't get me wrong,' said Tait quickly. He knew that his graduate entry to the police force, his special police college training and his accelerated promotion, was going to take some living down. He expected and accepted a certain amount of needling. He knew that in the first few weeks after he left Bramshill the old hands would be watching him intently, hopeful that he would make a fool of himself; at best he would be tolerated, at worst despised. But Tait was anxious to be judged on what he actually achieved in those weeks, not on an unguarded retort made in his first few days in the division.

'I haven't come here imagining that I can do any better than anyone else,' he went on. 'But since the girl disappeared from this division, and I've been sent here, I'm glad of the chance to join in the search. Isn't that how you'd feel?'

Godbold seemed mollified. 'Doesn't matter who finds her, does it, as long as she's found?' He sighed hugely, forgetting to be on the defensive; a father, consumed with vicarious anguish. 'Her parents must be out of their minds with worry . . .'

He drove on silently, presently turning to the right, off the main Breckham Market road and on to the minor road that led to Ashthorpe.

'You know what?' he burst our suddenly. 'I blame this motorisation. Oh, I like having the van, all right—it's a sight more comfortable than being out in all weathers on a pushbike. And the radio contact's very handy. But you lose the personal touch.'

Sergeant Tait had been in the police force exactly two and a half years. He turned in his seat and looked at Godbold with interest, as though the constable were the sole survivor of a dead civilisation. 'Did you really ride round on a bicycle?' he asked.

Godbold went dignified. 'Certainly. I started on a town beat, but I was village bobby at Ashthorpe for fifteen years, before they put me in this van and gave me a district to cover. Well, it's more efficient in a lot of ways, I can see that—but I don't know what's going on in my own village any more. And I reckon that if there'd still been a local bobby in Joy Dawson's village, she'd never have disappeared like that.'

4

'Oh, come on—that's expecting a lot of one policeman on two wheels!'

'Maybe,' conceded Godbold. 'All the same . . .'

He slowed as the road narrowed for Ashthorpe bridge.

'Take this bridge we're coming to,' he went on. 'I used to bike down here of a summer evening and sit on the parapet for a smoke, and I could reckon to see most of Ashthorpe going by. I'm not an Ashthorpe man myself, but you learn a lot about a place in fifteen years. I'd know who was sneaking past in a car with someone else's husband or wife, and who was mooning about alone and miserable, and who was looking for mischief. Now I don't know half what they're up to—I'm too busy dashing about all over. And I can't even stop when I do come by, because there's no room to park the van. Hold tight for the bump.'

The road rose over the sharp hump of the bridge. Tait caught a glimpse of gold in the meadow below, a flash of sunlight on water. He also had time to notice that there were tyre marks in the damp earth at the roadside just over the bridge, where a gap in the hedge led down to the river meadow.

'Looks as though somebody parked there recently,' he commented.

'Duzzy fool,' said Godbold dispassionately. 'It's asking for an accident, parking so close to that blind hump. Hadn't better let me catch him doing it again.'

The road climbed gently towards the village, between creamy hawthorn hedges and verges misted knee-high with cow parsley in full bloom. At the top of the rise was a tall-towered church, all flint and flushwork, with a neighbouring rectory that had been built for a family of Georgian size. Then the road dipped down again: past the pantiles and pink plaster of Church Farm and the thatch and white plaster of the Chequers, past a row of mean-windowed inter-war council houses, past a wooden shed that proclaimed itself the post office, past the willow-shaded pond and along the length of the narrow green with the war memorial in the centre; then sharply round to the left and past more thatch and plaster, some of it tatty; past a red brick nineteenth century terrace, a garage offering quadruple trading stamps on petrol, a county council Gothic school, a Georgian manor house, a general store, a gaunt Baptist chapel, an eruption of new bungalows and finally a post-war council estate, more generous as to windows but meaner with gardens. Godbold drew up outside the only detached house on the estate. The name County Police was incised above the doorway, and Tait's own car was parked on the lay-by.

'Care to come in for a cup of coffee?' Godbold offered.

'No thanks,' Tait replied, a shade too promptly. 'I'd better get back to the station.'

'Toffee-nosed pipsqueak,' thought Godbold, but without malice; the invitation had been no more than a polite formality.

Tait realised that his refusal had been interpreted accurately. 'Thanks very much for your help, though,' he added quickly, softening his fair sharp features into amiability: 'I'd never have found my way round the farms without you.'

'Nor persuaded the farmers to talk, neither,' thought Godbold; but since he was within a few months of half-pay retirement and already had a nice little security job lined up at a plastics factory on the industrial estate at Breckham Market, he could afford to be cordial. 'Any time. Now then, if you keep straight on from here you'll get to Breckham what we call the back way, through Lillington and Fair Green. But if you want the quickest way, it's back through the village and over the bridge to the turnpike. All right?'

'Thanks again. See you.' Tait gave him a nod, then did a quick U-turn in his small, aspiring Citroën. 'A real old-timer', he thought disparagingly, as he left the village and slowed for the hump-backed bridge. 'Bobbies on bicycles, for heaven's sake!'

Downstream from the bridge the flies clustered and hummed, and the flowers that were caught in the dead girl's hair began to wilt under the sun.

# TWO

Breckham Market divisional police headquarters, a monument to the Festival of Britain taste for neo-Georgian architecture embellished with spiky ironwork balconies, stands beside the main road that divides the old town from the new. Its neighbour on one side is the fire station, on the other the local branch of the county library; there were grandiose plans for a new town hall, but the money ran out.

And no bad thing either, thought Detective Chief Inspector Quantrill as he left the Victorian Italianate town hall in the market place and walked briskly through the streets towards his office. Not that better courtroom accommodation wouldn't be useful, but the five minute walk was good exercise and gave him the opportunity to sniff the atmosphere of the town, to keep in touch at street level.

He listened with patient sympathy to an indignant town councillor's story of vandalism in the public park, and noticed with interest that two apprentice layabouts turned and walked smartly in the other direction when they saw him coming. He passed the time of day with a number of market traders, acquiring from one the side-of-the mouth information that a local villain was newly out of prison, and from another a hint that a rival's cut-price groceries might well have fallen off the back of a lorry.

The market was busy. Quantrill had a wide acquaintance, and he tipped his hat impartially to the wife of the Methodist minister and to a retired prostitute who, feeling the lack of an occupational pension, tried to supplement her social security by selling information.

She accosted him with an eager greeting: "Morning, Mr. Quantrill!'

"Morning, Marje. How are you?'

'Fine, thanks.' She was thin, her wig and clothes girlish; her

7

voice was hoarse and her seamed upper lip was stained nicotine yellow.

'I say.' She glanced round, then leaned towards him conspiratorially, breathing stale gin. He turned his face away, as if to offer her his ear. 'I might have something to tell you later in the week, Mr. Quantrill.'

He doubted it. 'Well then, you'll know where to find me,' he said pleasantly, evading a detaining claw. He stepped into a tobacconist's to buy a tin of small mild cigars, then set course for the office again, tweed hat in hand, enjoying the mid-morning air.

The sunshine of early May warmed the streets, drawing out the shop window blinds and the middle-aged women in their white cardigans and summer dresses. A pity, Quantrill thought, that so many girls no longer bothered to wear pretty dresses; jeans and skinny tops were more revealing, but he found them less alluring than the tight-waisted, full-skirted summer dresses that girls had worn twenty-odd years ago.

River water gleamed tantalisingly at the foot of Market Hill. Nice to be going out into the country now, he thought—on an enquiry, of course, strictly on duty, but nice to be able to stay out in the open air with something positive to pursue, instead of having to return to his office and face the paper work that would have accumulated during the past two days while he was at county headquarters.

That was the trouble with promotion, he decided, resisting a passing temptation to have a word with the landlord of the Coney and Thistle. The higher you climbed, the further removed you were from the action; just as, the older you became, the more remote were the girls in their summer dresses.

Which made it all the harder, he remembered, returning to one of his perennial irritations as he waited to cross the main road which took the heavy flow of traffic between London and Yarchester, that the council should have planted a row of such feminine double-flowering pink cherry trees outside police headquarters. Not that he had anything against ornamental cherry trees in their proper place, a park or a small garden. But here, outside the bulk of the fire station and the police station and the library they were merely pathetic, ridiculously out of scale. Why couldn't the council have planted two or three proper trees, something that would grow to a reasonable

8

height and make a positive contribution to the area, instead of these pink frilly things that dropped their blossom like fistfuls of confetti all over the steps of the police station?

He dodged impatiently between a chemical tanker and a refrigerated TIR truck with a Dutch registration and strode, ruffled, through the main doors. The desk sergeant, a prematurely grey forty-year-old, heaved himself to his feet. 'Morning, sir.'

'Morning, Larry. Get the cleaner to brush those steps down, will you? Wretched blossom makes the place look like a register office.'

'Right, sir. How did it go in court this morning?'

Quantrill cheered up. 'Remanded in custody for a week,' he said with satisfaction. 'Just what we wanted—get word through to Inspector Howell, will you? And when you've a man to spare, send him to take a look at the damage that's been done to the children's playground in the park. Oh, and tell him that it wouldn't hurt to find out what Bert Framsden's youngest and his mate have been up to recently. Is the new Ds in, by the way?'

'Out on enquiries.' Sergeant Lamb, who had taken a dislike to the new detective long before he met him, drew himself up and began to enunciate in his best courtroom manner: 'When last seen, Detective Sergeant Tait was proceeding in the direction of a pig farm, wearing a pink suit with flared trousers and a pair of shoes with heels this high.'

Quantrill's thick dark eyebrows shot up an astounding inch, and Sergeant Lamb amended the gap between his outstretched finger and thumb. 'Well, *this* high, anyway. But the suit's definitely pinkish.'

A slow, countryman's grin spread over Quantrill's face. 'And going to a pig farm, was he?' he chuckled. Then he checked himself. 'Now hold hard,' he said severely, 'we've got to give this chap a fair deal. Oh, I know it gets up your nose when a man's given rank before he's got the sense to keep his feet dry. How long did it take you to make sergeant?'

'Seven years, sir,' said Lamb gloomily, 'and that was six years ago . . .' He was up for the next promotion board, but was not confident.

'Only seven?' asked Quantrill briskly. 'You've been quick, man! It was ten before they made me up, and then another eight before I got as far as inspector. You and I are doing it the hard way. But Tait won't have had it easy, you know. The selection board's tough, I hear, and Bramshill's tougher. If he's survived that, he's got all the right qualities. What he needs now is experience, and that's what he's here for—and it's up to us to help him. He's not used to the country, so if you see him making an obvious mistake, give him a bit of friendly advice. Don't wait to laugh behind his back—lend the man a pair of rubber boots if you know he's going to need them.'

'Sir,' agreed Lamb, subdued. 'He's not easy to talk to, though.'

'Well, try a bit harder,' snapped Quantrill. 'You're the same rank, aren't you? Have a bit of friendly conversation. You don't have to treat him like a lord, just because he's been to university and police college—but neither is there any call for you to go needling him deliberately. Treat him as you would any other new sergeant, and we'll see what he's like when he's had time to find his feet. Right?'

'Sir.'

'All right, then. Send him up when he comes in, will you, Larry. I'd better have a word. And if you could organise a cup of coffee? Thanks.'

As Quantrill went up to his first floor office, he admitted to himself that his own instinctive reaction was much the same as Sergeant Lamb's. He was actually apprehensive about meeting the new sergeant, who would almost certainly resent being sent to this rural division. If Tait had been in the uniformed branch it would have been easier; you knew where you were with a uniform. Besides, a uniformed Tait would not have been his responsibility. But to have foisted on him a university graduate who had been hand-picked and intensively trained for accelerated promotion—well, it was a bit hard on a working detective who had left school at fourteen.

Quantrill entered his narrow high-ceilinged office, hung his hat on the stand provided for the use of officers of the rank of chief inspector and above, and smoothed back his springy hair, dark lightly salted with grey. A young constable knocked and brought in a cup of coffee, and Quantrill sipped it as he glanced through the files in his in-tray.

Paper work. Ironic, really, when you stopped to consider it. Because he was a reasonably good detective—good with people, that is, good at understanding how they felt what they felt and why they did what they did—he had been promoted to a job that entailed spending most of his time in the office. And Quantrill was wistfully conscious, every time he found himself obliged to set down sentences that tended to slip awkwardly from his pen and twist their meaning, of his lack of formal education.

He sighed, put down his cup and picked up his ballpoint pen. Five minutes later he was absorbed in his work. Presently a word eluded him, and he began to chase it through the well-used pages of his dictionary. There was a knock on the door, he called an absent 'Come in', and started almost guiltily as a sharply blue-eyed young man walked into his office and looked him over, dictionary and all.

'Detective Sergeant Tait reporting, sir.' The sun was in Tait's eyes and he couldn't see Quantrill's expression, nor identify the book that the chief inspector slapped shut and pushed quickly into a drawer.

Tait stood still, waiting, his eyes lowered against the sun. Chief inspectors had been two-a-new-penny at Bramshill, but he knew that out here in the sticks they rated high, and should be deferred to accordingly. It was for this reason, knowing that Quantrill would be in the office today, that Tait had chosen to dress formally in a suit instead of in casual clothes; for this reason he had had his thick fair hair trimmed. Modest eagerness, he had decided, would be the appropriate line to take.

Quantrill surveyed the young man guardedly, but with a growing sense of relief. Larry Lamb had been exaggerating. The lightweight suit was an unexceptional pale clover, the heels of the shoes were no more than an inch higher than was strictly necessary. The clothes wouldn't suit Quantrill himself, nor yet Lamb, but on a man of Tait's age and figure they were perfectly acceptable; trendy, as Quantrill's daughters would describe them, but not way out. There was nothing objectionable in the sergeant's attitude, either; he looked, Quantrill thought, positively respectful.

The chief inspector stretched a welcoming hand across the width of the desk that, like the hat-stand and the carpet, came in a certain size according to rank.

'Glad to have you with us, Sergeant Tait. Sit down. Sorry I wasn't here at the beginning of the week, when you arrived.'

Now what on earth had made him say that? It wouldn't have occurred to him to apologise to any other newly promoted, newly arrived sergeant. Quantrill twisted in his swivel chair to the window behind him, and altered the louvres of the blind to keep the sun out of Tait's eyes. 'You're probably not too pleased about being sent here,' he went on quickly. 'I understand that you should have spent a year as station sergeant at Yarchester or Bishops Port as soon as you left Bramshill. But we're badly under strength in this division. We haven't had a CID sergeant since your predecessor retired a month ago, so as you'd had some CID experience before going to Bramshill . . .'

Tait smiled kindly. The DCI was talking too much; rattled, for some reason. It would be interesting to find out why. 'I quite understand, sir,' he said.

He looked speculatively at Quantrill's square, heavily handsome face. The eyes were the colour of hard green plums, and Tait reminded himself that even out here in the sticks it wouldn't do to underestimate a chief inspector. 'Frankly, sir,' he added, 'I wasn't looking forward to being a station sergeant and dealing with lost dogs and drunks. I much prefer CID work, so I'm very glad to be here. It'll be good experience.'

Quantrill relaxed. It was a great relief to find that Tait hadn't come out to the country disgruntled. 'Good,' he said heartily. 'Well, you've got a nice day for a smelly job. Pig trouble, I believe!'

Tait looked down quickly. The ends of his trousers were still dark with damp, and there were splashes of dried mud on his shoes. 'Does it smell? I'm sorry, I thought I'd wiped my shoes clean.'

It was Quantrill's turn to be kind. 'It's not too bad.' He opened the box of cigarettes that he kept on his desk for use at interviews. 'Do you smoke?'

'No thank you, sir.'

'Very wise.' Quantrill snapped the box shut, opened his tin of small cigars and lit one to drive away the faint but definable smell of pig. He was not particularly fond of cigars, but had forced himself to give up cigarettes after reading in a newspaper article that any man over the age of forty who had a tendency to overweight, took too little exercise, smoked heavily, ate irregular meals and worked under stress, was inviting a coronary.

He smiled cordially at Tait through the cigar smoke. 'What you want to do,' he added helpfully, 'is to carry a pair of rubber boots in your car.'

'That's what Pc Godbold suggested.'

'Oh, you've been out with Charlie Godbold, have you? He's a good man. You might call him old-fashioned, I suppose, but he's a good practical copper. I always find his advice worth listening to.'

'Yes sir. Stupid of me not to go prepared, but it was a lovely morning when we left the town.'

'Ah, but it had rained hard in the night. You have to watch that, in the country. Pavements dry soon enough, but the grass was bound to be wet, and it's always mucky round the farms. If you keep a pair of wellingtons and an old raincoat in your car, you'll be ready for anything.'

Tait did not possess a raincoat, of any vintage. He had thought that detectives in raincoats were extinct, a species recorded only on old film, and was intrigued to find one alive and apparently detecting well in East Anglia. But he continued alert and polite: 'I'll remember that, sir.'

'And have you found the pigs you were looking for?'

Quantrill's question came quietly, drifting out in the slow deep voice that had a Suffolk sing to it, but his eyes were suddenly difficult to evade. Taken by surprise, Tait floundered for a moment.

'Er—well, not actually *found* them, sir. I've one or two leads—'

To Tait's surprise, the chief inspector chuckled. 'Hi-jacked from outside a pub, I hear. Couple of young pigs, netted in the back of a pick-up truck, eh? That's the kind of crime that's going to keep you busy in this division, Sergeant Tait.'

It sounded, unfairly, like mockery.

'Well, two pigs are quite valuable, sir,' protested Tait. 'And then there's the truck itself . . . Anyway, it's the principle. To-day it's pigs, tomorrow it might be whisky or cigarettes. It's a crime, whatever's involved.'

'Quite so . . .' Quantrill sat back, staring meditatively at Tait through a drift of smoke. He had found the new sergeant unexpectedly easy to deal with; the young man's modesty and diffidence had taken him agreeably by surprise. Almost, he had been disarmed.

But the fact was that a policeman of Tait's calibre had no business to be diffident and modest. Quantrill leaned forward, his elbows on his desk, frowning at the tip of his cigar as he rehearsed, for Tait's benefit, the talk he had been asked to give at the next meeting of the Breckham Market Rotary Club.

'Crime patterns,' he said, 'are related to mobility. Now in this division, we get very little large-scale crime. The modern villain, the professional, is highly mobile. He operates in places he can get into and away from quickly, and since we've no motorways running through the Breckham Market division, we don't attract the big-time crooks. We'd catch 'em in a traffic jam before they got outside the county. Oh, we've got crime, all right, thefts and burglaries and assaults and vandalism, but very little organised crime. From a police point of view it involves hours of tedious, painstaking investigation, and it needs a lot more men than we've got.'

Quantrill looked up quickly, nailing Tait with a hard green stare as he added a rider he would not offer the Rotarians: 'But from an individual detective's point of view, it's not what you might call an intellectual challenge. Tell me, Sergeant Tait—would you describe yourself as an ambitious man?'

Too late, Tait saw the pitfall. Impossible, given his background, to deny his ambition; but to affirm it would hardly be consistent with the character he had been at pains to build. The chief inspector had caught him neatly.

He sat straighter. 'Sir,' he conceded.

Quantrill left his cigar in the ashtray, got up and walked to the window. Then he turned, scowling. He was a big man, six feet tall and broad with it.

Sergeant Tait thought it advisable to get to his feet and stand to attention, but Quantrill began mildly enough. 'It's not that I mind your being an actor. It's a very useful thing for a policeman to be, a detective especially. But let's get this straight—'

Quantrill placed his hands flat on his desk and leaned across it intimidatingly. 'I am not having any of my men putting on an act for my benefit—is that clear? If you're going to work with me, I want to know what you're thinking and why you're thinking it. Of *course* you didn't want to come to this division, a man with your background—but I'd have a hell of a lot more respect for you if you'd said so, instead of trying to soft-soap me.'

Sergeant Tait, who was barely half an inch above the stipulated minimum height for members of the county force, declined with steely courtesy to be intimidated. 'I told you the truth, sir. I was glad to be sent to this division.'

Quantrill straightened warily. 'You were, were you?' He thought for a moment, then bent across the desk again. 'Is this the reason, by any chance?' His hand went out to a large framed photograph that stood on his desk. He turned it to face the sergeant.

Tait had assumed that the frame would contain a photograph of the chief inspector's wife. In his experience it was an ostentatious assertion of connubial harmony that most policemen affected when they reached senior rank, as much a status symbol as the hat stand and the carpet and the swivel armchair. But as soon as he saw the photograph, Tait knew that he had misjudged the chief inspector.

He knew, too, that he had an answer more effective than words. Taking a snapshot from his wallet, he placed it silently on the desk next to the framed photograph.

They were the same, except that Quantrill's was a bigger blow-up of the original. They showed a girl of about fifteen years old, dark curly hair blowing round her cheeks, laughing into the camera.

Quantrill slumped down, and waved Tait back to his chair. 'Hoping to find her, are you?' he asked heavily.

'Hoping to help, sir.'

Quantrill picked up his cigar, took a puff, grimaced and stubbed it out. 'Yes, I understand. Joy Dawson's disappearance is the biggest unsolved case in the whole county at the moment. It's had national publicity. Naturally, you'd like to have a go at it . . . and it wouldn't do your career much harm if you were the one who found out what happened to her, would it?'

Tait gave him as blunt an answer as he'd asked for. 'No, sir. And I think it can sometimes help, when an investigation gets bogged down, if someone who hasn't been involved takes a look at it—'

'Involved!' Quantrill slammed his hand angrily on his desk. 'Involved . . . my God you're right, we are involved, all of us who've been trying to find her! You're not married, are you?'

'No sir.'

'Well when you are, with children of your own to be fearful

for, you'll begin to understand. You don't need to tell me that one of the rules of good police work is never to become personally involved in a case, but there are times when you can't help it. When a youngster dies, whether by accident or murder, it's tragic—but death happens all the time, and we have to learn to come to terms with it. Disappearance is different, though. It's a terrifying thing . . .'

Quantrill shook his head, as if to clear it. 'Maybe you're right,' he went on slowly, 'maybe it will help if someone new takes a look at it, someone who can read the evidence more objectively than any of us—though God knows there's little enough evidence. Still, you're welcome to read the file when you've got time. Take a look at the area when you're over on that side of the division, and then let me know what you think. But *don't* interview any of the witnesses.'

'Oh, but sir—'

'You heard what I said, and that's an order. The parents have had enough, they're ill with worry. The last thing they want is a cool, uninvolved young detective trampling about all over their feelings for the sake of furthering his own career, and I won't have them badgered. If you can see a possible new line of enquiry from the file, bring it straight to me.'

Tait's jaw tightened. 'Selfish bastard,' he thought.

'Sorry,' went on Quantrill, not unsympathetically, 'but I've got my orders too. The moment I get a new lead, I'm to tell the chief super—it isn't a divisional matter any more, there's a line of senior officers interested in the case and I'm afraid that detective sergeants go to the far end. So it looks as though you're stuck with the missing pigs—'

The internal telephone rang. Quantrill answered it, sat up abruptly, then relaxed. He put down the receiver, and began to scratch the side of his jaw with his forefinger.

'Radio message from Charlie Godbold at Ashthorpe,' he said conversationally. 'When you were out with him this morning, did you happen to go over Ashthorpe bridge—narrow stone hump-backed affair?'

'Yes, we did.'

'Ah.' Quantrill had learned to be a bit of an actor himself, and the opportunity to upstage his new sergeant was irresistible. 'Didn't happen to see a dead body in the river there, I suppose?' he asked casually.

Tait looked gratifyingly astounded. 'Sir—?'

Quantrill raised an understanding hand. 'But you don't go round looking for dead bodies, do you? That's all right, sergeant, it wouldn't be reasonable if you did. But it's there all right, a girl, been there some hours in Godbold's opinion. No sign of foul play, though. He's pretty certain it must have been an accident.'

Tait was alert, impatient. 'Do you mean it's Joy Dawson?'

'No—and in a way I'm sorry. Like I said, you can come to terms with death—and you know as well as I do that she could have come to a far worse end than death by drowning . . . No, this is an Ashthorpe girl, Godbold knows her. He'll break it to the relatives, so at least you'll be spared that. Just satisfy yourself that there are no suspicious circumstances, and then make the usual enquiries about when she was last seen.'

Tait stood up eagerly. He had thought that Quantrill meant to keep him permanently on lost pig duty, by way of retaliation. 'You're sending me, sir?'

'Who else? You can send a constable after the pigs. But sergeant—'

'Sir?'

'Try not to look so pleased about it, will you? The poor girl didn't die to provide you with a welcome change from routine. And don't go there hoping that it'll turn out to be murder, either. It's enough that she died—don't wish for it to be any worse than it is.'

Tait sobered. He hurried from the office, down the stairs and through the main hall. Sergeant Lamb looked up as he passed the desk.

'Hey—er—mate . . .'

'Can't stop,' said Tait. 'Fatality.'

'I know, girl found drowned. Want to borrow a pair of wellies?'

Tait hesitated, then looked down at his maltreated shoes. 'Thanks very much,' he said, 'I'd be glad to.'

# THREE

Chief Inspector Quantrill believed in delegation. He had no intention of trying to cramp an ambitious young sergeant; and surely a police college graduate could be relied on to deal with a simple case of accidental death?

But the Joy Dawson case was heavy on his mind. Because she had disappeared on a sunny February mid-morning, from a quiet country road within a mile of her own home, Quantrill had allowed the usual missing juvenile routine to take its course. It was five hours before he had appreciated that the disappearance was desperately serious, and in that time dusk had fallen and the trail—because there must have been a trail, there simply couldn't have been no evidence at all—was ice-cold.

Well, there was no reason to suppose that there was any connection between the death of the girl in the river at Ashthorpe and the disappearance of Joy Dawson twenty miles away and three months ago. But suppose there was some kind of connection? Or suppose that, despite Pc Godbold's assurance, this death was not accidental?

Quantrill gave Tait a half-hour's start, then took his hat and his car and made for Ashthorpe. As he neared the turning from the main road to the village the mortuary van came towards him, travelling in the direction of the county hospital; obviously Tait had found nothing suspicious, but even so his Citroën was still at the scene of the fatality, parked on the grass verge well before the approach to Ashthorpe bridge.

The chief inspector pulled his solid Austin in behind Tait's car. The grass had dried but he changed into his rubber boots, tossing his hat onto the car seat in acknowledgement of the sunshine before he walked to the bridge.

The shallow valley of the Dunnock was warm and quiet. A

18

good place to be on a heady May morning: river running, insects humming, sun shining, buttercups gleaming, lark rising. Only the reason for being here was sober, with death all the more a tragedy for coming young, at the height of spring.

He looked upstream. Some heifers, standing flicking their tails in muddy craters at the water's edge, stared back and blinked their maiden lashes. In the river a dead branch had wedged itself across the upstream arch of the bridge, forming a surface dam which held back a jumble of castaway plastic ware embedded in a creamy-brown scum, and left the water to run through the arch clean and clear.

Quantrill walked to the crest of the bridge and leaned on the downstream parapet, feeling the stone warm under his hands. Sergeant Tait, shirtsleeved and knee-deep in borrowed wellingtons, was searching the shallow river ten yards downstream.

'Nice day for a paddle,' called Quantrill austerely.

Tait looked up with a frown, irritated by the prospect of working with a DCI who didn't know how to delegate. But on the other hand, now Quantrill was here it would be that much easier to make his point forcefully. He waded nearer.

'Pc Godbold has gone to take the girl's father to the mortuary for a formal identification, sir. He knows the family well. The girl's a student, Mary Gedge, about seventeen or eighteen years old. Her parents keep a general store in Ashthorpe. I believe that Godbold reported that it looked as though the girl had slipped into the water and drowned while she was gathering flowers—and I agree that there's nothing to indicate foul play.'

'Well then? I saw the van going back to Breckham and I expected to find you in the village, establishing when she was last seen alive. What's kept you here? You know we're up to our ears in work.'

'There's an interesting query, sir,' said Tait smoothly. 'Since you're here, I'd be very glad of your opinion.'

Quantrill wavered. He suspected Tait of manufacturing the interesting query, but since the sergeant made no move to return to the road, he left the bridge and joined him in the meadow. Tait had climbed out of the water, and his wet boots were rapidly acquiring a lacquer of buttercup yellow.

'Who found the body, and when?' Quantrill asked.

'It was found about eleven thirty, according to Godbold, by two local boys who came down here to play.'

'Half a minute. It's Friday, isn't it?' Quantrill tried to remember where his own schoolboy son would be that morning, and failed.

'Yes, sir. Last day of Easter holidays, so Godbold tells me.'

'Ah.' Of course, the school holidays, late on account of a very late Easter. He'd promised to take a few days off while Peter was at home; get to know the boy better, do something together—take him angling for bass from Southwold beach, perhaps, as his own father had taken him . . . Another good resolution down the drain. 'Go on, then.'

Tait pointed. 'The body was just there, facedown. She was wearing a long dress, she was barefoot, and there were gathered flowers floating round her in the water. No sign at all of violence or interference, and no way of telling how or where she entered the water. The ground's damp, and the bare patches on the bank are covered with the prints and skid-marks the children made. But I suppose it's possible that she could have slipped in while she was reaching for those yellow flowers growing at the edge of the water.'

'Kingcups,' said, Quantrill absently. 'Yes, I see. But I get your point—if she did slip in, how did she come to drown in water this shallow?'

'Exactly, sir.' Tait had more to say, but he saved it.

Quantrill scratched the side of his jaw. 'Hit her head on a stone, perhaps?'

'That's just what I've been looking for. I haven't found one.'

Quantrill thought for a moment. 'There are one or two wilted buttercups lying on the parapet of the bridge. If she'd leaned over too far and fallen from up there she might have hit her head on the stonework.'

Tait frowned. He hadn't stayed long enough on the bridge to notice the wilted flowers. 'No head injuries that I could see, sir. And then, the water's hardly deep enough to float her down this far. It's all bends and shallows.'

The chief inspector agreed. 'Suicide?' he asked reluctantly. 'Any personal possessions left on the bank?'

'Nothing I've found so far. There might be a note at the girl's home, of course—but then, this river's hardly deep enough for suicide.'

'Depth's not essential. I agree that it'd be difficult for a normal person to drown deliberately in shallow water—the instinct for self-preservation's too strong, however much you may think you want to die. But depressives have been known to drown themselves in a few inches of water. Is there any suggestion that the girl was subject to depression?'

'Not according to Godbold. He says she was a normal, happy girl; she'd just left school and was going to university in October—looking forward to it very much. Everything to live for.'

'Unhappy love affair, perhaps?'

'Nothing that Godbold had heard of. A possibility, of course.'

Quantrill flapped some persistent insects away from his face. He was uncomfortably hot in his dark courtroom suit, but since he had no intention of lingering—nothing to linger for—there was no point in removing his jacket. 'Well, see what your enquiries turn up,' he said briskly. 'But the coroner won't consider suicide unless there's a note or some other definite evidence of intention. He'll order a post-mortem, of course, but if nothing unusual emerges from that he'll probably bring in an open verdict.'

'But there is another query, sir.' Quantrill was already turning away, and Tait spoke quickly. 'I can't find her shoes. She was barefoot, and I can't find any shoes either on the bank or in the water.'

The chief inspector shrugged. 'What makes you think she was wearing any? Some girls don't, especially when they're in those long dresses.' He spoke disparagingly. He'd sometimes seen the womenfolk from a nearby rural commune, cotton skirts flapping round their ankles, padding barefoot along the dirty pavements of Breckham Market. Townies playing at country life, he thought; countrywomen had more sense—except that you could never be sure, with young girls.

'Oh, I agree. I had a girl-friend last year who liked to go barefoot. It attracted me at first. Bare feet under a long dress are very sexy. But then I saw the soles of her feet—'

Quantrill could imagine, but Tait spelled it out for him.

'They were revolting, like grey leather, cracked and ingrained with dirt. It turned me right off. But Mary Gedge's feet weren't like that at all—I made a point of examining them.'

'Callous young devil,' Quantrill thought. His own first corpse, a suicide, had terrified him, and still had power to give him bad dreams; it had been a long time before he had been able to look at another with equanimity. But perhaps the preliminary examination of dead bodies was a routine part of the Bramshill curriculum.

'I'd say that Mary Gedge had never made a habit of going barefoot out of doors,' Tait continued. 'Her feet—the toes especially—were quite badly grazed, as though she'd scrabbled to keep her footing in the gravel bed of the stream. Otherwise they were far too unmarked to indicate that she was used to going without shoes. Apparently it's over a mile from her house, and I simply don't believe that she walked here barefoot. What I would really like, sir, is to get a man out here in waders to search the river thoroughly. If we can't find any shoes, then she must have come here in a vehicle, with someone else. And that suggests that it would have been some time during the night, perhaps after an evening out. And that's not the time when people usually gather flowers.'

Quantrill stared at him uneasily. 'Now hold hard—' he protested.

'When I came past this morning,' went on Tait firmly, ignoring the interruption, 'I noticed that a vehicle had been standing at the side of the road, just by that gap in the hedge. The tyre marks were quite clear. I've since checked with Godbold, and he tells me that it had been dry here for several days, but that it had begun to rain hard just after eleven last night, as he was taking his dog for a walk. He could hear that it was still raining at midnight, but when he got out of bed an hour later it was fine and the sky was clear. So it's likely that the vehicle was parked by the bridge some time after one o'clock this morning.'

'And what evidence have you got to connect that with Mary Gedge?' demanded Quantrill.

Tait was unabashed. 'None at all, sir. And of course we need to check on her movements. But it will be interesting to hear the pathologist's expert opinion as to whether the girl could have walked over a mile barefoot to get here; and if he says she didn't, and if we can't find her shoes, it'll then be a bit late to start making enquiries as to how she came.'

Quantrill stood dark and heavy among the buttercups, silent except for some disgruntled breathing, shoulders hunched, hands deep in his jacket pockets. Tait, waiting for his reaction, was prepared for resentful scorn; but although Quantrill found it difficult to like the new sergeant, his respect for a Bramshill training was increasing by the minute.

'How long would you say she'd been dead?' he asked after a pause. He knew better than to make such guesses himself, but heaven knew what esoteric sciences were taught at police college.

'I've no idea, sir,' said Tait promptly. 'It's a matter of body temperature—an expert job for the pathologist.'

Quantrill's opinion of Bramshill soared. It was even better to know that its graduates were taught that their knowledge had clearly defined limits.

'Pc Godbold did suggest that she died early this morning,' added Tait sceptically. 'In his opinion, she probably came down alone to gather flowers at sunrise—an old country custom on May Day, he said.'

'Hmm. Well, it's possible. But what you're trying to make out is that she was brought here in the early hours—'

'I'm not "trying to make out" anything, sir,' Tait retorted. 'I do suggest, from the available evidence, that she may well have come by car—and if so, then someone else was with her. The most likely time for that would be after an evening out. There's another point, too: the girl's fingers and knees were badly grazed. I agree that this doesn't necessarily indicate foul play, because if she fell in she'd obviously try to save herself. But if she fell in as a result of some fooling about, it's possible that her companion—or companions—panicked and left her. The significant point is, sir, that if she didn't walk down here alone, then someone else almost certainly knows something about her death. Don't you agree?'

Tait looked enviably, irritatingly cool in his grey shirt and dusky pink tie. Quantrill pulled off his own jacket, slung it over his arm and waded through wild flowers to the water's edge. The river bank at this point, under a willow tree, was bare with long-established use but the only identifiable prints on the damp earth were those of juvenile wellingtons.

The chief inspector stepped heavily down into the water and swished out to the place where the body had lain grounded, brushing past a clump of thick-stemmed yellow kingcups and stirring up the smell of river-rotten vegetation. The bed of the stream was gravelly, reedy and weedy in patches, but with no stones large enough to cause concussion. The water ran cool against his wellingtons, no more than eighteen inches deep. It was difficult to see how a simple fall into the Dunnock could kill anyone.

He sighed. 'She could have been dead before she got here, if it comes to that,' he said gloomily, without any expectation that Tait would have overlooked the possibility.

'Quite. And either way, the flowers could have been thrown in afterwards in an attempt to make it look like an accident. There's another point, though, sir. If we assume that she was here with a friend or friends and fell in accidentally, it still doesn't explain how she drowned in such shallow water. But if the post mortem revealed that she'd been drinking, or taking drugs . . .'

Quantrill clambered up the bank. 'If if if—' he growled irritably. 'It's nothing but supposition!'

'Based on the fact of the missing shoes,' Tait reminded him. 'All right, I'm speculating, I agree. The post-mortem may well show up a simple death by drowning, and if it does I'll be satisfied that it was an accident—as long as we can find the shoes. But I don't see that we can wait for the pathologist's report before *looking* for the shoes. If they're in someone's car, the sooner we know about it the better. So if I could have two men with waders—'

Quantrill rounded on him, an indignant figure in size twelve wellingtons that had suddenly, incongruously, turned to gold. '*One* man and that's all!' he snapped. 'Good grief, you know how under-strength we are—if it's a two-man job you'll have to stay here and help him while I make a start on the enquiries myself.'

Tait assured him that one man would be perfectly adequate.

'Carry on, then,' said Quantrill. He hesitated, remembering his intention to delegate. Sergeant Tait was obviously more than competent to carry out routine enquiries into the dead girl's last movements, and to follow up anything that might seem significant. But Quantrill could never forget Joy Dawson.

He'd left those preliminary enquiries to his sergeant too. Not that he blamed the sergeant, or that he himself could have done anything more to find the missing girl; but his lack of immediate concern, his preoccupation with paper work at the critical time, stabbed at his conscience as frequently as cold air strikes the exposed nerve of a decaying tooth.

'Might as well come along with you, since I'm here,' he explained, almost apologetic.

Tait gave him a cool smile. 'Please do, sir,' he said politely, 'if you can spare the time.'

# FOUR

'A cup of coffee, Mr. Quantrill?'

'Thanks very much, Mrs. Godbold. Very kind of you.'

It had been Quantrill's intention to meet Pc Goldbold at the Ashthorpe Chequers before going to interview the dead girl's parents, but the constable had forewarned his wife to provide coffee and sandwiches. Preferable, anyway, on this occasion, to a pub snack; bad enough to have to go badgering the bereaved, without breathing beer all over them. Quantrill bit into a cheese and pickle sandwich and waited patiently for the constable's stout wife to stop fussing and leave them alone in the front room of the police house, where family photographs stood on top of the official filing cabinet.

'Very tasty, Mrs. Godbold. Just what we needed, thank you.'

'My pleasure, Mr. Quantrill, I'm sure. I hope your—' She saw her husband's scowl and abandoned her attempt at conversation, but retained her dignity. 'I hope you'll let me know if there's anything else you want.'

'Very good of your wife,' said Quantrill as the door shut behind her, firmly putting down the apologies that Godbold looked as though he might be about to make on her behalf. 'We appreciate this.'

Sergeant Tait, making a cautious first acquaintance with a drink concocted from bottled essence of coffee with chicory, hot water, two spoonfuls of white sugar and a dash of evaporated milk, declined to comment.

'Now then,' Quantrill went on, 'the thing is, Charlie, that we think—' he caught Tait's sharp blue gaze '—Sergeant Tait thinks, and I'm bound to say I agree with him, that it's possible that someone was with Mary when she died.'

He explained Tait's theory about the missing shoes. 'Was she a girl who liked to go barefoot, do you know?'

Godbold shook his head, bemused. He had a stubble of greying hair, and without his uniform cap he looked a much older man. He had been distressed to find that the dead girl was someone he knew, and by the melancholy duty of breaking the news to her parents, he felt depressed and weary. He swallowed his wife's coffee, but what he really needed was a large whisky.

'Not that I've ever seen or heard,' he answered huskily. 'But then, like I told Sergeant Tait, now I'm in the van I'm not as close to touch with people as I'd like to be.'

'I know. Tell us what you can about the girl, though, Charlie—the more we can get from you, the less we'll have to ask her parents. You've known her a long time?'

Godbold smiled with sad reminiscence. 'Since she was a toddler, ever since I've lived in Ashthorpe. A really nice girl, she was—called out "Hallo Mr. Godbold" whenever she saw me. Pretty, too. Helped her father in the shop, always a pleasant word for everybody . . . clever, though, she was going to university after harvest. Cambridge and all, same as her brother would have gone to a couple of years ago. Only Mary wasn't going to one of the everyday colleges, she was going to King's, where they do the Christmas carols. A famous place. It was a real achievement for her to be going there. Not that she put on any airs about it, though, she was serving in the shop when I called in for cigarettes at the beginning of the week: "Hallo Mr. Godbold," she said, "here you are." She knew what I'd come for, you see, and the brand I smoke.' He shook his head uncomprehendingly. 'Oh, it's a tragedy, it really is. Just as she'd got the world at her feet, as you might say . . .'

Tait, who had a Sussex degree, looked unwillingly impressed at the mention of Cambridge. And the girl had been attractive, he hadn't failed to notice that. For the first time he began to think of her as a person, rather than as an interesting corpse.

'A terrible waste,' he agreed. He pushed aside the cup of warm, pungent glue. 'Tell me, is her brother dead too? You said he "would have gone" to Cambridge.'

Godbold lit a fresh cigarette from the butt of the old one, and relaxed a little. 'Blast, no, Derek's not dead!' He raised a half-hearted chuckle. 'No, Derek's a married man—case of having to be, of course. He was clever too, but not a patch on Mary in a lot of ways. A lazy young devil, never lifted a finger to help in the shop. His mother doted on him, though, you know what mothers are with boys—'

Quantrill knew.

'Anyway,' went on Godbold, 'seems Master Derek had been carrying on with a local girl on the quiet. Then she found she was pregnant, so that was the end of Cambridge for him.'

Tait made a strangled, incredulous noise. Godbold looked to the chief inspector for support.

'Well, he had to see her right, didn't he? Had to be man enough to take the responsibility. And with a family to keep, he had to get a job. I mean, he'd had his fun . . .'

'Quite,' agreed Quantrill. He too had been brought up in a village which maintained a relentless communal belief in the duty of lying on the bed you had made, however uncomfortable.

'What's his job?' Tait demanded.

Godbold gave his answer to the chief inspector. 'Oh, he was lucky. There's been a fair bit of redundancy in Breckham, as you know, sir. Jobs haven't been easy to come by in the last year or two. But his wife's uncle managed to get him fixed up at the chicken factory, down at the old railway station here in Ashthorpe.'

'Good God,' said Tait.

Quantrill turned on him sharply. 'What's the matter with you?'

'Well for heaven's sake . . . ! Poor devil, being expected to give up university and go to work in a chicken factory, just because—'

'*Just because!*' Quantrill fumed. 'Where's your sense of decency, boy? What about the poor girl—she's the one to be sorry for, isn't she? Talk about selfish young bachelors . . .'

The two older men, both fathers of nubile daughters, looked belligerently at Sergeant Tait. It occurred to him that he had undoubtedly been lucky never to have lived in a small and righteous community, and he prudently said no more.

'Mind you,' added Godbold fairly, 'I don't know as many Ashthorpe folk would have blamed Derek if he *hadn't* married Julie. I mean, there's plenty as don't get married these days. The girls don't seem to expect it, they can always get social security. And Derek wasn't Julie's first, everybody knows that, whatever her mother liked to make out. Trouble was, Derek's mother's very—' Godbold lowered his voice, as though he were speaking of some shameful disorder '—religious. Very strict chapel. She was the one who insisted on the marriage, and I hear she hasn't spoken to Derek since.'

'There was a family upset, then?' Quantrill commented.

'A real bust-up. And Mary got involved too. She was properly upset when her brother got married, and that put her on bad terms with him and her mother an' all. A shame, because she was very close to her brother before that. He's been living at his mother-in-law's ever since, and I doubt if Mary ever goes— ever went round to see him. Not that you could blame her. They're a slummocking family, the Pulfers, always have been.'

'So Mary wasn't happy at home?' asked Quantrill uneasily. He hoped very much, for the sake of the girl's family, that there would be no evidence to suggest suicide.

'Ah, I wouldn't say that, sir.' Godbold, knowing the family, was even more anxious that Mary's death should prove to be a simple accident. 'The row was eighteen months ago, and she'd have got over it by now. And she'd always been a happy girl. I don't know that she was ever close to her mother—Mrs. Gedge was always very strict with her, very unbending. But Mary and her Dad got along well. If you'd seen them working and laughing together in the shop, like I saw them only a couple of days ago, you'd know she was happy enough at home.'

Quantrill felt relieved. He loved his own two daughters very much, and had felt bereft when they left Breckham Market to live in London. The fact that Alison, the younger, sent him a personal weekly letter was a heartwarming source of pride. He tried to imagine Mary Gedge's father's desolation, and was ashamed to feel instead a sense of thankfulness that his own daughters were alive.

28

Tait asked the constable for Derek Gedge's address, and wrote it in his notebook. 'Did Mary have any other relatives in the village? Well then, can you tell us who her friends were?'

Godbold brushed a grey caterpillar of cigarette ash from the front of his tunic. 'To be honest, I can't tell you about her friends. I'm not in the village enough to know who Mary went about with. But I reckon most of her friends would be the ones she'd made at school, in Breckham.'

'A boy-friend?'

'Not an Ashthorpe one, not to my knowledge.'

'How did she travel to school?' Tait asked.

'There's a special bus that goes round the villages. My own boy travels on it.'

Quantrill forced a genial smile. 'Ah, Trevor. How's he doing?'

Trevor Godbold, having passed the eleven plus, had gone to Breckham Market boys' grammar school, to his parents' manifest pride. Quantrill had congratulated them wholeheartedly. Both his daughters had gone to the girls' grammar school, and he was confident that his son, three years younger than Trevor, would take the examination in his stride. It had been difficult to conceal his chagrin when Peter was, in the humiliating official phraseology, selected for education at the Alderman Thirkettle secondary modern school.

Since then—in pursuit of an equality that, however much he might approve of it in theory, Quantrill would not have welcomed in practice when his daughters were at the grammar school—the Breckham Market secondary schools had been put under one head and re-labelled comprehensive. Peter had settled into the new system cheerfully enough, and Quantrill's pride was soothed. But he had never been able to rid himself, whenever he met Pc Godbold, of the feeling that he had to take an exaggerated interest in the progress of Godbold junior in order not to be thought resentful of his ability.

The constable beamed modestly. 'He's doing well, thank you, sir. Taking O levels this summer. Would you like to see him, by the way? He's at home now, just had his dinner. He could very likely tell you who Mary's friends were.'

'Good idea,' said Quantrill heartily. 'I'd like a chance to meet the boy.'

Godbold left the room. Quantrill got up and peered at a large-scale map of the district, trying to ignore an altercation that was taking place elsewhere in the house; it sounded as though young Godbold was as reluctant to meet the chief inspector as Quantrill was to meet him.

When the boy entered the room it was fast, as though he had been propelled. His father stood close, blocking the door, breathing hard.

Trevor was an awkward sixteen: legs too long for his body, hands and feet clumsy, nose and ears too big for his face, voice creaky, eyes sullen.

'Hallo Trevor, nice to meet you again.' Quantrill thrust out a genial hand but the boy shied away from the overdone greeting and Quantrill found himself flapping his hand, instead, towards his sergeant. 'This is Detective Sergeant Tait.'

'Hi,' said Tait pleasantly, hoping to God that he had been less unprepossessing at that age.

Trevor looked at him contemptuously. 'Seems the house is overrun with the fuzz, then,' he commented.

Tait compressed his lips and turned away, ignoring him. Quantrill fumbled in his pocket for a cigar and made a business of lighting it while Pc Godbold scolded his son in a stage whisper: 'Trevor! Behave yourself! Mr. Quantrill often asks after you—the least you can do is to be civil. And Mr. Tait's been to university and police college, so don't you be cheeky to him. Stand up straight, boy,' he entreated, 'and just try to answer a few questions.'

Trevor lounged lower against the wall, his hands stuck as far as possible in the pockets of his jeans. 'Questions about what?' he asked suspiciously. Then: 'Oh yeah, don't tell me. Mary Gedge is dead. I didn't do it, honest.'

Quantrill snatched the cigar out of his mouth, took two strides and stood over the boy. 'Do what?' He asked it quietly, but with such intensity of eyes and voice that Trevor straightened, his face reddening.

His father caught at his arm. 'What didn't you do?' he whispered hoarsely, suddenly afraid.

Trevor wriggled. 'Why, nothing . . . nothing at all . . . honest.' He gave a placatory laugh. 'Look, it was only a joke—I didn't mean anything by it. I just know she's dead, that's all. I heard it in the village. She fell in the river and drowned, that's all I know.'

'Are you sure, Trevor?'

The boy looked up at the chief inspector, moistened his lips and answered with evident sincerity: 'Yes, sir.'

Quantrill turned away, tense with anger. Pc Godbold followed him, still trembling from his moment of anxiety. 'I'm sorry, sir, he's a good boy, really he is, it's just a difficult phase he's going through, you know how it is at that age . . .'

Trevor made for the door, muttering something about a job he had promised to do for his mother, but Tait reached it first and slammed his hand against it.

'Not just yet, Trevor,' he said, fixing the boy with a look that stilled him instantly. 'I need to ask some questions. I'd hope to do it informally, but if you're determined to make things difficult for yourself you'll find me very co-operative. I'll be happy to take you to the station, and keep you there until I can get some straight answers from you. Is that what you want? Is that what you'd like me to tell your mother I'm going to do?'

Trevor flicked a horrified glance in the direction of the kitchen. 'No sir,' he gulped.

Tait took out his notebook again. It was a useful part of the policeman act; time someone sorted out the wretched boy.

'What's your full name?' he snapped. He wrote it down slowly. 'And when did you last see Mary Gedge?'

'Er—er—' The boy was nervous, thinking hard in a desperate effort to be exact. 'When I went to the shop for Mum—Wednesday, I think.' His voice shrilled. 'No—no it wasn't, Mr. Tait, it was Tuesday. Tuesday afternoon.'

'And have you seen her—even caught a glimpse of her—since then?'

'No sir!' He looked as though he might begin to cry. Tait ease the pressure.

'All right, Trevor. Now as far as we know, Mary's death was purely an accident. But the coroner will want to know how the accident happened, so we have to try to piece together the events that led up to her death. That means talking to her family and friends, and since you go to the same school it would be a help if you can tell us who her friends were.'

The boy shook his head cautiously. 'We're all split up. There are three parts of the school, you see. The sixth formers are in what used to be the boys' grammar school, the first year are next door in the old girls' grammar. I'm in the middle school, and we're across town in the old Alderman T. We all go to the sixth form part for science and they come to ours for drama, but I didn't often see Mary.'

'What about friends in the village, then? You all go to school on the same bus. Who did Mary sit with?'

Trevor shrugged. 'No one special. Anyway, she didn't go on the bus all that often. Most days she got a lift.'

Quantrill had been listening, his back to the boy. Now he turned: 'Who with?'

Young Godbold had recovered from his fright. His voice was back in its lower register, his eyes were sullen again. But he elected to reply to Sergeant Tait rather than to Chief Inspector Quantrill. 'Sometimes Miller, sometimes Ma Bloomfield.'

'They're both teachers at the comprehensive, sir,' explained Godbold. 'They both live in Ashthorpe. *Mr.* Miller teaches English and Drama, doesn't he, Trevor? He lives at the Old Bakery. *Mrs.* Bloomfield is the deputy headmistress. She lives in one of the houses on the edge of the green.'

Quantrill knew Mrs. Bloomfield. He could have told Tait her exact address, even though he had never been there, but he left it to the constable. 'Did they give lifts to anyone else?' he asked the boy.

'No. Well, Mary was older than anyone else from Ashthorpe. Anyway, the rest of us would rather go by bus, we see enough of teachers when we're in school.'

'I understand,' said Quantrill. 'Well, that's been a help, Trevor, thank you. We'd simply like to talk to the people who knew Mary, you see.'

Trevor looked up. 'Hey, she wasn't—?' he said excitedly, but immediately he dowsed the gleam in his eye. 'Nothing. Doesn't matter.'

Quantrill glared at him. 'She wasn't sexually assaulted, if that's what you mean.' He turned away angrily.

Pc Godbold was shocked, and quick in his son's defense. 'I'm sure Trevor didn't mean that, sir, it would never have occurred to him—'

Tait stretched out an arm and drew the boy aside. Since he'd been the one to raise the subject . . . 'Nice looking girl, Mary, wasn't she?' he asked, man to man.

Trevor's enthusiastic nod disproved his father's evident hope that burgeoning sexuality might somehow manage to miss a generation.

'And she was one of the seniors, so most of the boys must have noticed her?'

Trevor's guard was up. 'I suppose so.'

'Did they talk about her?'

Trevor shook his head decisively. 'She wasn't like that.' He glanced cautiously towards his father and added, 'Not like some of 'em . . . Anyway, Dale Kenward kept everyone else away from her. He's one of the seniors, over six foot tall, and he once knocked another boy down for saying that he fancied her.'

'Some of the other boys were interested in her, then?'

Trevor gave a throaty chuckle: 'Who wasn't?'

Pc Godbold, pushing forward to listen, appealed anxiously to the chief inspector. 'Sir, it's not right! The boy's barely sixteen—'

His son shrugged, sullen again. 'Oh well, she's dead anyway. Too bad. Can I go now?'

Quantrill nodded, tight-lipped. Godbold jerked his head at his son. The boy escaped, wrenching the door open and banging it behind him.

'Time we moved.' The chief inspector clapped a friendly hand on the constable's shoulder. 'They grow up before we can turn round, Charlie, don't they? Anyway, it's been a help talking to the boy. Sergeant Tait and I are going to see the parents now, and I'd be glad if you'll go down to the river. I've sent for a man in waders to search it. Get him to take a look in the muck that's dammed against the upstream arch of the bridge, will you? Remember, if it was an accident—and if Mary was alone, as you think she was—we need to find those missing shoes.'

# FIVE

The name Manchester House was lettered boldly above the Victorian double-front of the shop in the village street: Manchester House, R. J. Gedge, Draper and Family Grocer. The door blind was pulled down, and a notice said 'Closed Even for the Sale of Esso Blue,' but through the windows they could see a figure in a brown dustcoat working alone at the counter.

Quantrill tapped on the glass. At first the man in the shop failed to hear; when he finally looked up and came towards the door he seemed to find motion difficult, as though he were a sleeper wading through a bad dream.

Quantrill roused him gently. 'Good afternoon, sir. Chief Inspector Quantrill and Sergeant Tait, county CID. We're very sorry to have to trouble you at a time like this . . .'

Mr. Gedge blinked and swallowed, his Adam's apple bobbing. He was lean, stooping, his thin remnant of hair appearing to be slipping off the back of his shiny head. He pushed his glasses up on the bridge of his nose with his forefinger out of nervous habit as he answered.

'Oh . . . Oh yes, Charlie Godbold told me that you'd want to see me.'

'It's purely routine, sir. Just a few questions we have to ask. We won't keep you long.'

Mr. Gedge backed clumsily. 'Yes. Yes of course. You don't mind talking in here, I hope.' He pushed sideways round a stack of cardboard cartons in order to get behind the counter, on which he had been assembling a pile of groceries. 'I'm all behind, you see, on account of having to go—to go out this morning.'

'You're working today, Mr. Gedge?' asked Tait, surprised.

The shopkeeper gave a thin smile. 'Well, I'm not open, of course, the customers couldn't expect that. But I must get the deliveries ready, I can't let my regulars down. It's the goodwill, you see, the personal service—it's the only way I can try to keep them out of the supermarkets in Breckham.' His hands moved blindly, assembling packets and cans. 'You don't mind if I carry on, do you?'

Quantrill knew the therapeutic value of it. 'Don't let us hinder you, Mr. Gedge. We just have to ask a few questions about Mary.'

'Yes, of course.' The dead girl's father paused in his work to push his glasses up onto his forehead and run a finger along the lower lids of his eyes. 'Excuse me.' He turned away, pulling a handkerchief from his pocket.

Quantrill, hating the necessary intrusiveness of his job, glanced round while he gave the man time to recover. It was a tall thin shop with a heavy mahogany counter, which must have been part of the original fittings, down one side. The rest of the shop had been modernised, with open shelves and a deep freeze cabinet containing the staples, fish fingers and frozen peas; but there was still an old-fashioned bacon slicer and a cheese cutter, and the shelves behind the counter were filled with jars of sweets that reminded Quantrill of the village shop of his boyhood. And hanging from a high rack over the counter, even more reminiscent of the shop he remembered from the nineteen-forties, was the drapery section: cotton pinafores, children's socks, women's blouses, men's working shirts, tweed jackets and flat caps, all in a choice of shades and sizes. Been there ever since the 'forties too, some of them, from the look of the styles.

Mr. Gedge polished his glasses, pushed his handkerchief away and added a jumbo packet of cornflakes to the goods on the counter.

'We're not sure, Mr. Gedge,' Quantrill said gently, 'when the accident happened. We have to try to establish that. Have you any idea?'

The shopkeeper looked puzzled. 'Why, early this morning, wasn't it? Sunrise time. That's what Charlie Godbold said. She must have gone out to pick flowers—you know, May Day . . .' He began to sound not entirely convinced.

'Is that what she said she was going to do?' asked Tait.

Mr. Gedge looked blank. 'Well, no. No, she didn't say anything about what she was going to do. She often went for walks though, she liked it down by the river.'

'And you saw or heard her leaving the house early this morning?' pursued Tait.

'Ah, well, no . . . But then, I wouldn't. Mary sleeps—' a spasm of grief contorted his face, but he managed to change tense without breaking down '—slept out in the old trailer at the far end of the orchard. Has done for the past eighteen months, except in the very worst of the weather. Liked to be a bit independent, you know how it is. Came and went as she pleased.'

Tait's head lifted with interest. Quantrill spoke quickly, before the sergeant could put too sharp a question.

'Yes, of course, understandable at that age. But you do know for sure, Mr. Gedge, that Mary slept in the trailer last night?'

'Well, yes—I mean, where else—?'

'At a friend's perhaps?' Quantrill suggested lightly, anxious not to alarm him.

'Why, no. I mean, she'd have said, wouldn't she? She didn't say anything about going out last night at all. She was a quiet girl, you see, not one for racketing about. Not much opportunity, anyway, out here in the village. Besides, she always had a terrible lot of school work to do. She's—she was very clever, did you know that? Going to one of the oldest colleges in Cambridge, where they've only just started taking girls. She was so thrilled—but there, she deserved it, she'd studied night after night . . . only her mother didn't like her to keep late hours reading, and that's why Mary enjoyed having a bit of independence. I expect that's what she was doing last night, reading in the trailer. If she's been going out with anyone, she'd have said.'

Quantrill had never had any illusion that his own daughters, when they lived at home, had given him an accurate account of their activities and intentions. But Mary's father had grief enough; it would be cruel to shake his conviction that she had always taken him into her confidence.

And perhaps she had. But her use of the trailer as a home worried Quantrill just as much as it interested Tait.

The sergeant was already coming in with the next question, and Quantrill was glad to hear that he phrased it kindly.

'Perhaps you wouldn't mind telling us when you last saw Mary, Mr. Gedge?'

The shopkeeper had been looking from one policeman to

another with a deepening frown. Now he forced himself into activity again. He ticked an item on a grocery list, and then began to weigh out half a pound of rum and butter toffees while he talked.

'Yes, let me see . . . that would have been early yesterday evening. Mary brought—' his voice tripped, but he managed to continue on a higher note '—she brought me a cup of tea, and stayed to serve some customers while I drank it. Thursdays and Fridays are my late opening evenings, I'm open till eight. Trying to provide a service, you see—so many women are out at work during the day. But things went quiet about half past six, and she left . . . Yes, that would be the last time I saw her.' He fumbled for his handkerchief again. 'Mrs. Gedge probably saw her later, she may be able to help you more than I can.'

'We'd certainly like to talk to your wife, if she's not too distressed.'

Mr. Gedge mopped his eyes and managed a smile. 'Oh, she'll be ready for you. She's got a lot more courage than I have, she's taken this very bravely.' He lowered his voice, as Pc Godbold had done when referring to Mrs. Gedge. 'She's religious, you see. It sustains her, it really does. I sometimes wish I had it, but there . . .' He polished his glasses with a dry corner of his handkerchief. And then a sudden imperious rapping at the window made them all turn.

Tait went to investigate. A dark strapping middle-aged woman was peering into the shop, mouthing and gesticulating. Tait pointed to the Closed notice and waved her away, but still she rapped. Irritated, he turned the key and stepped outside, closing the door firmly behind him.

'The shop is closed, Madam,' he said, choosing a pompous role. 'Mr. Gedge has been bereaved.'

The woman gave him a hostile stare. 'Well I know that, don't I? Everybody in Ashthorpe knows that. And I'm sorry for him, I really am, but there . . . life's got to go on, and I've got nothing for my man's supper.'

Tait's professional irritation turned to genuine indignation on the shopkeeper's behalf. 'You can hardly expect to worry Mr. Gedge when his daughter has just died. I suggest that you go to one of the other shops in the village.'

The woman flushed, puce as the stripes on her nylon overall.

She stood eye to eye with the sergeant. 'Don't you tell me what to do, Sunny Jim—I'm one of Bob Gedge's best customers, and if he can't serve me during shop hours that's a rum 'un! I wouldn't intrude if he was in the house, but I know he's in the shop, I saw him, and if he's not too bereaved to get his grocery deliveries ready—'

'Madam,' said Tait coldly, 'we are police officers. I must ask you—'

Behind him, the door was tugged open. Mr. Gedge peered out, his bald head and scrawny neck poking like those of a tortoise from the ill-fitting collar of his dust-coat.

'Ah, there you are, Bob,' cried the woman. 'I was only just saying—' she remembered to lower her voice: 'Well, there, I'm ever so sorry about Mary, I really am, ever such a nice girl, and I wouldn't trouble you for the world only you weren't here this morning and I've got nothing for my man's supper and I knew you wouldn't mind.'

Mr. Gedge looked worried. 'I'm sorry, Daph, but I've got the police here you see . . .'

The woman peered over his shoulder, agog with interest, to see who else was in the shop. Quantrill kept his head well down.

'Purely a routine visit,' the sergeant pointed out firmly. 'Now if you'll please—'

'Oh. Oh well, I'll just take half of bacon for now, Bob, seeing as you're busy,' said the woman graciously, 'and a tin of rice pudding. The rest'll do tomorrow. Better take a tin of Chum an' all, though, can't let the poor dog starve.'

'If you could just come back in half an hour, Daph,' pleaded Mr. Gedge. 'I haven't had time to bone the bacon yet, you see, and with the police here . . .'

'Back in half an hour! Now look you here, Bob Gedge, I've been up and down this street like a yo-yo today, trying to get served—' She found herself impaled on one of Sergeant Tait's ice-pick glances, and changed her theme. 'Well, all right, then, I'm sure I don't want to hinder the police. Tell Hilda I'm ever so sorry, Bob, will you? And I'll see about a whip-round for a wreath.' She backed from the door. 'An accident, was it?' she asked Tait confidentially. 'Only you never know what these young girls get up to these days, and you do hear such things . . .'

Tait shut the door on the bereaved father and caught at her sleeve as she turned to go. 'What things?' he demanded.

She shook him off indignantly. 'Well, things in the papers. Not that I've got anything against Bob's Mary, mind. Never heard a word of talk against her. But that's what I mean, it's not natural for a girl of her age not to have a bit of fun, and you can't tell me she spent all her time studying. After all, look at her brother. Butter wouldn't have melted in Derek's mouth, no interest in anything except his books—but we all know what *he* got up to on the quiet. Makes you wonder, eh? Makes you think. You know what they say, still waters run deep.'

Tait turned his back on her, went into the shop and locked the door.

Mr. Gedge was sitting on the bentwood chair by the counter, passing his handkerchief over his face. 'I'm sorry about that,' he was telling the chief inspector. 'Sorry about the interruption. Only it's the goodwill, you see, you have to try not to offend.'

The policemen exchanged grimaces. 'Of course, Mr. Gedge,' said Quantrill. 'I'm sorry we're keeping you so long, but we do have to try to build up an accurate picture. Did Mary receive or make any telephone calls yesterday?'

'Not as far as I know.' The shopkeeper pushed himself up wearily from his chair, and began to pack the groceries in a cardboard box.

'Can you tell me what sort of mood Mary was in yesterday evening? Was she depressed at all, or worried?'

'Why, bless you no!' said Mr. Gedge warmly. 'That wasn't Mary's nature. She was quiet, yes, but she wasn't moody. And yesterday she was happy, just as usual. I mean, she'd got nothing to be worried about. She'd passed all her exams, and left school at Easter. I was going to pay her for helping me in the shop during the summer, so there was no call for her to be worried about money. She was on top of the world.'

'Any—' Quantrill sought for the most delicate way to put it '—any family problems?'

Mr. Gedge shrugged. 'I suppose Charlie Godbold told you about Derek?' he said slowly. 'He had to get married instead of going to Cambridge, and Mary was very upset about it at the time. She'd got over that, though.'

But had Derek? wondered Tait. He spoke casually: 'Would

your son have gone to the same college as Mary? To King's?'

'Oh no.' Mr. Gedge cut a piece of cheese, absently slipping a sliver of it into his mouth before weighing and wrapping it. 'Derek was going to one of the other colleges, Selwyn.' He looked over his shoulder, then leaned forward and lowered his voice. 'I'd be greatly obliged if you didn't mention Derek to Mrs. Gedge. She can't bring herself to forgive him, you see.'

Tait changed the subject. 'Could Mary drive?'

'No. Some of her friends could, I think—they'd sometimes come and pick her up by car if they'd got anything planned. But Mary always mentioned it if she was going out.'

Quantrill, conscious of the heaviness of Mrs. Godbold's cheese and pickle sandwiches, helped himself to a packet of mints and placed the money on the till. 'Did you know any of her friends, Mr. Gedge?'

'Why yes. One of them came over here sometimes, Sally somebody, a nice girl. She was a school friend—most of them were, I think. I can't tell you anything about them, though. Mary spent a lot of time helping me here in the shop at weekends and holidays, and she'd chatter away about plays and tennis matches and swimming, and all these names would come out: Sally and Liz and Dale and Dusty and Miggy or Moggy or some such—to tell you the truth, I didn't listen half the time. It was all a bit beyond me. But whatever she was doing, I knew that I had nothing to worry about—Mary never gave me a moment's anxiety.'

It was a great deal more than Quantrill could say of his own daughters; and small enough comfort for the man, now that Mary was dead. The chief inspector would have liked to leave it at that but, recalling what young Godbold had said, there was one more question to be asked.

'Do you happen to know if your daughter had a boy-friend, Mr. Gedge?'

His conviction was absolute. 'Oh, she didn't. Not a boy-friend in the sense of—of going courting,' he said, offering an expression that must have been current in his own youth. 'Well, they'd had boys at the school since last year, so naturally she knew some of them. Dale, for one. But there was nothing serious. She didn't have any love affairs.'

Then, as though anxious not to appear to be denigrating his

daughter, he added quickly, 'Mind you, it's not that she wasn't pretty. Here—'

The colour print must have been on the counter in front of him all the time, propped up against a pyramid of canned fruit so that he could see it as he tried to work. It trembled between his fingers as he held it out for the policemen to see, and neither of them attempted to take it from him even for a moment.

Mary Gedge had been very attractive. Her drowned hair had looked brown to Tait, but now he saw that it had been blonde. Blonde shoulder-length hair, blue eyes, delicate features, a slight figure; not pertly pretty, but almost beautiful, with a look of serene happiness.

Quantrill said nothing. He thought of Alison, who was just a year older than Mary, and of how he might feel if Alison died, and he knew that there was nothing he could say.

'I took the photo this spring,' Mr. Gedge said in a thickening voice. 'It was just after she'd heard she was going to Cambridge. She was so happy—it was what she'd been working for all these years at school, and why she hadn't minded not having much of a social life here. She'd set her heart on Cambridge—she once said to me, "That's when I'll really start living, Dad."'

He stood with his head bowed over the box of groceries, trying to hold his shoulders rigid in an attempt to conceal his tears.

'Thank you very much, Mr. Gedge,' said Quantrill gently. 'You've been very helpful. If we could just see your wife for a few moments, please, just to confirm . . .'

Mr. Gedge straightened, blew his nose, and invited them round behind the counter. 'Yes, of course. You'll find her down at the trailer. Through this door and across the yard and the lawn, and then you'll be able to see the trailer at the far end of the orchard. Mary always liked to keep it private, you see, and my wife thought she'd go and give it a bit of a turnout. Get rid of the rubbish, like.'

Quantrill's eyes bulged. 'She *what*?'

He broke into a heavy run but Tait was ahead of him, the ends of his clover-pink trousers flapping as his legs scythed through the orchard grass.

# SIX

The orchard was vulgar with colour. Only a bad amateur painter would have sprayed so much pink and white apple blossom against so blue a sky, and splattered so many brilliant sunbursts of dandelion yellow against such vivid green grass. The old trailer was the sole drab feature, erupting like a weather-stained giant puff-ball from a patch of buttercups near the boundary hedge.

As Tait ran up, a hand emerged from the open doorway of the trailer to shake out a duster. It was followed by a suspicious head.

Mrs. Gedge was a smaller version of her husband, but unmistakably tougher: back straight, hair scraped into an uncompromising knot, glasses flashing formidably in the sunlight.

'And who may you be?' she demanded.

'Detective Sergeant Tait, county police. This—' as his superior pounded up '—is Chief Inspector Quantrill.'

She nodded, partially reassured. 'As long as you're not from the newspapers.'

'Mrs. Gedge,' said Quantrill, trying to control his panting breath, 'may I ask what you're doing?'

An ugly red flush spread upwards from her throat. 'If it's any concern of yours, I'm sorting out my daughter's things.'

Her voice was steady. At first glance Quantrill had thought her remarkably unmoved by Mary's death, but now he realised that what he had assumed to be bifocal lenses were in fact two small pools of tears, trapped against her high cheekbones by the frame of her glasses.

He took a deep breath and started again. 'I'm sorry, Mrs. Gedge. I'm very sorry about your daughter's death, and I apologise for this intrusion—but I'm afraid that what you're doing is very much our concern. In a case of sudden death it's our duty to investigate the circumstances, and we'd have liked to see your daughter's belongings just as she left them.'

The girl's mother stood straight and proud in the doorway of the trailer. 'There's nothing here to interest you, Chief Inspector. My Mary's dead. Let her rest.'

' 'I'm afraid that we have to find out how she died before we can do that,' Quantrill pointed out quietly.

'It was an accident. She went out early to pick flowers, slipped in the river and was drowned.'

'How do you know that?' Tait asked. 'Were you there, Mrs. Gedge?'

She turned on him. 'Of course I wasn't there! But what else could it have been? She didn't jump in deliberately, if that's what you mean—that would be sinful. And you've not come here to tell me that somebody killed her, because I know different. Charlie Godbold came and told us himself. A clean death, he said—she wasn't harmed in any way.'

'Yes. But we still need to know exactly what happened,' Quantrill explained patiently. 'There might have been witnesses, you see, and we have to find them.'

Mrs. Gedge shrugged. The movement released the tears from behind her glasses. They rolled down to her chin, gathering there for a moment before plopping singly onto the flat front of her cotton dress. 'That's no concern of mine. The Lord gave her to us, and in his wisdom he's taken her away again. I don't question his works, Chief Inspector.'

There were times when the chief inspector wished that he didn't have to question them either. 'May we look inside the trailer, please?' he asked.

'If you must. Not that you'll find anything. Mary was a good girl, and there's nothing here will tell you any different.'

'Then may I ask what you were doing here, Mrs. Gedge?' said Tait.

She raised the corners of her downturned mouth, giving a momentary impression of satisfaction. 'I was tidying up. She never let me give it a good turnout, and I wanted to be sure that she'd kept it clean. And she had. Even folded up her sleeping bag and washed her crockery before she went out.'

Mrs. Gedge stepped down from the doorway and let the policemen in. She followed them. The trailer was old-fash-

ioned, small-windowed and cramped with fittings, but scru-
pulously tidy. All the lockers and cupboards were open, their
contents laid out for inspection: clean crockery, a jar of instant
coffee and an opened packet of biscuits on the sink unit, a
sleeping bag folded on the bunk beside a pile of clean under-
clothes, an assortment of blouses and skirts and jeans hanging
from wire hangers on the outside of the wardrobe door, a heap
of folders and books stacked on the table beneath the window.
Apart from a transistor radio, and a calendar 'With Compliments and Thanks from R. J. Gedge, Draper and Family
Grocer, Ashthorpe,' hanging from the knob of a locker, there
was nothing else at all.

'Sellotape,' muttered Tait, who spotted it first. Quantrill
nodded.

'What have you taken down, Mrs. Gedge? Oh, come now.
Look, there are bits of sellotape on the walls—obviously things
were stuck here. What were they?'

'Rubbish!' she said vehemently. 'Just rubbishy photographs.
Actors and so-called singers.'

'Any photographs of real people? I mean, friends?'

'No.'

'Why did you take them down?'

'So that I could put them on the bonfire. Best place for
them. A lot of silliness, not suitable for a girl of her education.'

Quantrill riffled through the folders, but they appeared to
contain nothing but essays and school work. 'And what else did
you remove? Any personal letters?'

Two bright splotches warmed her cheeks. 'A few. Just ordinary letters from school friends. No point in keeping them.'

'Was there a letter from Mary herself? A note of any kind?'

Her chin lifted. 'No.'

'A diary?'

'No.'

Tait intervened. 'Where are the photographs and letters that
you're going to burn, Mrs. Gedge?'

Her mouth moved upward again, almost achieving the hori-
zontal. 'I've already put them on the bonfire. It's in the middle
of the orchard. Burned out by now, I should think.'

Quantrill jerked his head to Tait, but the sergeant was already on his way out of the trailer. The chief inspector looked
hard at the woman, trying to balance compassion against anger.

'I must point out to you, Mrs. Gedge, that it's a serious offence to conceal evidence from the police.'

She trembled with anger. 'Evidence of what? What have you got against my daughter? I'll tell you—nothing at all! She lived clean and she died clean, and there's nothing here will tell you any different!'

Quantrill could believe her. She had done her job with appalling thoroughness, destroying—with or without criminal intent—all evidence of her daughter's private life.

He stepped down from the trailer and walked over to the thickly blossomed hawthorn hedge. A gap, closed by a tattered section of wicker fencing, led on to a narrow country road; the fencing was wired to a branch of the hedge on one side, forming a crude gate. There were no houses within sight. On the opposite side of the road, as far as the eye could see, stretched a prairie farmer's lush green acreage of winter barley. It was an ideal back gate for someone who valued independence, a private exit where Mary could have come and gone without the knowledge either of family or of village gossips.

Quantrill turned again to the orchard. Tait was returning from the bonfire, and the chief inspector went to meet him.

The sergeant pulled a face. He held out a plastic evidence bag containing a few charred scraps of paper. 'Not much chance of turning up anything there,' he said in a low voice. 'It's a big permanent bonfire, a mound of ashes about six feet across—I should think they burn cartons and posters and the rest of the shop rubbish on it. I salvaged these pieces because they still felt warm, but forensic may find that they're just advertising material. Mrs. Gedge made a thorough job of it.'

They both glanced at her. She was standing outside the trailer, surreptitiously wiping her eyes as though ashamed to be caught displaying her grief. As soon as she saw them turn towards her she resumed her glasses and flashed them a challenging look. Quantrill sighed, and walked over to her.

'Can you tell me?' he asked gently, so as not to arouse her antagonism, 'when you last saw Mary?'

She tucked the handkerchief into the sleeve of her hand-knitted cardigan, folded her hands together and answered steadily: 'Last night, about half past seven. She helped her father, then came in and had supper and watched something on television. I didn't watch it myself, I've got better things to

45

do. The programme changed about half past seven, and she switched it off and went.'

'Back to the trailer?'

'I suppose so, I didn't ask her.'

'Did she say what she was going to do?'

'No.'

'Did she say she was going out?'

'No. I didn't beg for her confidences. You must ask her father, she talked enough to him.'

'Did you see a light in the trailer last night?' Tait asked.

Mrs. Gedge looked at him contemptuously. 'How could I? It's too far to see from the house when the leaves are on the trees. I didn't pry into Mary's affairs. Not that there was any reason to, she did nothing I could be ashamed of, nothing.'

'But you must have been worried when she didn't come in for breakfast this morning,' Quantrill commented.

Mrs. Gedge shrugged. 'I didn't expect to see her. She never ate breakfast, just made herself a cup of coffee in the trailer.'

Tait brought out his notebook. 'Did you know any of Mary's friends, Mrs. Gedge?'

'Yes, she brought one of them here. Sally Leggett—she seemed a decent kind of girl.'

'Do you happen to know her address?'

'She lived somewhere in Breckham Market, that's all I know. She hasn't been here since last summer—I don't know why not, I always made her welcome.'

'What about the other people Mary knew?' Quantrill asked. 'Did she have any special friends here in Ashthorpe?'

'No. All her friends were girls from the school. I've told you, Chief Inspector, Mary was a respectable girl. There's nothing for you to find out about her.'

Quantrill decided that it would serve no useful purpose to suggest that Mary had had a boy-friend. 'One last question,' he said. 'What was your daughter wearing when you last saw her?'

'A pair of jeans,' Mrs. Gedge answered, tight-lipped with disapproval. 'I never liked them, but she wouldn't listen to me.'

The chief inspector softened his voice. 'Did you know that she was wearing a long dress when she was found?'

Mrs. Gedge looked up at him, and for the first time during the interview the lines on her face quivered and crumpled.

She shook her head, closing her eyes. 'I did wonder,' she said in a whisper. 'I couldn't find it here, and I didn't like to ask her father . . .' She dragged her handkerchief from her sleeve and blew her nose fiercely. 'A shameful extravagance, that dress,' she declared, 'no sense in it at all, but her father *would* indulge her. Well, then, she got up very early this morning and put on the dress to go out and pick flowers for May Day, and she slipped and fell in the river just like Charlie Godbold said. You don't need to waste your time looking for any other cause.'

She turned away dismissively. 'And a final question from me, Mrs. Gedge,' said Tait quickly. 'Would Mary have been wearing shoes when she went out?'

She stared at him with indignation. 'Of course Mary would have been wearing shoes! What do you think we are, heathens? Well, not shoes, but a pair of flip-flap sandal things. She lived in them during the summer.'

'You haven't found them here?'

Mrs. Gedge went back into the trailer and checked her inventory. Quantrill followed her. She shook her head: 'No, they're not here. Like I said, she'd have been wearing them . . . why—wasn't she?'

Quantrill shook his head. She closed her eyes and swallowed hard.

'Charlie said she wasn't harmed,' she said hoarsely. 'It's true, isn't it?'

'Quite true,' Quantrill said, with a confidence that he felt obliged to qualify: 'as far as we know.' He offered as much reassurance as he could. 'She was fully clothed, apart from her shoes, and we may well find them somewhere else in the meadow. Well, thank you for answering our questions, Mrs. Gedge. I'm sorry we had to bother you at such a distressing time.'

He waited for her to leave the trailer, then gathered up the pile of folders and passed them to Tait. He closed the door of the trailer behind him and turned the key in the lock. 'I'm afraid that I shall have to take these papers, and keep the key for a day or two—we may need to take another look inside. I hope we shan't have to trouble you again, but I must warn you that we may have some more questions to ask about the things you've destroyed. You understand?'

'Perfectly, Chief Inspector.' She stood straight and self-contained under the apple blossom, her hands folded in front of her; only the red patches on her cheeks and the pools of tears that had collected again behind her lenses gave evidence of her emotion. 'You'll find me at home whenever you want me.'

'Yes—well, thank you. We'll see ourselves out by the back way.' Disconcerted by her composure, Quantrill fumbled clumsily with the loop of wire that fastened the makeshift gate. Tait came to his rescue with deft fingers. They stepped out into the narrow road, and fastened the gate behind them. To their left, the road wound away across the vast open field of young barley towards the church tower of the next village. They turned right, walking beside the hedge that bounded the orchard, on a course roughly parallel with the village street.

'Interesting. . .' said Detective Sergeant Tait.

'I don't like it,' said Chief Inspector Quantrill. 'Not,' he added quickly, 'that I think that the mother was concealing a suicide note, or anything like that. Though she would have done, of course, if she'd found one. What did you make of her?'

'I agree, sir. I don't believe that there was a note of that kind, or her attitude would have been different. I very much doubt whether Mrs. Gedge found anything that seemed to her significant at all—though whether the things she burned would have been useful to us is another matter. I'd like to have seen those letters and photographs, but from what that bag Daph said to me outside the shop, it seems that Mary Gedge had certainly led a virtuous life. There's no gossip in the village about her at all.'

'Don't you believe it,' said Quantrill sardonically. 'There'd be gossip in a village about the Archangel Gabriel. If nothing's known against Mary, it'll be a matter of nods and winks and "Still waters run deep" and "What's behind it, eh?" Villages can be unpleasant places to live in. I expect you think that country life's idyllic, but you'll soon find that there's a surprising amount of spare hatred about.'

Tait, who had always found the idea of country life as attractive as that of a meal of limp lettuce, was interested to hear that it had more substance than he had supposed.

'You can see what worried Mrs. Gedge,' Quantrill went on. 'She didn't know what her daughter got up to, and so she suspected the worst. After all, her son had let her down badly. In a village, you see, everybody is expected to be the same—

48

anyone who gets on in the world is disliked for it. When I was a boy, a family of three girls in my village worked their way to grammar school and university, and you should have heard the envy and nastiness there was about it! I reckon there must have been a lot of righteous glee in Ashthorpe when Derek Gedge was caught and tied down, and the gossips would have had a marvellous time if it turned out that his sister hadn't been virtuous either. No wonder her mother wanted to sort her things out before we came! Oh, she knew the burning was wrong, but she was more relieved than guilty. I agree with you, I don't think she found anything to Mary's discredit.'

The road swung sharply to the right, rounded the back of some farm buildings, passed between the walls of the garage and the junior school playground, and then formed a dusty T-junction with the main street of the village. There were no cars in the garage forecourt, no children in the playground. A dog barked in the distance, but otherwise all was quiet. Across the street, in front of the Ostrich inn, was an island of grass, and on it an old man sat on a seat beneath a white-candled chestnut tree; like Ashthorpe, he dozed in the early afternoon sun.

The policemen stood surveying the scene. 'So Mary Gedge went out on the quiet, wearing her long dress and a pair of sandals, some time after seven thirty last night,' said Tait with relish. 'Well, someone must know a great deal more than either of her parents . . . the boy-friend, Dale Kenward, for one. But while we're still in the village, I'd like to have a word with her brother.'

'According to Godbold,' Quantrill pointed out, 'Mary and her brother haven't been seeing each other since he married.'

'According to Godbold,' said Tait briskly, 'motorised policemen no longer have any idea of what's going on in their own villages. If Mary and Derek were once very close, I think it would be worth having a word with him while we're here.'

'We need to check with anyone who might have seen her,' Quantrill agreed. 'Certainly the boy-friend, and the girl Sally Leggett too.' He hesitated. 'Since the school's on holiday, we can probably get their addresses from Mrs. Bloomfield, the deputy headmistress. She'll be able to tell us where to find the school secretary, anyway. We might as well call, since we're so close.'

'Would it save time, sir,' asked Tait, 'if I go to see Derek Gedge while you call on Mrs. Bloomfield?'

The question was innocuous enough, but Tait observed that an extraordinary change seemed to be coming over the chief inspector: the back of his neck was reddening; he looked uncomfortable, almost embarrassed.

'Well, no,' said Quantrill hastily, 'as a matter of fact I think it will be quicker if you come with me. Mrs. Bloomfield can probably give us some useful information, a number of names, and it'll be simpler if you're there to write them down. Come on, we might as well walk, it's only just round the corner.'

He squared his shoulders and strode down the road and round the corner to the green. Tait followed him, hitching Mary Gedge's folders underneath his arm and raising a thoughtful eyebrow. So the chief inspector knew Mrs. Bloomfield, and was embarrassed by the prospect of being alone with her . . .

Not only were there significant enquiries to be made about Mary Gedge's death; it seemed that an interesting sidelight on Chief Inspector Quantrill's personality was about to be uncovered too.

Detective Sergeant Tait took a deep breath of country air, and found that it tasted unexpectedly piquant.

# SEVEN

Two small detached early Victorian villas stood side by side on the far edge of the narrow village green, almost opposite the war memorial. They were as neat, pretty and symmetrical as the houses that small girls used dutifully to cross-stitch on contemporary samplers. Each house had two chimneys, one at either end of the shallow slated roof, a central front door, a sashed window on either side of the door and three sashed windows above. They were faced with grey brick and bright with white paint except for their doors, one of which was dark blue, the other primrose yellow. Both had neat front gardens behind iron railings, though the owner of the blue door went in for time-consuming bedding plants while his neighbour preferred the simplicity of gravel and hydrangea bushes.

Chief Inspector Quantrill, having made up his mind to the visit, marched determinedly across the daisied green, crossed the narrow unmade access road, passed Saxe Villa and came to a halt at the yellow door of Coburg House. Detective Sergeant Tait, his arms filled with folders, stood a pace behind and watched with amusement as Quantrill smoothed down his hair, adjusted his tie and buttoned his jacket before ringing the bell.

'You know Mrs. Bloomfield, sir?' Tait probed politely.

'Yes—she was headmistress of the girls' grammar school while my daughters were there. She was very kind to them. I was a sergeant at the time, divisional crime prevention officer, and Mrs. Bloomfield invited me to give a talk to the sixth form.' Quantrill eased his collar and rang the bell again. 'She said the talk was very good,' he added defensively.

'Does her husband work locally?' enquired Tait, all blue-eyed innocence.

'She's a widow,' said Quantrill shortly.

'Ah.' Tait sucked in his cheeks to hide his grin. 'An elderly lady, I imagine?'

Quantrill saw from the corner of his eye that Tait's lips were twitching, and glowered; there were clearly going to be drawbacks to having a sergeant who didn't miss much. 'She's out, anyway,' he said with regretful relief. He lingered for a moment on the doorstep and a spare ageing man, straight-backed but just beginning to weaken at the knees, emerged from the door of Saxe Villa with a straw shopping basket in his hand.

'Good afternoon,' he called across the narrow intervening side gardens. 'Mrs. Bloomfield is out.'

The policemen left Coburg House and joined the man on the access road. His vertically creased face had a yellowish tropical tinge and he spoke in a dry, gravelly voice, as though he were permanently thirsty.

'Good afternoon, sir,' Quantrill replied pleasantly. 'County police, just making some routine enquiries. Do you happen to know whether Mrs. Bloomfield is likely to be back this after-noon?'

The man's cloudy eyes brightened, as though even a routine police enquiry had added zest to his day. He stood taller. 'M'name's Finlay,' he said briskly. 'I haven't actually spoken to Mrs. Bloomfield since she returned this morning from her holiday, but I saw her go out just after two o'clock. Wearing tennis clothes, so I imagine she won't be away long. Does that help at all?'

Quantrill smiled at his keenness. 'Very much, thank you, sir. We'll come back later, then.'

'Can I be of any help with your enquiries?' Mr. Finlay offered.

'I'm afraid not—it's a matter of finding the addresses of some of Mrs. Bloomfield's pupils.'

Mr. Finlay nodded glumly, knees going again, the zest departing from his day. 'Yes, I see. Well, I'm sure Mrs. Bloomfield won't be late. I was surprised that she'd want to go out playing tennis so soon after she got back from France, but obviously her holiday must have improved her health. And then, of course, she's young . . . I only wish I had her stamina.'

The policemen thanked him and walked away. Tait's grin broadened. 'Do you play tennis yourself, sir?' he asked with wicked courtesy.

Before Quantrill could make an appropriately forceful reply, a police van came bucketing up the dirt road behind them. Pc Godbold put his head out of the window.

'Been trying to contact you, sir. We've found the sandals—in that muck just above the bridge, where you suggested. And Mrs. Gedge has identified them as Mary's.'

'*Both* sandals?' Tait asked, disappointed.

'Both.' Godbold was relieved, thinking that Tait's theory had been demolished. 'And they're definitely Mary's, because she'd put her initials on the inner sole.'

'Good,' said Quantrill. 'Thank you very much, Charlie, that's a great help. I don't think we'll need you any more. Well—' he turned to Tait, relief in his own voice. 'So there's no reason why Mary couldn't have walked down to the river on her own. Took her shoes off when she got there, balanced them on the parapet, perhaps, while she picked flowers, and a passing vehicle knocked them off.'

Tait was unimpressed. 'Perhaps,' he agreed. 'On the other

hand, the fact that she was wearing shoes doesn't prove that she was alone, or that she didn't go by car. After all—'

'I know,' conceded Quantrill. 'We still haven't accounted for her movements after half past seven last night.'

He paused for a moment. They were just passing the war memorial, a tall granite cross erected on an octagonal stepped base, which stood on the edge of the green a few yards back from the main road. The names of the fallen in two world wars were incised on the shaft of the cross, and a wreath of British Legion poppies, battered after a winter of exposure and of mishandling by village children, leaned crookedly against the upper step. Beside it lay a bunch of wilted buttercups.

Quantrill picked up the flowers. They flopped over his hand, as wild flowers do when they have been gathered and left waterless in the sun for several hours. By tomorrow they would be dead. He held them for a moment, thinking that they must have been gathered at about the same time as the ones that had floated round Mary Gedge's body; but then, there were buttercups asking to be gathered on the roadside verge just opposite the memorial. He replaced the flowers tidily.

'All right,' he said to Tait, 'we'll go and see whether Mary's brother knows what she was doing last night.'

They collected the chief inspector's car from outside Mr. Gedge's shop and drove to the address that Godbold had given them. Derek Gedge lived with his wife's family in Jubilee Crescent, a row of terraced houses that had been erected to commemorate the twenty-fifth year of the reign of King George the Fifth by a local council which had more concern for keeping down the rates than for the convenience of its tenants. The houses in Jubilee Crescent had been built with neither bathrooms, kitchen sinks nor indoor lavatories. But Ashthorpe was now high on the council's list for the provision of twentieth-century plumbing, and it had begun to seem possible that the tenants might be able to celebrate the Silver Jubilee of George the Fifth's grand-daughter by walking to the privy in the rain without getting their feet wet.

The houses all had large well-kept gardens, with flowers and grass in the front and vegetables at the back; with one exception. Quantrill, remembering Godbold's description of the Pulfer family, made unerringly for the house whose front garden was a wreckage of rank grass, rubbish and weeds. He was not surprised to find the garden ornamented by a rusting bicycle, upside down, tyre cover off and inner tube hanging limp, abandoned half-way through some long-ago repair operation.

The most prominent feature of the garden was, though, a pram. It stood near the front door, vibrating with sound; from its interior, a fruity masculine voice belted out a pop song with a crashing drum and guitar backing. The policemen peered suspiciously into the pram and found it occupied by a toddler, flushed but soundly asleep, with a transistor radio for company.

Tait was appalled. He put his hand out to the radio, but Quantrill pulled him back. 'When they're asleep,' he advised with paternal wisdom, 'leave 'em alone.'

Tait shrugged, and pressed the front door bell. He heard no ring, and banged the knocker.

A thin ginger woman, with prominent eyes in a flat round face and a small turned-down nose, peered at him owlishly through a narrow gap between the door and its frame. 'If you've come about the rent,' she said, 'it'll be paid right up next week.'

'We're police officers,' said Tait briskly. 'Is Mr. Derek Gedge here?'

The woman opened the door further and stuck out her head, goggling with interest. 'What's he done?' she shrieked. 'What's he gone and done?'

'Nothing, as far as we know,' said Tait. 'We'd just like a word with him. May we come in?'

The woman looked disappointed. She opened the door wider. 'Suit yourselves,' she said. 'Derek's at work, though. Here, mind our Kevin's motor bike.'

Quantrill would have preferred to ask directions to her son-in-law's place of work, and leave; he'd met plenty of families like the Pulfers. But Tait was eager to see the kind of life that Derek Gedge had settled for as an alternative to Cambridge. He followed Mrs. Pulfer into the main room of the house, where a gleaming Japanese motorcycle stood just inside the door.

The room was hot. Despite the warmth and brightness of the day the window was closed and a fire burned in the hearth.

The room was littered with discarded clothes, abandoned newspapers and grubby soft toys. There was greasy plates on the table, and the smell of chips and vinegar lingered on the air. A plump girl of about twenty sprawled on the settee, wearing jeans and a thin sweater of knitted material that revealed only too clearly that she was not wearing a bra. She was flicking through a magazine called *True Confessions*.

Tait sized her up. She had lovely hair, red rather than her mother's shabby ginger, and full pouting lips. No wonder Derek Gedge had been attracted.

Aware of Tait as he was of her, the girl pretended to ignore him. She got up from the settee, pulled her sweater modestly down over her hips so as to make her nipples even more prominent, went to the mantelpiece and lit a cigarette. As she turned her back, the men saw the message patched on to the well-filled seat of her jeans: 'Make love not babies.'

'A bit late for that,' thought Quantrill caustically. Poor Derek Gedge . . . the girl's mouth reminded him of the big devouring lips of one of the occupants of his son's tank of tropical fish. He averted his eyes with an effort and, since Tait seemed to be temporarily silenced, spoke to the girl's mother.

'Sorry to disturb you, Mrs. Pulfer, but we thought your son-in-law might be at home today. I believe he works at the old station—can you tell me where that is?'

Interest replaced disappointment on the woman's face. She pushed her small beak confidentially up towards the chief inspector. 'Oh, he knows about his sister, if that's why you've come. He heard it at work and biked back specially to tell us at dinner time—only we knew, of course, my next-door heard it at the butcher's.'

'But he went back to work?' Tait asked.

Mrs. Pulfer's eyes rounded in incomprehension. 'Nothing for him to stop away for, was there? No sense in losing pay. Mind you, he was upset, eh, Julie? Couldn't fancy any dinner. Still, he was a bit off colour this morning, couldn't eat his breakfast neither. He's got a weak stomach, Derek has. Up with it half the night. Julie'll tell you.'

Julie, having lost Tait's interest, had flung herself back on the settee and picked up a copy of *Intimate Stories*. She inhaled deeply, and tapped ash from the end of her cigarette onto the floor. Mrs. Pulfer fumbled in the pocket of her ginger-brown cardigan, pulled out her own packet of cigarettes and tucked one into her mouth with a pecking motion of her head.

''Course,' she went on, '—chuck us your matches, Julie. Ta—we're sorry about Mary. Wouldn't have wished it on her for the world, but there . . . Fell in the river and drowned while she was picking flowers, Derek said.' Her unlit cigarette waggled with amusement. 'Picking flowers, I ask you, a girl of her age! But then, that's just about typical of Derek's sister, eh, Julie! Turned eighteen and still at school, I ask you!'

'Did Mary come here to visit her brother yesterday evening?' Tait asked.

Mrs. Pulfer was so indignant that she let the match burn out in her fingers. She snatched the cigarette from her mouth. 'Did she . . . ? You must be joking! That Mary's never been here in her life—too stuck up to visit us, wasn't she, Julie? Julie'll tell you—just the time of day if we happened to see her in the street, that's all we got from Mary Gedge, just as if we hadn't been related at all.'

'Perhaps they met somewhere else', suggested Tait. 'After all, they had a lot in common.'

'What would they want to meet anywhere else for?' demanded Mrs. Pulfer, her flat face blank. 'If they'd got so much in common, why couldn't she come here? I'll tell you why, we weren't good enough for Mary's precious brother, that's why. Not that I believe in speaking ill of the dead, but she tried to persuade Derek not to marry our Julie, I know that for a fact. The cheek of it, when my poor daughter was expecting his baby—'

She paused to concentrate on lighting her cigarette. From outside, the music from the transistor was augmented by a loud wailing. Mrs. Pulfer nodded vigorously, coughing over the smoke and pointing to the window. 'Derek's boy, her own nephew, that poor little child out there is—eh, Julie? But his own aunt didn't care tuppence for poor little Jason. Fatherless, that innocent child would have been, if Mary Gedge'd had her way. Julie'll tell you.'

Julie yawned delicately, arching her back and eyeing Tait. He ignored her. She shrugged, smiled to herself, moistened her full lips with the tip of her tongue and cuddled down with a copy of *True Romances*.

Quantrill asked the way to the chicken factory and quickly left the house, pausing as he reached the noisy, shaking pram. Its occupant, a little over a year old, was sitting up; nappy steaming, eyes screwed tight, face crimson, mouth cavernous, apoplectic with misery. The chief inspector bent down, grimacing over the long-forgotten ammoniac smell of wet nappies, and snapped off the transistor. The child stopped crying instantly, closing its mouth and opening a pair of eyes that were, like its hair, almost black—considerably darker than any eyes or hair the men had seen so far on either side of the family.

They returned to the car. 'My God, what a set-up,' said Tait. 'Are you still on the girl's side, sir?'

'Poor silly young Gedge,' Quantrill agreed. 'Ten to one the kid's not his.'

'It'll be interesting to see how he's taken his sister's death,' Tait said. 'You turn left here, and then keep straight on through the village, past the police house.'

'I know,' snapped Quantrill, 'I heard what she said, I'm not deaf.' And then, remembering the advantage Tait had taken of him on account of Mrs. Bloomfield, he made a jocular attempt to redress the balance. 'And not blind, either. Not wonder Julie's had the men after her—she's quite a piece, isn't she?'

Tait wrinkled his nose fastidiously. 'Did you think so, sir? Not my kind. She smells like a dirty ashtray.'

Quantrill drove in heavy silence to the site of the old railway station.

It was a mile out of the village on the Lillington road, the back way to Breckham Market. The railway line had been abandoned so long ago that sugar beet grew where the track must once have been. A gang of freelance beet-hoers, their cars left by the roadside, worked their way across the field chopping out the weeds that threatened to smother the young plants. As they bent over their hoes, they reverted to an age-old stance; no longer unmistakable citizens of the last quarter of the twentieth century, but archetypal agricultural labourers in a landscape.

In the middle of the beet field, the old station buildings stood in an isolated cluster, all smoke-stained brick and ornamental barge-boarding. The former station yard was crowded with cars and lorries, some of which were stacked high with wire crates containing what Tait assumed to be dead chickens; white feather and yellow claws protruded from between the wires.

The policemen walked past what had been the booking hall and waiting rooms, now occupied by the office staff, and made for the centre of activity, a former engine shed. It blared at them, loud with canned music and shouted voices and the hum of extractor fans.

At one end was an unloading bay. As they approached it, one of the lorries backed in and three or four youths began unloading the crates of chickens, heaving them from hand to hand and finally banging them down at the back of the ramp, where they were wrenched open one at a time.

A whistling youth thrust his hand into a newly opened crate and dragged out a crumpled bundle of feathers. To Tait's surprise and disgust, the bird was alive. It squawked and flapped in its moment of freedom from confinement, but the youth promptly seized its legs and swung the bird upside down, shackling its claws with nonchalant expertise on to the clips of a conveyor chain that moved at shoulder height into the engine shed.

'Enough to turn you vegetarian, places like this,' Quantrill said gloomily into Tait's ear. His work in rural police divisions had taken him often enough into slaughterhouses, but he had never overcome his sense of depression at their sights, their sounds, their smells, their frighteningly casual doing-to-death. 'Ah, that looks like the foreman.'

They approached a harrassed-looking man in a long white coat and a white trilby hat. He scowled at them over the clipboard he was writing on.

'County police,' said Quantrill briskly. 'We'd like a quick word with Derek Gedge, please.'

The man's scowl deepened. 'Why—has he done anything?' he demanded. 'Because if it's just about his sister, he knows. One of the girls in the office had a phone call this morning from her mother, and I passed the news on to him. I offered him the rest of the day off, but he knows we're short-staffed and he said he'd go on working.'

'We'd still like a word,' said Quantrill.

'The line's running,' objected the man. 'He's on the killing machine—I can't stop the whole line, we're behind as it is.'

Quantrill disliked having to pull his rank, but there were times when it was undeniably useful. 'Chief Inspector Quantrill,' he said quietly. 'Will you get someone to take his place in the line, please. We sha'n't keep him long.'

The man looked taken aback and turned away quickly, shouting instructions above the din. In a few moments, a young man came towards them. Like the other workers he wore rubber boots, a long white coat and a white cotton cap; like theirs, his whiteness was fouled. There was blood all over him, blood on his face, blood on his cap, blood on his coat, blood on his hands.

# EIGHT

Quantrill kept his eyes steadily on Derek Gedge's, trying to ignore the splatter of blood on the young man's forehead and the chicken down that clung to his unkempt hair. Like his dead sister, Derek was blond and blue-eyed; like hers, his features were attractively regular. But he looked unwell: his face was pale and moist, his eyes heavy.

'You want to see me?' His light, colourless voice was strangely at odds with his bloodied appearance.

Quantrill beckoned him out into the sunshine, away from the worst of the noise, and introduced himself and Tait. 'Sorry to bother you, Mr. Gedge, but we have to clear up one or two matters about your sister's death.'

Derek Gedge looked from one to the other and wiped his forehead with the back of his hand. 'Oh yes?' he said dully.

Quantrill decided to go straight to the point: 'Did you see your sister last night?'

'No.'

'At any time yesterday?'

'No. We don't—we didn't meet.'

'But you live in the same village,' Tait pointed out. 'You couldn't help meeting her occasionally. When did you last see her?'

Derek Gedge was irritated out of his composure. 'I don't know!' he snapped. 'A week, ten days ago—how the hell do you expect me to remember a detail like that? Yes of course we saw each about the village sometimes, and when we met we'd say "Hallo". But we didn't socialise, and I certainly didn't see her yesterday. OK?'

'Yes, thank you.' Quantrill spoke pleasantly, to take the edge off the questioning. 'We have to try to trace your sister's movements yesterday evening, you see. Your mother-in-law told us that Mary didn't go to Jubilee Crescent, but we wondered whether you might have seen her elsewhere.'

At the mention of Jubilee Crescent, Derek's mouth twisted. 'You've been there, have you?'

'We thought we might find you there,' said Quantrill, 'in the circumstances.'

Derek gave an abrupt, unamused laugh. 'Well, now that you've had a look at my domestic life, you'll know why I prefer being at work.'

'But in a place like this?' asked Tait. 'When you've just heard of your sister's death?'

Derek Gedge stared at the sergeant with dislike. 'Look,' he said with pale intensity. 'I loved my sister, OK? Just because we had a family row and didn't meet any more, it doesn't mean that I'm not upset by her death. I'm shocked, sick, numbed— oh for God's sake leave me alone.'

He turned away, distressed, but Quantrill called him back. 'I'm sorry, Mr. Gedge, but the point is that someone might have been with Mary just before her death. We've spoken to your father and he says that she often went for walks down by the river. Tell me, who would she be most likely to go for walks with?'

Derek stood with his eyes stubbornly downcast. 'I don't know.'

'But surely she wouldn't go alone?' said Tait. 'An attractive girl like Mary—come on, you must have some idea.'

'I don't *know*!' Derek Gedge pulled off his stained cotton cap in a gesture of exasperation and rubbed it over his damp forehead. 'I haven't talked to Mary since I got married—that's nearly eighteen months ago, she'll have done a lot of growing up since then. It's no use asking me anything about her.'

'But you haven't been completely out of touch,' said Tait. 'You must have heard things about her, whether you met her or not; that she was going to Cambridge—to King's—for example.'

The bitter grin returned. 'Oh yes; I heard about that, from several sources. You'd be amazed how many people wanted to be sure that I knew where she was going.'

'Right—so you do hear about your sister. Come on, then, tell me—did she have a boy-friend in Ashthorpe?'

'I *don't know!*' Derek Gedge was sweating freely. He rubbed his cap over his smeared face again, and appealed to Quantrill. 'Look, it's no use your badgering me, I honestly can't tell you anything about Mary. I'm shattered, that's all I know. Can I go back to work now?'

Quantrill nodded, but walked beside him towards the old engine shed. The powerful beat of the music and the barbaric smell of freshly fallen blood met them even before they reached the building.

Tait came up quietly on Derek Gedge's other side.

'Lovely place, Cambridge,' mused the sergeant, 'particularly at this time of year. Delightful to be in a punt on the Backs just now, with a good friend and a couple of intelligent, attractive girls . . .'

Gedge whirled on him with a look of hatred. 'All right,' he snarled, 'don't rub my nose in it! God, don't you think I hate working here? But I'll tell you something: everyone in Ashthorpe thinks that my mother made me give up Cambridge and marry Julie Pulfer against my will, but it isn't true. I married her because I wanted to. I was blindly in love with her and I felt—well, chivalrous, if you want to know. Proud to be shouldering a man's responsibilities. That's what I tried to explain to Mary, but she didn't understand. That's why we had the row.'

Tait raised a sardonic eyebrow. 'You mean you've no regrets about your marriage?'

Gedge answered him contemptuously. 'Don't be a fool, man! I was telling you what I felt at the time, what made me give up Cambridge. But now—you've seen for yourself the pig-sty the

Pulfers live in. And have you seen Jason, my unaccountably dark-eyed son? Have you taken a good look at this place? Well, all of this is the price I'm having to pay—not, as everyone thinks, for the sexual experience, but for being a romantic idiot. My sister told me that I was too young to marry and that I'd regret it, and I've never been able to forgive her for being right. That doesn't mean that I don't grieve over her death—but you know something? Even after what's happened to her, even though she hasn't lived to enjoy her success, I'm not sure that she isn't still the lucky one.'

He strode away, jamming his cap back on his head. The policemen watched as he leaped up onto the concrete platform at the end of the shed, the continuation of the ramp where the chickens were unloaded. The conveyor chain entered the shed at this end, dangling the wriggling black-eyed birds at regular intervals and bearing them to a place where a machine stood, and attendant youths with knives.

Derek Gedge stood shoulder to shoulder with one of the youths, watching the sudden flurry of activity as each bird arrived, waiting to get back into the rhythm of the production line.

Quantrill, knowing the process, would have left; but Tait lingered, watching with incredulous distaste as the birds, stunned by an electric shock from the machine, had their throats slit. The dead chickens flapped and jerked violently in their final nervous spasm, their wings beating the youths about the face, their down rising in a dusty cloud to cling wherever their falling blood had splattered.

Sickened, Tait stood as though his shoes had been cemented to the bloodstained concrete floor. The grotesque chorus line of dead birds dipped and swayed on their hooks across the shed, plunging into tanks of scalding water, entering a plucking machine, and then emerging naked to be slapped down on another conveyor belt for evisceration and packing by a team of women. In a matter of minutes, living creatures were being transformed before his eyes into hunks of graded, quality controlled, hygienically packaged, inexpensive protein.

Quantrill pulled at his sergeant's sleeve and led him outside. They stood for a few minutes by the car, and the chief inspector considerately looked away to give Tait time to recover.

'All right?'

Tait nodded. The delicate green had disappeared from his cheeks, though he was almost as pale as Derek Gedge had been.

'I know what you're thinking,' said Quantrill. 'Yes, it's a brutalising job. God knows how anyone as sensitive as Derek Gedge could have contemplated it in the first place.'

'If he's stuck it for eighteen months,' muttered Tait, 'his sensibilities must be pretty well blunted by now.'

They sat in the car and clipped on their seat belts. Quantrill glanced at Tait again and grinned.

'There's a lot to be said,' he suggested, 'for a station sergeant's job in Yarchester . . .'

But Tait was determined not to concede a single point. He swallowed. 'Do you think so, sir?' he said heroically. 'I've found this a very interesting experience—I wouldn't have missed it.'

Quantrill accelerated out of the yard, still grinning. This was one he had to win. 'But you won't fancy eating chicken for a while,' he prophesied confidently.


Alan Denning, BSc (Econ), headmaster of Breckham Market comprehensive school, lived in one of the detached houses that had been built in the 'sixties along Mere Road. Formerly, when Breckham was nothing but a declining market town, the road had been simply a farm track that skirted a circle of murky water in a rough meadow on the outskirts of the ancient borough. But then an arrangement with the London County Council had brought to the town an influx of factories, people and relative prosperity, and the meadow had quickly spawned an estate of desirable freehold properties.

The houses on the Mere estate were built in a variety of sizes and designs, none of which harmonised in either style or materials with the original buildings of the town. The new roofs were pitched too low, the windows were disproportionately large, the brickwork was either too yellow or too pink; there were too many spurious external features in white plastic shiplap and simulated Cotswold stone. The developers seemed not to know, and the planning authority of the time not to care, that the local building materials were flint and grey brick.

The largest of the houses on the estate, the executive type with separate dining-room and downstairs cloakroom, had been built on Mere Road itself, facing the attractively tree-lined, dredged and deodorised Mere. Unfortunately for the owners of these houses, the Mere had immediately become a local beauty spot. On summer evenings and at weekends, strange cars were parked outside every house and the air pulsated with chimes from prowling ice-cream vans trying to steal each other's pitches. Litter proliferated.

As a consequence, the Mere Road residents felt themselves beleaguered. Quantrill was not entirely surprised, when he drew up outside the Dennings' house, to see a whiskered face glaring at him supiciously from over the white ranch fencing. It was a face that he had seen on numerous occasions, in photographs in the local newspaper; Mr. Denning was not averse to publicity, for himself or for his school.

Denning reluctantly led the policemen up the weedless drive, past a regimented area of grass. He was, Quantrill knew, in his late thirties: of medium height, inclined to be porky, but dapper in neat, plain, casual clothes. His hands and feet were small and constantly active.

'*Chief* Inspector, did you say?' he demanded as he opened the front door.

Quantrill confirmed it, and Denning looked slightly mollified. A sergeant on his own, both policemen guessed, would have been offered short shrift. Tait was sorry not to have been given the opportunity to take up the challenge.

Denning darted in ahead of them, stopping abruptly to wipe his shoes on the mat with an exaggerated care that Quantrill interpreted as a hint and passed on to Tait, who chose to ignore it.

'Quantrill,' said Denning. His voice was crisp, authoritative. 'I know the name.'

'My son's at your school,' said Quantrill, without any expectation that the head of a school of nearly a thousand pupils would be personally acquainted with any particular thirteen-year-old; it was simply the name that people remembered.

'Ah yes.' Denning nodded rapidly, stroking his whiskers. He had a carefully groomed luxuriant brown growth on either side of his jaw, compensating for the prematurely bald swathe on either side of his crown. 'Yes, now, let me think. Yes, Quantrill— a good lad, you must be pleased with his progress.'

The chief inspector was not deceived. He could understand

that a headmaster faced by a succession of importunate parents might well be tempted to deal, like an astrologer, in bland generalities. But Quantrill had not come in his rôle of parent, and he found the headmaster's glib response distasteful.

But then, he acknowledged, he was not predisposed to like the man. It had been assumed in the town that when the three secondary schools were amalgamated, the headship was likely to go to the head of either the boys' or the girls' grammar school. Quantrill had been a discreetly ardent supporter of Mrs. Bloomfield. She had held her appointment for five years, was well-qualified, liked and respected in the town. It had seemed to him—and to most of the other parents he knew—a matter of natural justice that Mrs. Bloomfield should be appointed in preference to Mr. Denning, who was a newcomer to the area, no better qualified, slightly younger, and had been headmaster of the boys' school for only a year.

Quantrill still felt aggrieved about the man's appointment; less, now, for the sake of the school, which seemed to be settling down tolerably well, than on Mrs. Bloomfield's behalf.

'Come into my study,' Denning said. It was a command rather than an invitation.

He led them into what must have been designed as the dining-room of the house; Mere Road executive houses were not, like the managerial type overlooking the golf course, in the separate study bracket. It had been made into a masculine room, dark-toned, well-ordered, furnished with PVC leatherlook armchairs and a polished desk considerably larger than Quantrill's own.

Denning stood with his hands clasped behind his back and looked hard at Quantrill, while he rose and fell impatiently on the balls of his feet.

'Well, Chief Inspector?'

He made no suggestion that they should sit down, and Quantrill's dislike increased. He studied the whiskers, deciding that they were less an expression of a naturally flamboyant personality than a consciously contrived feature, like the Cotswold stone cladding on the front of the house. But if Denning's conservative style of dress ruled out natural flamboyance, there was no doubt about the man's nervous energy; he fizzed with it.

'I'm afraid,' said Quantrill quickly, before Denning's impatience could boil over, 'that we have some bad news about one of your pupils.'

A car slowed outside. Denning hurried to the side window and craned to see it. The car picked up speed. He turned back and sat at his desk, motioning his visitors to sit down.

'Mary Gedge?' he asked, grooming his whiskers rapidly with small fingers. 'Ah, I thought that might be the reason for your visit. Yes, I heard about the accident. My deputy, Mrs. Bloomfield, lives in the same village, and she very properly rang me as soon as she heard the news. She thought that there might be some press enquiries. In fact I had a local reporter here just before you came.'

He stood up abruptly, glaring out of the window again as a passing ice-cream van gave a quick burst of 'Oranges and Lemons.' 'Mary's death,' he went on, as smoothly as though he were repeating a prepared statement, 'is a great shock, of course. A tragedy. I am deeply grieved, as I know the rest of the school will be.'

'You knew her well, Mr. Denning?' Quantrill asked.

'Not socially, Chief Inspector.' His right hand went instinctively to the broad wedding ring he wore, twisting and turning it. 'But in school, yes, of course. Mary was one of my most outstanding students.'

'She was at Mrs. Bloomfield's school until last summer,' Quantrill pointed out, irritated by the 'my' and unprepared to let the girl's new headmaster attempt to hog all the credit. 'My daughters were at that school too—Mrs. Bloomfield is an excellent teacher.'

'She certainly brought Mary along very well, I agree. I have heard a number of reports of what a good teacher she used to be.'

'"Used to be?"' demanded Quantrill.

Denning gave a deprecating shrug: 'One doesn't, of course, wish to criticise a colleague's work, but frankly I've seen remarkably little of the great teaching ability that I'd been told Mrs. Bloomfield possessed. I realise that her failure to get the headship of the comprehensive must have been a great disappointment to her, but it was not unexpected. She has considerable responsibility as my deputy, and I would have thought that this was ample recompense. But possibly she feels inhibited by the presence of male colleagues—she'd have done better, I think, to move to another small girls' school. She seems to find it difficult to adjust to the new circumstances—but then, perhaps, her age . . .'

Quantrill fumed in silence. Mrs. Bloomfield was in her early forties, about the same age as his own wife, who would indignantly repudiate any suggestion that there was reason to make allowance for her on that account.

Denning saw the chief inspector's indignant look. 'As for Mary Gedge,' he went on quickly, 'she was handicapped in the way common to all girls in single-sex education. I could see the girl's academic potential as soon as I met her, but her mind lacked that—' he smiled confidently at the policemen, assuming a male consensus as he gestured with his right hand, bringing his fingertips close together '—that *edge*. You know? I think that my extra tutoring—the contact with a masculine mind—made a great deal of difference to her. After all, it was at my school that she gained her Cambridge entrance. That will still stand to the credit of the school, despite her death.'

Quantrill stared at him, bemused. He had heard his daughters talk about male chauvinist pigs, and had been confident that they exaggerated. Now it seemed that he had met one.

But Tait was not bemused. 'You gave Mary extra tutoring, sir?'

Denning stroked his whiskers. 'Oh yes, on a number of occasions.'

'*Private* tutoring, sir?' enquired Tait.

# NINE

Denning froze. The hairless areas of his face went white. His whiskers bristled.

'Yes, Sergeant,' he said, chipping each word out of ice. 'Private tutoring. *During* the autumn term, *in* my office at school, and *during* school hours. And not only to Mary Gedge, but to three other Oxbridge candidates. Do I make myself clear?'

'Perfectly, thank you,' said Tait equably.

Denning turned his attention to Quantrill. The chief inspector had by now realised the function of the whiskers: they could make an angry man of otherwise insignificant appearance seem formidable. No wonder his son held the headmaster in awe.

'Let me tell you, Chief Inspector,' said Denning, 'exactly what I told the newspaper reporter. Mary Gedge left my school at the start of the Easter holidays, two weeks ago. Her *death* has no connection with my school at all. I'm obliged to you for coming to break the news to me, but if that's all—?'

Quantrill had no wish to prolong the interview. He asked, stiffly, for permission to approach the school secretary for the addresses of Mary's friends, and stood up. Denning bounced out of his chair and darted to open the door, clearly glad that his visitors were going.

'You'll find my secretary at the school until five o'clock. I'll let her know what you want, and tell her to give you every cooperation. Er—my wife is away at the moment, I'm afraid, otherwise I might have offered you tea.' He gestured vaguely towards the end of the hall, as though the kitchen regions were located behind a green baize door which he himself never penetrated.

'That's quite all right, thank you,' said Quantrill, one hand on the front door. 'Oh, one other thing. We've had some instances in the town of young people being found in possession of drugs—usually amphetamines, but sometimes cannabis in one form or another. You'll have read the cases in the local paper, no doubt. I know that you would report it to us if any drug taking or pushing came to your knowledge, but it's a very big school and you can't know all your pupils. Do you think it's at all possible that any of the seniors *might* be involved?'

Denning's whiskers reinforced his fierce answer. 'Not in *my* school, Chief Inspector.'

Quantrill gave him a long, thoughtful look. 'No, of course not . . . Thank you for sparing so much of your time.'

As he opened the door, an orange mini turned on to the drive. Denning almost pushed the policemen out of the way as he hurried from the house and tried to wave the mini on towards the two-car garage, but the woman driver stopped and smiled enquiringly up at Quantrill and Tait from the open window as they edged past.

Denning joined them, looking embarrassed. 'Ah, there you are, my dear. These gentlemen are just going. Er—Mr. Quantrill, my wife.'

The chief inspector sent Tait out to his car to initiate a call to the school secretary, while he murmured politely to Mrs. Denning. To his surprise she scrambled out of the car to talk to him. She was her husband's age, small and dark and intense and breathy. A travelling case lay on the passenger seat of the car.

'Mr. Quantrill?' she gabbled. '*The* Mr. Quantrill—the chief inspector? I read about your promotion. Congratulations!'

Quantrill took the hand she thrust at him and returned a modification of her smile. He was susceptible, but wary, scenting a marital dispute. Denning's whiskers were making furious 'Where the hell have you *been*?' signals but his wife was deliberately ignoring him, chatting with brittle effusiveness in an obvious attempt to postpone her interview with her husband.

Denning took her arm and tried to draw her away. Her eyes darkened. His grip must have been hurting her, but she managed not to flinch. 'Are you here on business, Mr. Quantrill?' she asked. 'There's nothing wrong, I hope?'

'Nothing at all,' said Denning briskly. 'Come into the house, Sonia, I'll put your car away later. Good afternoon, Chief Inspector.'

Quantrill turned to go; other people's marital problems were an unnecessary reminder of his own. But Tait, who had returned and summarised the scene, wanted to discover whether it was anything more than anger at her apparent lateness that made Denning so anxious to get his wife away from their company.

'A very sad business, Mrs. Denning,' he said, ignoring her husband. 'One of the girls who left school at Easter has just died. We came to let your husband know. One of the senior girls, you might perhaps have met her—Mary Gedge.'

The effect on Mrs. Denning was more than he had bargained for. She went white. Her hand went up to her mouth. '*Mary* . . . dead?'

'An accident,' said her husband quickly. 'She fell into the river at home, at Ashthorpe, and was drowned.'

Mrs. Denning leaned against the car for support. 'Oh, what a tragedy! Such a pleasant girl, I liked her so much. We both did, didn't we, Alan? But it's incredible that she should be dead . . . I mean, she was here, alive and well, only yesterday evening. I met her at the gate, just as I was going out. She was bringing one of your books back, wasn't she, Alan?'

There was a pause. Denning found the policemen's eyes on him. He nodded.

'Can you tell us what time this was, Mrs. Denning?'

She looked from her husband's set face to Quantrill's stern eyebrows, and knew that something was wrong. 'Er—half-past eight?' she said uncertainly. 'That would be about it, wouldn't it, Alan?'

'It didn't occur to him that it was relevant, my foot!' snorted Quantrill. The policemen were leaving the Dennings' house for the second time that afternoon. 'He was scared stiff—not necessarily because he knows any more than he told us, but because he doesn't want to harm his public image. The man's a pig if ever I met one—I'm sorry for poor Mrs. Bloomfield, I can't imagine how she puts up with working as his deputy. As for Mrs. Denning, I don't blame her walking out on him— even if it was only for one night. Pity she rushed off before seeing the girl go, though.'

'Well, at least we've established that Mary was in Breckham last night, and wearing the dress she was found in. And according to Mrs. Denning, Mary said she'd been given a lift to Breckham by a friend.'

'But we don't know who, any more than we know what she proposed to do for the remainder of the evening, or how she was going to get back home.'

Tait clipped his seat belt. 'Assuming, of course, that Denning was telling the truth and Mary *did* leave here alone at about a quarter to nine.'

'We've no reason to suppose that he's not telling the truth, even though he *is* a pompous, self-centred bastard,' said Quantrill fairly. He pointed the nose of his car in the direction of the police station, scenting a cup of tea, but the radio began to burble information about Mary Gedge's school friends: Sally Leggett had gone to the United States for the summer; Dale Kenward lived at number three, Priory Gardens.

## DEATH IN THE MORNING

Quantrill pulled a face. 'Oh, one of *Councillor* Kenward's boys, is he?' He turned the car in another direction. 'The posh end of the town, then.'

'I didn't know there was one.'

'You'll be surprised. Right, let's see if it was Dale Kenward who brought Mary into Breckham last night.'

But Dale was out, in the new car his father had given him as an eighteenth brithday present a few weeks previously. He had gone to spend the afternoon and evening in Yarchester, with his friend Colin.

The information came from his mother, in a torrent of words expressing relief that the police had not come to tell her that her son had met with a fatal accident. Quantrill was sorry that as soon as her agitation had subsided, he had to break the news of Mary Gedge's death.

Mrs. Kenward was upset. The policemen waited patiently while she stumbled through the necessary expression of disbelief, shock and sorrow. Quantrill murmured practised sympathy, while Tait took the opportunity to smooth his hands over the armchair he sat on and confirm his impression that any furniture that looked like leather, in that handsome thirty foot long room, was genuine hide.

Priory Gardens was not an estate. It was an exclusive development of eight private houses, each with half an acre of landscaped garden airy with willow trees, situated between the edge of the golf course and the grey-fanged ruins of a former Cluniac priory. The houses had been individually designed by an architect who combined a sensitive appreciation of the local area with a shrewd appraisal of the priorities of incoming senior business executives, who were the only people likely to be able to afford to buy them.

The houses had been built, like most of the other new private houses in Breckham Market, by Dale Kenward's father, who had inherited from his own father a considerable scattered acreage of freehold land that, until the early 'sixties, was good for nothing but rabbits. Then, like an elephantine fairy godfather, had come the London County Council, homburg in hand; and Dale's father, who had made a point of taking a seat on the moribund town council, had been persuaded without difficulty to vote in favour of the expansion of the town.

By the early 'seventies, Councillor Kenward had made a tidy fortune. It was natural for him to want to enjoy his early retirement in one of the best of his houses, but unhappily the experience was unnatural for his wife. Mrs. Kenward was a small, shy, modest woman. Even after three years in residence, she found it difficult to know how to make use of the vast entertainment areas of their new house; the more so as her husband had employed an interior decorator, jovially consigning their own well-used furniture to a dealer. Secretly, she hugged the hope that she might one day wake up to find that it had all been a bad dream, and that they really lived in a snug bungalow near her sister and the shops.

Now, she perched like a nervous visitor on the edge of the six-foot long chesterfield—it was the only position in which she could sit with her feet on the floor—and babbled about the ending of a love affair between her son and Mary Gedge.

'Of course, I was glad in a way that they'd parted—they'd been getting too serious. Not that we didn't like Mary, but Dale's only just eighteen. It was silly to talk about marriage.'

'They planned to *marry*?' asked Quantrill, alarmed at the unexpected development.

Mrs. Kenward twisted her damp handkerchief in hands that had obviously been accustomed for most of her married life to hard work in a labour-making house. 'Oh, it hadn't got to that stage—it was just some silly talk of Dale's.' She lifted her head and looked at Quantrill with horrified appeal. 'You're not trying to tell me that she—that poor Mary drowned herself? I'm sure she wouldn't do that, not on Dale's account! You've got it wrong, it wasn't a matter of Dale throwing her over, the love was more on his side than hers—she wanted him more as a friend. I'm sure that Dale was far more upset about their quarrel than Mary would have been. If either of them did anything rash as a result, it would have been Dale, not poor Mary!'

Quantrill winced, appalled that the woman did not realise what her generous exculpation of her son's girl-friend could suggest to a suspicious mind. 'No, no, Mrs. Kenward,' he said quickly. 'As I told you, it looks like an unfortunate accident. But we know that Mary came into town yesterday evening, and I wondered if she might by any chance have met your son.'

She smiled damply, reassured. 'Oh no. Dale went out with

Colin yesterday evening—they've spent all their time together this holiday.'

Tait made a note of the friend's name and address. 'And can you tell us what time Dale came home last night?' he asked.

Mrs. Kenward looked at him with big moist innocent brown eyes. 'He didn't come home till breakfast time. He's a very keen naturalist, you see. Of course, he told me what he was going to do, so I didn't need to worry. He wanted to make recordings of some nightingales, and then the dawn chorus. He and Colin spent the night bird-recording.'

# TEN

'This,' declared Chief Inspector Quantrill, 'is ridiculous.'

Privately, Tait agreed with him. It was ridiculous that the chief inspector should insist on stringing along; perhaps the old man had at last had enough and would go back to his office.

Quantrill drummed his fingers irritably on the warm dusty roof of his car, thinking of the work that would be accumulating in his absence, and of the compensatory cup of tea. 'There are enough unsolved crimes in this division,' he went on, 'to keep us all working flat out until Christmas, without anything new. The chief super told me only yesterday that now you're here to fill the vacancy he'll expect a marked improvement in our detection rate. And yet here we are, spending hours making enquiries about something that as far as we know isn't even a crime, and getting suspicious without any justification of any man who happened to know Mary Gedge.'

'There's no need for you to stay, sir.' Tait pointed out. 'If you want to get back to the station, I'll carry on.'

'What with?' Quantrill demanded. 'I don't see any point in pursuing this any further, until we get the result of the post-mortem and know whether there's anything to investigate. The chances are that Mary and young Kenward had made up their quarrel, and that he'll be able to tell us where she was last night. I'll get one of the patrol men to keep an eye on this house and have a word with the boy as soon as he returns. Until then, we're both wasting our time.'

Tait, who had made it his business to look at the unsolved crimes file as soon as he arrived in Breckham Market, was not impressed. It was a wasteland of largely undetectable crimes: assaults, thefts and burglaries, vandalism, dismantling of cars, all still unsolved because they were without pattern or form, impulsive, mindless. A detective who set himself the task of solving that lot would be lost without trace, and Tait had no intention of sacrificing himself for the sake of the divisional crime statistics.

'Wouldn't you give a girl's death a rather higher priority than the enquiry I was on this morning, sir?' he asked reproachfully.

Quantrill scowled and turned away, his hands jammed into the pockets of his jacket. Why the hell, he asked himself, aggrieved, should he let the new sergeant spend valuable time trying to make a difficult case out of something that was almost certainly a simple accident, while the real, dull, seedy police work remained to be done by someone else? Why should Sergeant Tait, with his university degree and his Bramshill qualification, expect to be allowed to devote his time to discovering exactly how Mary Gedge came to drown, rather than to the tedious business of who pinched another man's pigs?

Quantrill found the answer almost before he had formulated the question: because Tait had his priorities right, that was why.

It was easy for Tait, of course. He didn't have the daily responsibility, the everlasting problem of too much work to be done and too few men to do it. Tait didn't have a disagreeable chief super nagging at him to improve the statistics. Tait could afford to take a detached view.

But that didn't make him any less right. People are more important than property. Quantrill had already acknowledged with bitter regret that he should have given more attention to Joy Dawson's disappearance than to a series of burglaries that had been preoccupying him at the time, and now he acknowledged the importance of investigating Mary Gedge's death, even though it should prove to be an accident. The pigs, and the crime statistics, could wait.

He turned back to the car. 'I'll have to give you a lift to Ashthorpe anyway, so that you can pick up your own car. And while we're there, we might as well take this a stage further. After all, we've no reason to doubt what Mrs. Kenward said, and if Dale and Mary really weren't seeing each other any more, then it was someone else who gave her a lift from Ashthorpe.'

'I was thinking along those lines myself, sir,' agreed Tait, whose pleasure at the chief inspector's capitulation was modified by the realisation that the old man still wasn't going to give him a free hand. 'I thought it might be worth having a word with the other teacher who sometimes gave Mary lifts to school—Mr. Miller.'

'Good idea,' Quantrill agreed, slipping a mint into his mouth to compensate for the lost cup of tea.

It was seven years since the Old Bakery at Ashthorpe had performed its original function. Everyone in the village gave lip-service to the idea of a bakery and professed to regret its closure; but since the majority of the inhabitants preferred to buy sliced bread—the country women for the very good reason that they had to make sandwiches for their menfolk to take to work every day, the traditional middle class for the equally good reason that it made the best toast—and the thrifty and the trendy preferred to bake their own, a village bakery could no longer be a viable business.

The Millers, Quantrill suspected unkindly, belonged to the trendy minority; a man who taught Drama could fit into no other category. Their property, a long low detached building with a flint façade and a wide Georgian shop window, had clearly been converted to domestic use by people with more sympathy than money. No plate glass, no carriage lanterns, no shining paintwork. A glazed upper window and a protruding stench-pipe indicated that it was no longer in its original state of innocence of plumbing, but otherwise the property looked as though it had hardly been touched during the past seven years; not so much neglected as never-been-got-round-to.

Tait made reluctant use of his knuckles on the scarred, flaking paintwork of the door. And again. There was the sound of movement from inside the house, and presently the door opened.

Tait made the introductions. 'Mr. Michael Miller?' he asked.

The man blinked and nodded, then winced as though he regretted the movement, and rubbed the back of his neck. He was late fortyish, tall and slim, with thinning red-gold hair and a long, mobile, actor's face, at present unshaven.

Miller was wearing shabby jeans, a T-shirt and a denim jacket. Quantrill told himself that it was pathetic that a middle-aged man—older than himself—should dress as though he were a quarter of a century younger; but had the grace to acknowledge that he was envious, not of the clothes but of Miller's ability to wear them.

'May we come in?' asked Tait, looking at the denims with the tolerant amusement of an unassailably young man. Miller grunted and grudgingly held open the door.

It led straight into a large room that must once have been the shop and was now used as a living-room. The sparse furnishings were a mixture of stripped pine cottage antiques and shabby Habitat. An assemble-it-yourself shelving unit leaned precariously against one wall, and a scatter of rugs went only part way to disguising the fact that the work of staining the floorboards had been abandoned before it was completed.

The predominant impression indoors, though, was less of work unfinished than of recent neglect. There was none of the squalor of the Pulfer household, no dirty clothes or greasy plates or smell of food, but instead a strew of newspapers, correspondence, books and tape cassettes. A pair of suede ankle boots stood on the pine dresser, next to a great pottery dish containing a few shrivelled oranges. Dust was thick on every surface, ashtrays overflowed, bottles and dirty glasses stood abandoned. A pile of children's toys had been shovelled into one corner. In the draught from the open door, skeins of dust rolled across the bare boards like tumbleweed.

To Tait, it was immediately identifiable: discounting the toys, a bachelor's pad on the day after a good party.

That it had been—in bachelor terms—a good party was obvious. Miller had all the symptoms of a hangover: bleary eyes, slack cheeks, an aversion to movement and noise and light. In his normal condition he would have been a good-looking, well-preserved middle-aged man, but at the moment his condition was abject. He closed the door behind them with exaggerated care and then stood swaying and blinking, rubbing his long fingers over the golden-grey stubble on his cheeks.

'Sorry,' he said. 'Had rather a thick night, and then topped up at lunch time—just been sleeping it off.' His voice was slurred, but still beautifully modulated; a deep, actor's voice. 'Sit down,' he suggested, as his knees deposited him abruptly on the crumpled colour-weave cushions of the settee. 'If you can find anywhere to sit,' he added, with a painful gesture at the cluttered room. 'My wife's away at the moment. Took the children to her mother's for a holiday. You know how it is?'

Quantrill knew how it was. He felt a totally unexpected sympathy. The newspapers that he shifted from a chair were a good three weeks' accumulation; too long for a normal holiday visit. Even though he despised the youthful Breton cap that hung on the back of the door, he could look with fellow-feeling at the dust and the drink and the pathos of the pushed-aside toys.

'I'm sorry to bother you,' he said, and meant it. 'We just wanted to have a word about one of your former pupils—Mary Gedge.'

Miller looked from one policeman to the other, without moving his head. 'She's dead, isn't she?' he said uncertainly. He massaged the back of his neck with his hand, grimacing over the discomfort. 'That's what they told me at the Ostrich at lunch time—that's why I got tanked up again. Or have I been dreaming it?'

Quantrill confirmed that he hadn't. Miller rubbed his hands over his slack face. 'Christ,' he said thickly. He pushed himself to his feet. 'Sha'n't be a minute . . .'

He stumbled from the room, and slammed the door. They heard a cistern flush, water being sluiced, a spluttering, more oaths. A few minutes later Miller returned to the room, his hair spiked and darkened by water, the front of his scalp showing pink, rubbing his face on a drab towel.

'Sorry,' he said, his voice less thick, 'that's better. I only wish I had been dreaming about Mary, though—just for a minute there I hoped that it had all been a nightmare . . . Well, what do you want to see me about?'

'Routine enquiries, sir,' said Tait. 'Did you know Mary well?'

He's at it again, Quantrill thought, as his sergeant darted in with the sharp question. This was obviously Tait's speciality: needling people, trying to make them indignant and flustered and angry, so that they said more than they might soberly intend. It could be a successful technique, if you suspected anyone of villainy. And Tait was obviously determined to suspect anyone who knew Mary, until such time as the post-mortem proved conclusively that there had been neither foul play nor untoward circumstances at the time of her death.

The chief inspector listened with half an ear to Miller's protestations that Mary was not a personal friend, that he never saw her outside school, and looked surreptitiously at his watch. The post-mortem would be bound to take a long time, since he'd allowed Tait to persuade him that he had grounds for requesting more than a primary-cause-of-death investigation.

Miller was getting annoyed now. One day, Quantrill foresaw, Sergeant Tait would go too far with someone of local self-importance, and find himself hauled before the assistant chief constable; and then he, Quantrill, would have to go to his defence. That was part of the responsibility of command, supporting a subordinate regardless of the fact that you didn't like him or his methods.

And the chief inspector disliked the deliberate provocation of anger. Anger can so easily lead to violence and God knows, Quantrill thought, there's enough violence about without deliberately stirring it. He'd once had a chief inspector who liked to play the hard man. One of his suspects, an inoffensive man who proved to be perfectly innocent, had become so incensed by the questioning that he went home and broke his neighbour's jaw in an argument over a garden bonfire.

Quantrill himself preferred a calmer approach in questioning, one which allowed him either to make a diplomatic withdrawal or to cut the ground from beneath a suspect's feet. But at least, with their different techniques, he and Tait should make a useful double act: the hard man and the sympathetic one; an effective combination.

'And did you give Mary a lift into Breckham Market yesterday evening?' Tait was demanding.

Miller objected vigorously, flinging his damp towel to the floor. The wings of his nostrils were white with anger. 'No I didn't! Why the hell should you think that I did?'

78

'Because we understand that you sometimes gave her a lift to school.'

Miller scowled. 'Is there a single thing you can do in this bloody village without someone informing on you?' he said bitterly. 'Yes, all right, I did sometimes give her lifts—so did Mrs. Bloomfield. So?'

'That's all right, sir,' Quantrill intervened pacifically. 'Mary was seen in Breckham Market last night, but as long as we know that it wasn't you who gave her the lift we can continue our enquiries elsewhere. Did you happen to see her in the village yesterday, though?'

Miller turned his back and began rummaging about on the dresser. He found what he was looking for in the fruit bowl and sat down again composedly, a battery shaver in his hand. 'Yes,' he said. He switched on the shaver and buzzed it up and down his cheek. 'Soon after six o'clock, I believe,' he said eventually. 'I went to the shop for some cigarettes and a bottle of whisky, and Mary was serving.'

'You talked to her?' Quantrill asked.

'Naturally.' Miller did some careful blind flying round his mouth. 'I reckon to have a civilised exchange of conversation with people I know when we meet. We talked about a play we'd both seen on television the night before.'

'And did she say what she intended to do yesterday evening? Did she say anything about meeting anyone?'

'No,' said Miller. He got up, blew the hairs out of his shaver, cased it and put it back in the fruit bowl. With his cheeks firmed and shaven and his hangover washed away, he began to look personable. 'There's nothing useful I can tell you, I'm afraid.'

'What about other people in the village?' Quantrill persisted. 'Can you suggest anyone who might have given her a lift into town?'

Miller combed his hair forward with his fingers to camouflage his scalp. 'Sorry, no. I'm not the right person to ask, though. I suggest you have a word with Jean—Mrs. Bloomfield. She was Mary's headmistress and she knew the girl a great deal better than I did. She was due back from the Dordogne today, so you'll probably find her at home by now. She lives—'

'Yes, I do know Mrs. Bloomfield.' Quantrill heaved himself to his feet from the low chair. 'Thank you for your help, Mr. Miller.'

Tait echoed him: 'Thank you.' He looked pointedly at the dirty glasses. 'Quite a party you had last night,' he said, smiling.

Miller ignored him. 'If you see Jean,' he said to Quantrill, 'tell her that I hope she feels better for her holiday, and give her my love.'

The policemen walked back to their car. 'Coburg House, sir?' enquired Tait. 'You'll try Mrs. Bloomfield again?'

Quantrill nodded and turned the car in that direction, refusing to allow himself to admit that he knew exactly why he felt suddenly disconsolate.

As he rang the bell of Coburg House for the second time that afternoon, Quantrill deliberately restrained himself from making a second nervous adjustment to his tie and his hair. It was not, he told himself, that he wanted to evade Tait's quizzical eye; not even that he knew that he could never compete with so personable a man as Miller. But he had now remembered that in the four years since he last met Jean Bloomfield, his circumstances had changed completely.

He was no longer a despondent, never-likely-to-be-promoted detective sergeant, with a rapidly breaking-up marriage and two teenage daughters to look after on his own. He was no longer so wretched that when an attractive woman showed him sympathy and understanding, he was liable to find himself in love. That crisis had passed. He was his own man again, with his family intact, his financial pressures eased by promotion, his career prospects strengthening.

It was true that, despite the improvement in his circumstances, he had never been able to recapture the glimpse of possible happiness that he had had four years ago. Detective Chief Inspector Quantrill was not a happy man. But then, he had been forced to spend the interminable Sundays of his boyhood penned in a Baptist chapel, where elderly lay preachers declaimed at length their Victorian working class nonconformist conviction that man is put on this earth to work and to suffer; happiness, they had propounded, was the reward reserved for the righteous in the hereafter.

# DEATH IN THE MORNING

Young Douglas Quantrill, bored and resentful in his best grey flannel suit, the short trousers held up by a snake belt, his knee-length socks gartered with itchily tight elastic, had subconsciously absorbed the proposition together with the smell of varnished pine pews and Victory V cough lozenges. Certainly, the adult Quantrill conceded in his gloomier moments, any happiness he had ever found in this life had proved as transitory as those old preachers prophesied. Go looking for happiness and you'd be bound in the end to get hurt.

As he waited for Jean Bloomfield to answer the door, Quantrill determined that this time he would keep his head. He would not repeat the follies of four years ago. There would be no craving for a smile from her, no wishful interpretation of light words, no fantasies; no fantasies, no painful withdrawal symptoms. This would be a short, straight interview, friendly but impersonal.

Probably she wouldn't even remember him.

He rang the bell again.

Perhaps it was the fact tht she drove up just as he turned away from the door that threw him; or perhaps it was her instant smile of recognition. Quantrill didn't stop to analyse the reason for his downfall. He hurried down the path toward her Renault, his breath catching in his throat, his heart seeming to trip its beat.

'Good afternoon, Mrs. Bloomfield,' he said, and knew that he had reddened like an adolescent.

She looked older, of course. Her sunburned face was thinner than he remembered, the incipient lines on her forehead and at the outer corners of her eyes more marked, and she looked very tired and very sad; but he thought her even more beautiful.

'Mr. Quantrill!' she said in a low, soft voice. 'How good to see you.'

Sergeant or chief inspector, Quantrill was lost again.

# ELEVEN

She was wearing a tennis dress, its whiteness making her sun-burned face and arms seem even browner. Her sunbleached blonde hair was held back by a blue cotton scarf, which empha-sised the flecks of blue in her dark-hollowed, dark-lashed grey eyes. A pair of sunglasses was pushed carelessly up on to her hair. She wore no make-up, but her lips were pink against her tan. Quantrill bent down so that he could talk to her through the open window of her car, surveying the contours of her face as avidly as a desert traveller, having at last topped a dune, might view the terrain that led to an oasis.

'This is Liz Whilton,' she said; and had to repeat it before Quantrill collected himself sufficiently to notice the girl sitting beside her. The chief inspector introduced Sergeant Tait who, whether from tact or inclination, went immediately to the other side of the car to talk to the girl.

Mrs. Bloomfield turned her head towards Quantrill so that her companion could not hear. 'Have you come about Mary—Mary Gedge?' she asked quietly.

'Yes, I'm afraid so. I'd like to have a word with some of her friends, and I thought you might be able to tell me who they are.'

'I'll be glad to help if I can—though Liz will be far more use to you. I'm sure she'll be able to give you all the information you need. Shall we go in?'

As she spoke, she slid off the white sweater that had been slung across her shoulders, and let it fall casually on her lap. Quantrill started back, reddening, suddenly aware that he had been staring down at her slim brown thighs. He wrenched clumsily at the door handle and stood aside, his eyes gallantly averted, while she got out of the car.

She seemed smaller. As he remembered it, she had reached the level of his jaw, but now her shoulders drooped a little from dejection and weariness. But she made an effort to smile generously at Quantrill as she stood on the path, holding her sweater negligently in front of her so that, without obvious intent, it compensated for the brevity of her tennis dress.

'Liz and I are longing for some tea,' she said. 'I'm sure you and Mr. Tait would like some too, if you can give me a minute to change first. Liz, would you take our guests round to the garden? I sha'n't be long.'

Liz was seventeen or eighteen, chunky, with dark hair and freckles, pleasantly upturned features, a very brief tennis skirt and no inhibitions at all about displaying her legs. Tait took her into protective custody and they disappeared round the side of the house, but Quantrill moved more slowly, making the most of the opportunity to watch Jean Bloomfield as she hurried up the path to the front door.

He admired her even more for her moment of self-consciousness, her instinctive modesty. And it was nothing but modesty, he was sure of that. From what he had seen in the car and from what he could see now, from the back, there could be no possible reason for her to be ashamed of her legs.

He looked at their length under the absurdly short white dress, their smooth unblemished skin, their suntanned firmness—and then turned away, hot and angry with himself.

It was unfair to make the comparison. His wife was the same age but she'd had three children, she was shorter and more heavily built, she hadn't the benefit of a French suntan and regular exercise. It was unfair to compare her fat white thighs, so heavily veined that they reminded him resistibly of the marble top of his mother's old wash-stand, with Jean Bloomfield's thighs . . . to compare anything about her with Jean Bloomfield.

Besides, he'd put on weight himself. He had no way of being certain that Jean had found him attractive four years ago, and even had she done so then, she might not now.

He made the best of his appearance, checking his suit and smoothing back his hair, and then walked round to the garden to join Tait and the girl.

They were sitting in the late afternoon sun on a garden seat on a stone-flagged terrace at the back of the house, closer together than was called for in the line of duty. Quantrill paused discreetly beside a lilac bush and watched his sergeant at work.

Tait might be hard with men, but with girls he practised a different technique.

'It's awful—' Liz was saying bleakly. 'I still can't believe that Mary's *dead* . . . I mean—' She hiccoughed with grief and a tear fell with a splat on to her plump knee. Tait took from an inner pocket of his jacket a handkerchief that he carried for the purpose of comforting attractive girls in distress but—prudently aware of what might technically constitute an assault—resisted the temptation to mop up the fallen tear. Instead, he put the handkerchief in her hand and slid his arm round her shoulder.

'I know,' he said gently. 'And you were one of her closest friends?'

The girl dabbed her eyes and sniffed. 'Well,' she said earnestly, as if anxious not to be accused of misrepresentation. 'I wasn't her *best* friend. That was Sally Leggett—she's gone to the USA to work in a summer camp, lucky thing.' She sniffed again. Tait decided that it sounded more like a deplorable habit than an emotional reaction, and unobtrusively retrieved his handkerchief while he continued his sympathetic questioning.

There was very little that Liz Whilton could tell him. She had just returned from a visit to her grandmother, and had not seen Mary since the beginning of the holidays; as far as she knew, Mary had not seen Dale Kenward since they parted; as far as she knew, Mary had no other boy-friend.

'But I live on a farm at Lillington, you see, I always get out of touch during the holidays. I think that was why Mrs. Bloomfield came to break the news to me this afternoon. She knew that I was Mary's friend, and she didn't want me to read about the accident in the local paper. And she made me go straight with her to Breckham Market to play tennis, to take my mind off it. Very nice of her, really, because she didn't get back from France until this morning. She crossed on the night boat and drove up from Southampton, so she must be awfully tired. I don't think she wanted to play tennis at all, really, it was just for my sake.'

Quantrill stepped forward. 'Mrs. Bloomfield *is* very kind,' he agreed. He smiled at the girl, trying to raise her spirits again: 'And so you beat her at tennis, I imagine?'

'Well, only because she was so tired, and out of practice. She used to play awfully well when we were at the grammar school, considering how old she is. She didn't run much, of course, but then she didn't need to—she had this tremendous first serve, and even Sally and Mary couldn't often beat her. Today was just a fluke—I'm useless, really.'

She gave a deprecating shrug, smiled at Tait and nibbled at a wandering strand of dark hair with engagingly gap-fronted teeth. Her brown eyes were huge and soft, thickly lashed. Tait decided to give her the benefit of the doubt about the sniffs, grinned and took out his notebook. 'I don't believe that for a minute! Well, then, if I could just have your name and address, in case I want to get in touch with you again—'

The girl gave them eagerly: 'And the number's Ashthorpe five eight six.'

Jean Bloomfield, who had come quietly from the house onto the terrace, caught Quantrill's eye and smiled. Instinctively, he straightened his shoulders and pulled in his stomach.

There had been little enough time for her to change, but she looked immaculate in white trousers and a coffee-coloured silk shirt, with her hair swept up into a knot. She had put on a touch of eye shadow and lip gloss, and Quantrill felt dizzy with the thought that it might be for his benefit. He strode to her side.

She nodded towards Tait and the girl, who were laughing and talking together. 'Your sergeant has done more for young Liz's morale in five minutes than I achieved in an exhausting afternoon,' she said ruefully. 'I wish I'd known you were bringing him. He'd be a great success at school, if you could spare him to come and talk to the seniors—as you once did, if you remember? Though of course I'm not now able to issue such invitations. I'd need to get the headmaster's permission first.'

She said it lightly, but there was an unmistakable undertow of bitterness.

'We've been to see Mr. Denning this afternoon,' said Quantrill, trying to convey in his tone his disapproval of the man.

She gave a dry smile. 'That was very—proper—of you,' she said, giving the word a slightly mocking emphasis, 'to call on the headmaster before you came to see me, I mean. He sets great store by protocol. Well—' she dismissed the subject diplomatically: 'Liz,' she called, 'would you be a dear and make us all some tea? The kitchen's the first door on the right—perhaps Mr. Tait wouldn't mind helping you?'

They went indoors, Liz Whilton with alacrity, Tait with an amused flick of one eyebrow as he passed the chief inspector. Jean Bloomfield apologised for the transparent manoeuvring.

'I wanted to ask you about Mary's death.' She tore a leaf from a lilac bush and shredded it restlessly as she spoke. 'I heard about it in the village, when I went out to do some shopping just after I got back from holiday. Everyone had heard that it was an accident, but there was a certain amount of innuendo—oh, you know what villages are like.' She looked up at him, her eyes dark with fatigue. 'Was it really an accident? Had she been attacked? I'm sorry to ask you, but when a girl is found dead . . .'

'I know. I understand how you feel.' Quantrill longed to be able to touch her, to convey his sympathy in something other than clumsy words. The white cones of lilac blossom were still tight but their scent was sufficient to tug at his senses, making concentration difficult. 'Mary wasn't assaulted, so please don't distress yourself on that account. So far as we know at present it was an accident, just as you heard. All the same, we're puzzled about her death. I don't know whether you know the river at Ashthorpe bridge, but it's very shallow—not an easy place to drown, even if she did fall in. So we wondered if perhaps she'd been to a party and had been drinking. Do you think that's likely?'

Mrs. Bloomfield shook her head. 'Definitely not. Lager and cider are the fashion at the moment, but most of the girls just sip their drinks—half a pint lasts them for hours. It would be completely out of character for Mary to drink anything stronger.'

'That's the impression I got. And I'm sorry to have to ask you these things, but have you any suspicion that Mary or any of her friends might possibly have been experimenting with drugs?'

She hesitated for a full minute before answering. Her shoulders had straightened when Quantrill reassured her, but now they drooped again. She looked dejected, almost defeated.

'I would dearly like to be able to say that nothing of that kind goes on among our pupils; but how can any of us be sure? I hope not—God, I hope not. But all I can say in truth is that I don't know.' She bit her lower lip, frowning, and then said slowly, 'But as far as Mary herself is concerned, and her immediate friends, I do feel confident that they wouldn't be interested in drugs. I'm sure—absolutely sure—that Mary would have been neither drunk nor drugged when she fell in the river.'

Her tone was so vehement that Quantrill felt that he had been accused of bad taste. 'I'm sorry I had to ask,' he repeated. 'It's just that we have to consider every possibility . . .'

She relaxed, and smiled. 'Yes of course—I understand. When someone dies suddenly, you have to investigate. You have to do your job, I realise that. But why are we standing here? Come indoors.'

The original separate dining- and drawing-rooms of the villa had been converted to one through room, connected by an arched opening. It was an elegant room, with a plain dark grey carpet and soft terra-cotta walls, the furniture a careful selection of Victoriana. The chairs, upholstered in fabric a shade darker than the wallpaper, had, as Quantrill discovered, been designed to accommodate voluminous skirts and prosperous Victorian behinds, and were remarkably roomy and comfortable.

He settled, watching Jean Bloomfield as she opened the windows to freshen the air that had staled during her absence. Understandably, a layer of dust had accumulated on the small table beside his chair, and on the silver-framed photograph that stood there.

Quantrill looked at the photograph. It showed the head and shoulders of a good-looking young RAF officer, with a pilot's brevet above his tunic pocket. Jean Bloomfield's husband had, he knew, been killed in a flying accident.

Quantrill himself had served in the RAF, but he had no illusion that his experiences gave him any common ground with the widow of an aircrew officer. He had performed his two years' compulsory national service at the beginning of the nineteen-fifties as a reluctant storekeeper on the permanent staff of a recruits' training station. His contribution to the defence of his country had been confined to issuing stiff hairy uniforms to bewildered recruits, and the highest rank he had attained had been that of senior aircraftsman. Jean Bloomfield would never have looked at him, then.

Sergeant Tait carried in a tray of tea. Quantrill noticed that, as she poured it, Jean Bloomfield's hands were shaking—understandably, he thought, with protective yearning. She must be emotionally as well as physically worn out: the long journey, the distressing news of Mary Gedge's death, an afternoon's tennis . . . and now she had to give a coppers' tea party. No wonder the strain showed.

But despite her tenseness, she was beautiful. It would be impossible for any man not to admire her appearance and her voice, but Quantrill's admiration was not confined to superficialities. He was captivated by her modesty, her kindness to the dead girl's friend, her sympathetic understanding; by the honest uncertainty she had shown when they talked of the drug problem, in contrast with Denning's self-centred denial; and by the loyalty she had demonstrated in refusing to criticise the headmaster despite her justifiable resentment of him.

'Has Liz been able to answer your questions, Mr. Tait?' she asked.

'Oh yes, she's been most helpful.' Tait grinned at the girl who coloured and laughed, momentarily forgetting the reason for his presence. 'Liz has given me the address of several friends Mary might have gone to visit in Breckham Market last night. It's a great pity that Sally Leggett is away, though.'

'Sally knew Mary better than anyone,' Liz confirmed, downcast again. 'She knew ages before I did that Mary had finished with Dale.'

'Could we get in touch with Sally, Mrs. Bloomfield?' Tait asked.

'I doubt it—she went to the United States with her brother, and I believe they intended to spend the first two or three weeks on a camping tour.' She turned to Quantrill. 'You're trying to check Mary's movements last night, is that it?'

'Yes. Someone gave her a lift into the town and someone brought her back, but we've no idea who or when. So anything that either of you can tell us about Mary's friends, her character or her habits would help us. Anything at all.'

Liz Whilton shrugged helplessly, having already given Tait her all in the way of information and her telephone number as further encouragement. Mrs. Bloomfield lit a cigarette, inhaling deeply. She looked puzzled.

'But why last night?' she asked. 'What I heard in the village was that Mary drowned early this morning, while she was out gathering flowers for May Day.'

'The time of death hasn't yet been established,' Tait explained. 'The gathering-flowers-for-May-morning bit is Pc Godbold's private theory.'

'Were there no flowers, then?'

'Oh, a meadowful of them,' said Tait cheerfully, 'and buttercups floating all over the river. But it does seem more likely that she would have been out last night rather than early this morning.'

'And in fact we know she was out last night,' said Quantrill, 'but because she slept in a trailer instead of in the house, we don't know whether she ever returned home.'

'Yes, I see.' Jean Bloomfield got up to fetch an ashtray from the table near Quantrill. She saw that his cup was empty, and raised an eyebrow. He nodded gratefully, and pretended not to notice that it rattled in the saucer as she carried it away. 'All the same,' she said, 'whatever Mary was doing last night, I don't see why you should want to dismiss Pc Godbold's theory. It made perfect sense to me.'

'It did?' Quantrill got up to collect his refilled cup from the tray and so save her the embarrassment of lifting it. For a moment his fingers touched hers. She gave him a grave smile that sent him back to his chair elated, remembering that he was now neither a pimply senior aircraftsman nor a dejected detective sergeant.

'Of course. I know that Mary liked going for walks alone, and this countryside's now such an agricultural factory that the river meadow is about the only place in Ashthorpe where one *can* walk without damaging crops. It seems to me quite likely that she woke early and decided to celebrate May morning by going out to gather flowers. After all, it's an old country custom—or at least it was when I was a village child in Suffolk. At Oxford we used to gather flowers after we'd been on the river at dawn to listen to the choristers on Magdalen tower, and I've no doubt the tradition continues. I'm sure that May Day still has a rural significance that's lost on the international socialists.'

Quantrill recalled his own schooldays, and the humiliation of being made to dance round a maypole with a sissy ribbon in his hand; but the little girls had loved the flowers and the fuss. 'I don't know whether they have May Day celebrations at Ashthorpe school,' he said, 'but I know they still do in a lot of villages round about.'

'They used to have a May Queen here in Ashthorpe until a few years ago,' confirmed Liz Whilton. 'I remember, because we didn't at Lillington, and we were really envious.'

'Well, then—isn't it reasonable to suppose that Mary went out early to gather flowers?' asked Jean Bloomfield. 'Perhaps in a moment of nostalgia for her childhood?'

'Maybe. But not in a long dress,' objected Quantrill, 'particularly after it had been raining. She was seen last night in a long dress, and that's how she was found this morning.'

Liz looked suddenly stricken. 'Oh—that would have been her Laura Ashley dress,' she said reverently.

'There's no reason why she couldn't have put it on this morning as well,' Mrs. Bloomfield pointed out. 'I agree that it would be more romantic than practical to wear a long dress in long grass, but gathering flowers on May morning *is* more romantic than practical. In fact, you know—' she stubbed out her cigarette with sudden vigour as her theory strengthened '—that may well be why she fell in the river! The hem of her dress would become heavy with damp and mud. It would get in the way. She might well have tripped on the river bank—'

'*Hey!*' Liz Whilton was sitting bolt upright, flushed, her eyes glistening with A level intelligence and tears. 'That must have been how she came to drown. Don't you see—the long skirt and the flowers . . . Mary must have drowned in just the same way as Ophelia did!'

Chief Inspector Quantrill was instantly alert: 'Ophelia who?' he demanded.

# TWELVE

Quantrill drove back to Breckham Market in a temper, so blinded by humiliation that afterwards he remembered nothing of the first part of the journey.

It was so bloody unfair. How was he to know who Ophelia was? He'd never had the educational advantages that Tait and the girl and Jean Bloomfield had enjoyed. Jean had been wonderfully tactful, offering more tea and changing the subject and emphasising his status by referring to him as a chief inspector, but there had been no mistaking Tait's derisive twitch and the girl's crow of laughter. 'Ophelia Shakespeare, I suppose,' she'd spluttered hysterically, 'or else Mrs. Hamlet-to-be,' and Quantrill had been so hot with embarrassment that he couldn't get out of the house quickly enough.

What would Jean Bloomfield, with her Oxford education and her handsome aircrew officer husband, dead or not, think of him now?

It wasn't that he was completely ignorant. If the wretched girl had mentioned *Hamlet* in the first place, he'd have known where he was. Douglas Quantrill had a great respect for education, and every intention of making up for his lack of it as soon as he had the time. To this end he had joined a book club, and was now the possessor of a series of handsomely bound classics that he had never realised he could buy much more cheaply in paperback. He proposed to read them all, Shakespeare and Dickens and *War and Peace* and a confusion of Lawrences and Brontës, just as soon as he had retired; and meanwhile, he drew them reverently from his bookcase when he remembered them, and flipped through a few of the pages. He wasn't so much of a fool that he didn't know that Shakespeare had written *Hamlet*, but he couldn't be expected to know all the characters in the play.

He smarted under the injustice of it all. Just because he'd

attended nothing but a Suffolk village elementary school, where one harrassed teacher had had to cope with thirty children whose ages ranged from five to fourteen, he'd been handicapped educationally from the start. Just because, from the age of fourteen, he'd had to earn his living, he had had no time to make up for the deficiencies of the old system by educating himself. Just because . . .

But Quantrill was a reasonable man, with a limited capacity for self-deception. As the angry mist cleared from in front of his eyes, and he wiped the sweat of humiliation from his forehead and guiltily reduced his excessive speed, he acknowledged that his resentment was entirely retrospective. He'd hated school, and had longed to leave. He'd heard that the parents of children who won a place at the local grammar school had to undertake to keep them there until they were sixteen; young Douglas had been so alarmed at this prospect of elongated boredom that when he took the examination he deliberately made no effort to get his sums right. His sole ambition, at the age of eleven, had been to work at the village garage and eventually become a driver with the local bus company, like this father.

He'd learned his respect for education far too late. He realised now that he could have done all the reading in the world while he was in the RAF, if he'd bothered. Heaven knew there'd been time enough, between bouts of kitting-out each week's new arrivals. If only he'd had the sense, when he'd skived off into his den at the back of the clothing stores, leaving Ac McClusky at the counter to act as a primitive early warning system, to read the complete works of Shakespeare instead of *Reveille* . . .

Sergeant Tait, sitting quietly beside him, let out a silent breath of relief as the chief inspector calmed down and began to drive with due care and attention. Far from deriding Quantrill, the sergeant felt a strong professional sympathy with him. Tait himself had read social science and his acquaintance with Shakespeare was limited to school set books which hadn't, in his time, included *Hamlet*. Certainly he'd heard of Ophelia, and had a sketchy knowledge of her fate; but only a pre-war fictional amateur detective would think of a corpse in Shakespearean terms, and Tait was contemptuous of fictional amateurs. He was interested in facts, not literary allusions. In Quantrill's place he might well have said the same thing.

He glanced at the chief inspector's glum, set profile. Mrs. Bloomfield wasn't at all bad, either—no wonder the old man was put out. Of course, as far as Tait himself was concerned, she was too old. Women a little older than himself, who knew what it was all about and didn't get emotional, yes; but as soon as the firmness began to go from under their chins and the lines deepened on either side of their mouths, he lost interest. But Mrs. Bloomfield had obviously been stunning in her day, and had kept herself trim. Trait could see that to a man of her own age or older, she would still be extremely attractive.

He glanced again at Quantrill. The old man had let himself go round the middle, but he must have been handsome enough when he was young. Whether Mrs. Bloomfield wanted the chief inspector as much as Quantrill wanted her, though, was another matter; she liked him, obviously, but from what Tait had seen of their relationship—and he had kept it under close but unobtrusive observation—the affair was principally in the chief inspector's mind, poor old devil. Wife trouble, Tait diagnosed, with the callous relish of an unmarried twenty-four-year-old who is convinced that no girl will ever catch him.

For his part, Quantrill was determined to put Jean Bloomfield out of his thoughts. He had made a fool of himself in front of her, and that was it; he could never hope to reinstate himself now, and the sooner he concentrated the whole of his attention on his job, the sooner he would forget her.

Except that she hadn't forgotten him, in four years. 'Mr. Quantrill,' she'd said, smiling at him, 'how good to see you.' And then he'd gone and said, like the oaf that he was, 'Ophelia who?'

Quantrill twisted savagely at the air intake on the dashboard, directing a jet of cold air full on his face. 'Sergeant Tait,' he said sharply, 'there are just two things I want you to do about Mary Gedge's death. First, get a patrol man to watch the Kenward house for the boy's return. If Dale admits to having seen Mary within the past forty-eight hours, I want to interview him. Secondly, keep in touch with the hospital and get the gist of the pathologist's report to me as soon as possible. Apart from that, you're to spend no more time investigating this fatality. Is that clear? There'll be more than enough work waiting for you in your office, and for me in mine.'

'Sir,' agreed Tait. But he had in his pocket the notebook that contained the names and addresses of Mary Gedge's Breckham Market friends, and on duty or off, he intended to follow them up. If the chief inspector was satisfied that this death was accidental, Tait wasn't. And no deaths on this patch were going to be left unexplained while he was divisional CID sergeant.

Quantrill worked at his desk for an hour without once thinking of Jean Bloomfield or of Mary Gedge. Soon after seven o'clock, with an evening's paper work in front of him, he rang for a cup of coffee and a sandwich.

It was brought by a pink and white complexioned probationary constable, who was so hideously embarrassed by a pair of squeaky boots that Quantrill felt obliged to address him kindly.

'Thank you very much,' he said as the constable, breathing heavily, set the snack down on his desk. 'Bedford, isn't it?'

Pc Bedford sprang to instant attention, with a thump and a creak at ground level. 'Sir!' he said, the pink rushing upwards to displace the white from his forehead.

Quantrill sat back in his chair, scratching his jaw thoughtfully. 'Busy at the moment, Bedford?'

The constable gulped, trying to decide the most politic answer. Eventually he said, 'Plenty to do, sir. But if you need anything done urgently, I could postpone the other things.'

'Good. If I remember rightly, you're an educated man, aren't you? A levels and so on?'

Pc Bedford looked apprehensive. He was proud of his A levels, but the chief inspector's question made him suddenly aware of the gaps in his knowledge. He was afraid that he was about to be asked something totally unfair, like the name of the French prime minister or the coefficient of the expansion of brass. 'Economics, Geography and English Literature, sir,' he admitted warily.

'English, good. You know *Hamlet*, then?'

Bedford would have shuffled his feet, if it weren't for the boots; it was far worse to be asked about something he once knew and had forgotten. And what on earth did the DCI want with *Hamlet*? Still, the constable had discovered that senior officers were alarmingly unpredictable and Sergeant Lamb, his mentor, had given him an invaluable piece of advice: humour them.

'I haven't read *Hamlet* since O levels, sir,' he apologised. 'I don't remember it all that well—but I could fetch you a Shakespeare from the library if you like, they stay open till eight tonight.'

Quantrill looked at him with approval. 'Good! Right then, nip round to the library and give my compliments to Mr. Bradshaw. We only need the book for half an hour but give him a signature for it, we don't want him to think that we're taking advantage of being next door.'

Pc Bedford was puzzled. 'Wouldn't it be simpler if I used one of my borrower's cards, sir?'

The chief inspector, who had never learned the library habit, glowered. 'Be off with you! Use your initiative, boy!'

Pc Bedford fled at a rapid squeak.

Quantrill took a gulp of coffee, looked at his watch and then put a call through to his home. He was relieved when the telephone was answered not by his wife but by Peter, who gave their number clearly just as his father had taught him.

'Hallo Peter.'

'Hi Dad.'

'Your mother in?'

'She's just changing. The Higginses are coming, worse luck—that means I'll miss *Kojak*.'

'The Higginses—oh Lord, I'd forgotten! Well, it's no good, I just can't make it.'

'Mum'll be mad.'

'Again . . .' Quantrill heard the boy's answering chuckle, and then a distant raised voice and the muffling of the receiver as Peter called a reply.

'She says what is it *this* time?' Peter reported. He tried to sound blasé, but Quantrill knew that he had taken to reading the local paper and had developed too great an interest for a thirteen-year-old in the more sordid cases that his father had to handle.

'Oh, mostly routine. Too much work and too few men to do it.'

'Who'd be a chief inspector?' sympathised Peter, who was secretly proud of his father's new eminence.

'Who'd be a chief inspector's wife, you mean,' amended

Quantrill, slapping a fresh piece of wallpaper in an attempt to hide some of the cracks. 'Listen,' he added quickly, anxious to conclude the conversation before his wife reached the telephone, 'don't let on that I forgot about the Higginses, there's a good chap. They understand that my time's not my own. Just tell your mother that I'm sorry, but I'll be late. I've no idea when, so she's not to wait up. Okay?'

'Ten-four, Captain,' confirmed Peter, using the jargon of the New York cops he seen on television. 'Hey, Dad, any chance of my having a portable telly for my birthday, so that I can watch it in my room without disturbing anybody? Just a small one? A miniature? Please?'

'No chance,' said his father firmly.

Quantrill was unenthusiastically eating a cheese sandwich when Pc Bedford returned. The constable offered a thick volume, but the sandwich gave Quantrill an excellent excuse to wave it away.

'You know your way round it better than I do. Read me what it says about Ophelia's death, will you?'

Pc Bedford, who hoped in time to transfer to the CID, had already been doing a little detective work on his own account. He had discovered from Sergeant Lamb what the chief inspector had been working on during the day, and had guessed why he had been sent for a copy of *Hamlet*. Bedford was most impressed to learn that the DCI was a literary man.

He blushed. 'Excuse me, sir,' he said diffidently, 'but do you mind if I ask whether you're thinking of the girl who was drowned at Ashthorpe?'

Quantrill paused in the act of lighting a small cigar. 'Did you know her?'

'No sir, I'm new to Breckham Market. But I've heard how the body was found, in a long dress with flowers scattered round her, and it *does* sound a lot like Shakespeare. I imagine that your theory is that she'd been gathering flowers and then, remembering Ophelia, acted out the part and took it too far. Is that how you see it, sir?'

Quantrill coughed as the smoke went the wrong way. Taking this for confirmation, Bedford riffled quickly through the pages. 'Yes, there's this touching scene where Ophelia offers her flowers to the courtiers; "There's fennel for you, and columbines; there's rue for you; and here's some for me." And she

96

sings very sadly. Well, the girl might have acted the scene and then climbed a willow tree, just as Ophelia did. That's in Gertrude's speech, Act Four Scene Seven. Would you like me to read the relevant bits, just to refresh your memory, sir?'

'Do,' said Quantrill hoarsely.

Bedford cleared his throat. He had never thought, when he joined the force, that he would find himself standing in a DCI's office reading Shakespeare; as the recruiting advertisements had promised, it seemed that a police constable's life really was full of variety. He selected some lines and started to read:

> *There is a willow grows aslant a brook,*
> *That shows his hoar leaves in the glassy stream;*
> *There with fantastic garlands did she come,*
> *Of crow-flowers, nettles, daisies and long purples . . .*
> *There, on the pendent boughs her coronet weeds*
> *Clambering to hang, an envious sliver broke—'*

'A what?' Quantrill interrupted.

'"An envious sliver," sir. He means a branch, don't you think?'

'Ah,' said Quantrill profoundly, suppressing the disrespectful thought that Shakespeare ought to have put what he meant, instead of wrapping facts up in words. It was the most obscure piece of evidence that he had ever heard. 'Go on.'

> *When down her weedy trophies and herself*
> *Fell in the weeping brook. Her clothes spread wide*
> *And, mermaid-like, awhile they bore her up;*
> *. . . but long it could not be*
> *Till that her garments, heavy with their drink,*
> *Pulled the poor wretch . . . to muddy death.'*

Quantrill sat in silence for a few moments. 'How deep would you say this brook was?' he asked eventually.

'I've always thought of it as being about waist-deep, sir.'

'Hm. The Dunnock's nowhere near that, at Ashthorpe bridge. Do you know the place?'

'No, sir.'

Quantrill stood up. 'Get your cap, then, we'll go and have a look.'

'Yes *sir!*' breathed Bedford, eagerness pinking his ears.

The evening sky had darkened to unpolished pewter. Rain was on the way, Quantrill smelled it in the wind; but still the sun shone, slanting low from under the clouds, turning the grass a vivid green and lighting every detail of the bridge and the willow trees.

Quantrill led the way down through the meadow, where the flowers had closed their petals for the night, to the place where the body had been found. The water looked dark now, its surface rippled by the evening breeze, but it was as shallow as he had remembered it. There could be no question of Mary Gedge's dress dragging her down, not if she were conscious.

Pc Bedford was clambering about in the nearest willow tree, with an enthusiastic disregard for his uniform that he was to regret when he returned to the section house. 'There's no evidence that she fell from up here, sir,' he said, disappointed; 'no coronet of flowers, or broken branch. But if she was acting Ophelia's mad scene she might quite well have climbed up here, and then tripped over her long dress.'

'Ophelia was mad?' asked Quantrill tentatively.

Bedford swung down to join him on the grass. 'Oh, that's arguable, I agree, sir. Just quietly out of her mind, I suppose. After all, with Hamlet spurning her and then killing her father—'

'Quite,' agreed Quantrill, fascinated.

'You've ruled out suicide in Mary Gedge's case, sir?'

The chief inspector returned to the mercifully less violent reality. 'No evidence to suggest it. And she was happy, by all accounts.'

Pc Bedford scratched his jaw, in unconscious imitation of Quantrill's habit. 'But so was Ophelia, when she drowned. Well, serene rather than actually happy. I mean, that was the form her madness took—when she fell in the water she simply floated along singing, didn't she? A kind of unintentional suicide, I suppose. Oh, I know it was just a device that Shakespeare used to keep the sympathy of his audience, because they would think that suicide was a sin. But could it have been unintentional suicide with Mary Gedge?'

'No,' said Quantrill. 'She didn't just float along serenely, she hurt her hands and knees trying to save herself. Still, you've reminded me that she didn't necessarily drown. Let's say it happened as you suggest—that she climbed the willow and fell in, hurting herself as she tried to prevent the fall. I've known one or two cases where the death of someone found apparently drowned has actually been due to heart failure, caused by the sudden shock of immersion in cold water. In that event, the depth of the water's immaterial. It's an interesting thought, Bedford, I'm obliged to you. Let's hope that we soon hear the result of the post-mortem, then we might begin to know where we are.'

The road by the bridge was too narrow for Quantrill to turn his car. He had to go up to Ashthorpe before he could find a turning place and having reached the village he drove on, almost defiantly, past the green. But if he had hoped to glimpse Jean Bloomfield outside her house, he was disappointed.

As he drove slowly along the length of the green, he passed the war memorial. On impulse, he stopped the car and got out. The buttercups still lay on the steps, dying now beyond revival. They were flanked by several empty beer cans, some crisp bags and the packaging from a Lyons individual fruit pie. Above the litter, immediately after the names of the men of the village who had been killed in battle between the years 1914 and 1918, was an exhortation to the survivors and their descendants:

*Sons of this place, let this of you be said,*
*That you who live are worthy of your dead.*
*These gave their lives, that you who live may reap*
*A richer harvest, ere you fall asleep.*

Quantrill had been taught in his boyhood to be respectful of his village war memorial. To his parents, the names of the fallen in the First World War were a harrowing memory, in the Second World War, a current grief. Mildly resentful on behalf of his father's decimated generation, Quantrill scooped up the rubbish and carried it a few yards down the road to an almost empty litter bin. Beside the bin was a public bench, ankle deep in lolly wrappers and cigarette packets and empty cans. The chief inspector looked at the mess with resigned disgust, and returned to the memorial. He felt strongly, intuitively, that there was some special significance in the bunch of buttercups;

that it was no coincidence that they had been placed there within the last eighteen hours.

As on war memorials everywhere, the list of names of the dead in the First World War was far longer than the 1939–45 list: nineteen names as against five. And in the first list was the common tragic recurrence of the same name. Ashthorpe had lost three Fletchers between 1914 and 1918.

It had also lost a Gedge.

Frowning, Quantrill drove on. He would not have disturbed the dead girl's father at home but Mr. Gedge was outside the shop, grey-faced, loading boxes of groceries into his van. Quantrill pulled up just behind him, and got out of his car.

'Forgive me for bothering you again, sir, but do you mind telling me whether the Gedge on the war memorial was one of your relations?'

The shopkeeper closed the van door, pushed his smudged glasses up on to his high forehead and rubbed his eyes wearily. 'Why, yes,' he said slowly. 'Yes, that's my Uncle Ralph. Not that I ever knew him, of course, he died exactly ten years to the day before I was born, that's how I know the date—first of July 1916, that's when he was killed.'

Pc Bedford, anxious to miss nothing, had been hovering at Quantrill's elbow. 'First day of the battle of the Somme,' he contributed promptly. The two older men looked at him, Quantrill in surprise, Mr. Gedge with a wan smile.

'Yes, Mary knew that too,' he said. 'She was very interested in the First World War, for some reason. Of course, they did it on telly a little while ago,' he added, as though the monstrous carnage of the Somme had been specially devised by the Outside Broadcasts department of the BBC. 'My Dad—he was Ralph's oldest brother—was alive and living with us then, and Mary used to badger him to tell her about it. She found some old photographs of Ralph up in the attic, and cards and things he'd sent home from France, and made a sort of little memorial to him.'

'I see . . . The reason I asked, Mr. Gedge, is that there's a bunch of buttercups lying on the steps of the war memorial. I wondered whether by any chance Mary might have put them there.'

Mr. Gedge frowned. 'Could have—I don't know, of course, but it's possible. I know that she got quite emotional about

Ralph. He'd volunteered at the beginning of 1915 and falsified his age, you see. He was only just eighteen when he was killed.'

His eyes focused on Quantrill. They were full of the pain of loss. 'Just eighteen,' he repeated. 'The same age as Mary herself.'

# THIRTEEN

$A$lone in his office again, Quantrill looked through the folders that he had retrieved from Mary Gedge's trailer. There seemed to be no personal information there at all; they contained nothing but school notes and essays, written in tiny but beautifully legible handwriting. The chief inspector pushed aside those in foreign languages and those dealing with international affairs, and was left with poems, notes about poems and essays about poets.

It was hard going for a working detective who had left school at fourteen, but he floundered through, comprehending where he could and trying to decide whether the selection of poems gave any clue to the dead girl's personality. It was some time before he realised that the physical discomfort he felt was not so much inability to digest the poetry, as hunger.

Quantrill looked at his watch. It was nearly nine. The canteen would have closed for hot meals, and he couldn't face another sandwich.

He went to the washroom, shaved hurriedly to freshen himself, put on his jacket again. 'I'm going to the Rights for a quick meal, Chalky,' he told the desk sergeant. 'Do you know where young Tait, the new Ds, is?'

'He went over to the mortuary about ten minutes ago, sir,' said Sergeant White. 'A bit impatient about the post-mortem they're doing on the Ashthorpe girl.'

'He's not the only one. Get word through to let him know

where I am, will you? I should be back in half an hour anyway.'

The rain had blown over, after a spit or two, but the streets were fresher for it. Dusk had begun to fall, and the sodium street lights were giving their preliminary red glow before fizzling into yellow brilliance. Quantrill hesitated for a moment at the open door of the half-timbered Coney and Thistle pub, longingly smelling the real, unpressurised Adnams Suffolk ale; but what he needed at the moment was hot food, not a pub snack, and so he turned the corner and entered the cobbled courtyard of the Rights of Man.

The Rights had begun life as the White Hart, an Elizabethan inn that had acquired a Georgian facade and stables in the heyday of coaching. The inn had declined with the long decline of Breckham Market, but the conversion of East Anglia into a vast United States airfield in the Second World War had brought an influx of new customers.

Long after the war had ended, some American air bases remained. A new generation of thirsty airmen had found their way to Breckham Market, augmented by increasing numbers of American tourists. Each summer, groups of greying, paunchy men would come on pilgrimage to East Anglia, to search among the camouflage of barley and sugar beet for the concrete runways from which they had once lifted off their Liberator bombers, and for the corrugated black half-hoops of their Nissen huts, inhabited now only by the wind and the silent ghosts of the slim young men who had flown from there and had never returned.

It was with an eye to the American tourist market, as well as to the rapid growth of the town, that the old White Hart had been bought by a big hotel combine. The inn had been modernised, considerably extended and re-named the Rights of Man; not in defiance of the proposition of the equality of the sexes but in commemoration of Thomas Paine, the advocate of American independence, whose ancestral connection with the town was a further encouragement to tourism.

Quantrill crossed the courtyard, by-passed the genuinely Tudor room that was so dark and low-ceilinged that it had been furnished with strip lighting and a juke box, named the Prior's Cellar and relegated to the use of the local lads, and entered the modern Tudor Buttery. Here, in the ferro-concrete new extension that had been built on the site of the stables, no expense had been spared to create a more comfortable six-teenth century. The walls of the spacious room were rough-plastered in white; steel girders, sited well above head height, had been covered with a laminate resembling ancient wooden beams. Each wall had a purely decorative row of latticed case-ments, lit softly from behind to display green whorls of imita-tion bottle glass. The hum of the air conditioning was as discreet as the perpetual Musak.

Quantrill was not enthusiastic about the way the old White Hart had been tarted up, but he was a practical man. The Tudor Buttery served grills at any time from nine in the morn-ing until ten at night, and he regarded the place with gratitude if not affection.

Tonight, he thought, he was going to indulge himself. He reached for the menu. A steak, that was what he would have, a good thick steak with all the trimmings, and hang the expense. After all, it had been a frustrating day, both professionally and personally: he was still no nearer to knowing whether Mary Gedge had died in suspicious circumstances; and as for Jean Bloomfield . . .

He shrugged irritably and set about trying to assuage desire with food. The menu was a new one since his last visit. Quantrill studied it and flinched. He was learning to live with inflation, but this was ridiculous; a steak meal would set him back over three quid.

It was out of the question, of course, for a man who had no expense account. He couldn't even begin to justify it, not with the mortgage and the rates and the electricity bill and the rental of the colour television set that Molly was dependent on because he was out so much. He sighed, and settled as usual for bacon, eggs and chips—French fries, in the intercontinen-tal jargon of the Rights—and a pint of their burp-inducing bitter.

While he ate, he concentrated his thoughts on a series of warehouse break-ins; he had reached the apple pie and coffee stage before he saw Jean Bloomfield, alone at a table for two. She must have been there for at least ten minutes, because a meal was on the table in front of her. But she was reading a book and, though she held a fork, hardly eating.

Quantrill felt all the physical symptoms that are associated with both love and indigestion, and invariably put the newly-in-love off their food: his chest tightened, his throat thickened. His heart began to thump. Oh God, had she seen him, gorging himself on chips and swilling beer? If she hadn't despised him before, this would be all that she needed. He pushed aside the remains of his pie and blotted the grease from his lips with a paper napkin. He felt hot, his stomach grossly distended, while she looked cool and remote behind the reading glasses that she wore.

She was dressed in a long skirt of some dark material, with a long-sleeved high-collared white blouse that emphasised her sunburn. Quantrill looked at her covertly, covetously. Oh, she was beautiful, even though there was nothing but gravity and weariness in her face.

He looked away from her and tried to will himself into invisibility. Presently he risked another glance from under his eyebrows. She was still reading, but now she had taken off her glasses.

Quantrill sat up, emboldened. Molly wore reading glasses too, and disliked being seen wearing them in public. He had always thought this an irritating piece of feminine vanity; but when the woman he was in love with took off her glasses in his presence, he found it wholly endearing.

He was insufficiently arrogant to be convinced of the significance of her action, but it gave him hope. If Jean had seen him, and minded that he should see her in her glasses, then it couldn't be true that she despised him. He stood up, squared his shoulders, drew in his stomach as far as he could, picked up his coffee cup and walked across to her table.

'Good evening, Mrs. Bloomfield,' he said boldly.

Molly, in similar circumstances, would have been coy: would have feigned surprise, started theatrically, blushed, flapped, said 'Well, fancy seeing you, I had no idea you were here.' But Jean Bloomfield gave him a sweet, sad smile that made his heart do a handstand. 'I hoped you'd come and join me, Mr. Quantrill,' she said. 'Do sit down, please.'

Her voice was as beautiful as ever, but slightly slurred. The omelette on the plate in front of her was hardly touched, the side salad not even disarranged, but the large carafe of white wine was half empty. She was not drunk, certainly, but she must by now be on her third glass; and that quantity, on an empty stomach after a long and distressing day, was bound to affect her.

Quantrill rummaged through his vocabulary for a word that would describe her condition, rejecting the vigorously vulgar masculinities and finally emerging with an expression favoured by his sister-in-law, a silly woman who, on her mercifully infrequent visits, got the giggles as soon as he uncorked the sweet sherry. Yes, that was it: Jean Bloomfield was gently sloshed.

And why not? he demanded of himself fiercely. He disliked women who drank anything more than a social glass before or with meals, because he'd seen too many pitifully drunken women. Molly, he was glad to recall, had eventually learned that she had a weak head, and stayed on bitter lemon. But if, on this occasion, Jean Bloomfield had chosen to get gently sloshed, he had nothing but love and sympathy for her.

He was gruff and protective, trying to persuade her to eat something when she admitted that she had returned empty-handed from her midday shopping expedition in the village on hearing of Mary's death. She declared that she was not hungry, but accepted his suggestion of coffee. Her hands shook as she took a cigarette from her packet; Quantrill flicked his lighter and held it out to her, wishing that he dared take her hands in his own and stop their trembling.

But at least he had a professional excuse for being masterly, for insisting on driving her home: 'I'm a police officer, remember—you're not allowed to refuse! Let me have your keys and I'll get someone to take your own car over to Ashthorpe first thing tomorrow.'

She hesitated, then surrendered her keys into his large, outstretched palm. He felt a surge of excitement, and glimpsed a fantasy in which he was already with her in her sitting-room, already holding her hands; but he controlled it with black, unsweetened coffee. Business first, pleasure—he hoped—later.

'If you don't mind talking about Mary,' he said, 'there is something that I'd like to ask you. Do you happen to know whether she kept a diary—a personal diary of her thoughts, I mean?'

Jean Bloomfield sipped at her coffee before speaking slowly and carefully, obviously aware that the wine had affected her sibilants. 'I'm sure that Mary didn't keep a diary. We were discussing famous diarists in school last term—some of the class admitted keeping diaries, but Mary said she wouldn't dream of it. She said she hated the idea of anyone reading her private thoughts after she was—'

She left the final word abruptly unspoken. Her eyes were brilliant with unshed tears and wine, and Quantrill made a business of lighting a cigar to give her time to recover. 'The thing is,' he said, his eyes on the flame, 'that we've been able to find very little personal information about Mary. And her death bothers me because I've been reading some of her school work and she seems to have had an obsession about dying young. Not that there's any evidence to suggest suicide—'

Jean Bloomfield stubbed out her half-smoked cigarette emphatically. 'I'm quite sure it wouldn't have been suicide! And I really don't think you need to worry about her taste in poetry—a good many poets have celebrated the idea of dying young, and some of them did just that, so their work has a particular appeal for people of Mary's age. It was something else we happened to be discussing in school last term. Mary was certainly interested, but that doesn't for a moment mean that she would deliberately go out and drown herself. I'm sure it must have been an accident.'

'We all hope that. But this Ophelia business—' he evaded her eyes, but went on doggedly '—I followed up the reference, and one of our young constables saw the point right away. He suggested that Mary might have been acting out the part of Ophelia, by herself, and that she might have climbed a willow tree and fallen in from there. Is it at all likely that she would have been play-acting, do you think?'

Jean Bloomfield looked up with interest, a new cigarette wavering in her hand. 'Why, yes—she loved acting. Mike Miller will tell you that—he teaches Drama, and Mary was the lead in a play he produced last term. And she did *Hamlet* at O level, so she might quite well think of Ophelia when she was gathering flowers, and act out the part. There's another thing, too—'

She absently picked up her glass and drank some more wine. The brightness of her eyes was almost feverish, and Quantrill remembered the message that Miller had asked him to take: 'Tell Jean I hope she feels better for her holiday.' Obviously she hadn't been well, and today had done her no good at all, poor girl. Not that he had any intention of passing on the message, least of all the bit about Miller's love, blast him.

'Do you mind, Mr. Quantrill,' she went on diffidently, 'if I put forward another speculation about Mary?'

He minded nothing but her formality. She knew his first name, he was certain of it. He wanted her to call him by it so that he could call her Jean. The use of his surname was a reminder that the barrier between them had not been dismantled.

'What I'm wondering,' she said, careful with her speech again, 'is whether Mary might have . . . might have allowed herself to drown without deliberately intending to take her life. Rather as Ophelia did.'

Quantrill frowned. 'My young constable suggested something of the sort, but that kind of accidental death in such a shallow river would only be possible if she were incapable of realising what was happening and saving herself. And you told me that you were quite sure—'

'Sure that she wouldn't have been either drinking or taking drugs, yes! But it's perfectly possible to be high—to be in such a state of elation that you temporarily lose your judgement—without any artificial stimulants.'

'Oh yes?' said Quantrill doubtfully.

'Yes, of course! Oh, don't look so disbelieving—you see, I know that Mary wouldn't think of drinking too much or taking drugs because she was naturally happy. Not merry-and-laughing or jolly, but serenely happy. Particularly so recently, because everything had gone right for her—she found life wonderful. And you can be just as high on happiness as on alcohol.'

'I'll take your word for it,' Quantrill said sceptically. 'But surely what you're saying is that Mary had everything to live for. If she was that happy the last thing she'd want to do would be to die.'

His words seemed to surprise Jean Bloomfield to such an extent that the trembling of her hand on the stem of her wine-glass slowed almost to a stop. 'Oh, no—perfect happiness is every bit as good a reason for seeking death as despair is!' she insisted. 'Better! No—not for *seeking* death; but for accepting it.'

Quantrill shook his head in disbelief. She leaned across the table and put her hand on his sleeve, and he realised that she was holding herself as taut as a trampoline. The wine glittered in her eyes but her voice was low and affectionate, anxiously willing him to understand and agree.

'But it's true—at least I've found it so. There were times when I was a young woman—not many, but all the more memorable—when life was so rich that I knew it could never be better. And I thought to myself then, in those moments, that it would be no hardship at all to drift away quietly into death at the very height of my happiness. Oh, surely you must—at least once—have experienced that kind of happiness too?'

'No,' said Chief Inspector Quantrill. 'I haven't.'

# FOURTEEN

Her false brilliance faded. She looked suddenly older, infinitely weary. 'I'm sorry,' she murmured uncertainly, taking her hand from his arm. She tried on a smile, but it was a lop-sided fit: 'I admit that it's been a good many years since I was as happy as that.'

Quantrill was disturbed by her look of desolation. 'Would you like to go home now?' he asked, lasciviousness forgotten.

She shook her head. 'I'd rather stay a little longer, if you're not in a hurry. I'll be glad of your company. No point in going home yet—I don't sleep well.'

'Have you been ill?'

'Oh, nothing physical. It's been a particularly difficult winter, that's all. The spring term's always a long hard haul, and the change to the comprehensive system made it seem worse.' She took another cigarette. 'Tell me, how are Jennifer and Alison?'

Quantrill told her in proud detail, and then hesitated before adding, 'I've never really thanked you for being so helpful and kind to them when we were . . . in difficulties.'

'If I was a help in any way, I'm glad. They were at such a critical stage in their education, and I admired you for undertaking to look after them single-handed so that they could stay on at school.'

Quantrill shrugged away three months of domestic confusion and remorse: 'Well, the girls were very good. We muddled through.' He looked at her with a big shy smile. 'It was an ordeal, I can tell you, going to see you at the grammar school to try to explain what had happened and to ask for leniency for the girls. I didn't expect the sympathy you gave me as well, though. After all, if a marriage gets to the stage where a wife leaves her husband and takes the youngest child home to her mother, it has to be the husband's fault. I was afraid that you'd think I'd been beating her, or running after other women.'

'But we'd already met, don't forget. I'd listened to the talk you gave to the seniors, and so I knew that you were a kind and honest man.'

Quantrill drew hard on his cigar and mumbled a disclaimer. 'I was a very inconsiderate husband, I realise that—working all hours, never on time for meals, hardly ever taking her out . . . She'd tried for years to get me to resign from the force, and threatened often enough to leave me if I didn't. Not that I ever thought she would. It really shook me when she did.'

'But she did come back—and you're still a policeman.'

'Oh yes, we compromised somehow. I can't do much about the odd hours I work, but Alison makes sure that at least I don't forget birthdays and wedding anniversaries any more. And of course the extra rank helps a lot—and not just financially. It seems that it's a good deal less humiliating when your absent husband's a chief inspector than it was when he was only a sergeant.'

He could hear the bitterness in his voice, and was ashamed of it. 'But at least we're a family again,' he added quickly. 'That's the main thing.'

'I envy you that,' she admitted. She gave him a sombre smile. 'And not only that. I was delighted to read about your rapid promotion—sergeant to chief inspector in four years!'

Quantrill tried not to glow at her approval. 'Oh, that's the way it often happens in the force, nothing for years and then a quick shove up the ladder in your forties. It's because of our early retirement system.'

One corner of her mouth twisted downwards. 'If only we had that in my profession! It's all very fine to be brilliant at the beginning of one's career, but it's very hard to adjust to the fact that the majority of one's working life is going to be spent going downhill. For you, though, the prospects are excellent, aren't they? What comes next, superintendent? Then chief superintendent?'

'Hold hard,' Quantrill protested modestly. 'I probably sha'n't get any further than this. I'm just an old-fashioned uneducated copper, one of the original Pc Plods. It's the clever ones who'll get top rank in future. Young Tait, now—he's been to university and police college, he'll be a chief super by the time he's thirty. He's a high-flyer if ever I saw one.'

'Yes, I can believe it. And obviously he's lucky, to have chosen a career in which high-flyers don't lose their status and become failures in early middle age—'

Her voice, as well as her hands, had begun to tremble, and Quantrill was indignant on her behalf. 'You ought to have been made head of the comprehensive,' he said warmly. 'Everybody I know thought so, I can tell you.'

She shook her head, unconsoled. 'It's not just that. I was an enthusiast for the comprehensive principle, you see. I thought it wrong that the great majority of children should be regarded as second-class citizens and offered less than the best. I wanted to use my skill and experience to give all the Breckham Market children the benefits of the kind of education we used to give the grammar school girls. And I've failed completely.'

'I don't see how you can possibly say that,' Quantrill objected, 'not after only two terms!'

'But it's true,' she said bleakly. 'I've been put in charge of the middle school, and it's all so different. I can't communicate with most of the children. They aren't even local, most of them, they've been brought from London to live on the new estates. They've been uprooted, disoriented, and they feel anonymous and unwanted. They hate the town, and they hate school because what we try to teach seems irrelevant. Nearly a quarter of them find reading difficult, and so they're bored and idle and aggressive and destructive. I used to be a good academic teacher, but I seem to have nothing to offer these children at all. I'm as confused as they are . . . and I've another eighteen years of it before I retire. Oh God, another eighteen years of Breckham Market middle school—and to think that I was once a high-flyer, an Oxford scholar with a brilliant future . . .'

So that was the trouble, thought Quantrill: that accounted for Denning's snide remark about his deputy's lack of ability. Well, no wonder she was finding it difficult to adjust, poor girl! Bad enough to have to try to teach a large number of children as noisily unenthusiastic about school as his own Peter, let alone the ones who could hardly read. And let alone the ones—by no means the ex-Londoners exclusively—who had been known to the police since junior school, who stole and lied and vandalised the town and terrorised the housing estates. No wonder Jean felt that her career had turned to failure. No wonder her nerves were raw.

He made what he hoped were understanding and consolatory noises, but she hardly seemed to hear. She sat with one elbow on the table, her chin propped on her hand. Her blue eyelids were lowered, and the lighting was so kind that the sweep of her dark lashes hid the lines and hollows under her eyes. She looked for a moment younger, more remote.

'I was thinking,' she said softly, almost to herself, 'of my husband. Life can turn out to be such a cheat and a disappointment for high-flyers, and that's what Philip was, literally. He was an RAF pilot, a member of the crack aerobatic team. He was killed twenty years ago, when he and another pilot collided while they were rehearsing their display.'

Quantrill had not known the occasion of her husband's death. He murmured conventionally, inadequately.

'It was terrible, of course,' she said, 'but twenty years is a long time . . . What finally consoled me was the thought that my sorrow was merely for myself—there was no need for me to grieve on Philip's behalf because he died doing exactly what he wanted to do. He'd had a brilliant RAF career and he loved flying, lived for it. But military flying is strictly for young men; he knew that, and dreaded the thought of being grounded. If he'd lived, he would be forty-five now. About your age?'

Quantrill nodded.

She smiled at him. 'But not, like you, forging ahead in his career. He'd never have made senior rank, he was too much of a rebel. No, if he'd lived, Philip would by now have been either bored and frustrated in a minor RAF desk job, or bored

111

and disillusioned as some kind of civilian sales representative. Or quite possibly unemployed and unemployable.' She took a cigarette. 'One of the friends of Rupert Brooke, the poet who died in the First World War, said that it was just as well that he died young, because he was magnificently unprepared for the long littleness of life. That was Philip, too.'

He watched her thin cheeks hollow further as she accepted the light he offered. 'It must have taken a very long time for you to get over the shock,' he said.

She considered the matter objectively, from a distance of twenty years. 'It was the *violence* of his death that was so hard to come to terms with. But my other consolation has always been that our marriage was wonderfully happy. We'd been married less than a year, and we were still very much in love. We never had time to take each other for granted. I can look back now on our marriage as a time of perfect happiness—and that could never have lasted, not with that degree of intensity. Philip had his share of vanity, and he would probably have tried to compensate for the disappointments of being middle-aged and grounded by running after girls. But as it is, he died young and happy. That's enviable, when you come to think of it, isn't it?' She touched the thick paperback that she had been reading. 'Do you know Dorothy Parker?'

No connection with Shakespeare, even he knew that. He admitted his ignorance of the name.

'She was an American writer,' Jean Bloomfield explained. 'She was young and rich and brilliant and famous in the nineteen twenties and thirties. She welcomed the idea of dying young—she hated the thought of middle and old age. She said that people ought to be one of two things, young or dead.'

Quantrill looked surreptitiously at his watch, wondering how much longer it would be before the post-mortem result on Mary Gedge came through. 'In my job,' he said heavily, 'I see far too many people who are both.'

'Yes—yes, I imagine you do. Can you tell me, is there any news of the girl who disappeared a few months ago, Joy Dawson? I know my headmistress, and she tells me how disturbed and distressed everyone at her school is. Is there any hope?'

'Hope of what, after this time?' asked Quantrill glumly. 'That instead of being brutally murdered, she was picked up and taken to London, and that she's now on drugs and the game? We've simply no idea—and it's the not knowing that's the worst thing of all for the parents. You'll think that this is a terrible thing for me to say, but when I heard that a girl had been found drowned but otherwise unharmed at Ashthorpe, I really hoped that it would be Joy Dawson.'

'I know exactly what you mean. Death—as long as it isn't violent—is preferable to disappearance. At least Mary Gedge's parents have the consolation of knowing that she hadn't been molested. At least they can bury her body. It won't lessen their immediate sorrow, of course, but after the burial and the mourning they'll gradually be able to come to terms with their grief, in a way that Joy Dawson's poor parents never can. And I think that in time the Gedges will be glad that they can remember their daughter as being always young and happy . . . just as I can remember Philip . . .'

Her eyes had softened, and her smile of reminiscence was so unexpectedly tranquil that the chief inspector felt a rush of envy. Not of the dead pilot; as Jean had said, twenty years is a long time, and Quantrill did not imagine that fidelity to his memory would keep her—had, for all he knew, kept her—from taking a lover if she wanted one. But he envied her acquaintance with perfect happiness.

They were silent for a few moments. 'Why are you looking so sad?' she asked gently. 'You've no need to. You have a family, and a very successful career. You're a lucky man.'

He was tempted to confide in her, to tell her about his marriage; to explain that, gratifying as it was, success in his career seemed to be merely a consolation prize for the absence of personal happiness. What a wonderful wife Jean would make, he thought. Not just in bed—he had no proof of that, of course, but no doubts either—but as a lifetime companion, an intimate friend whose idea of conversation was not confined to comments about the neighbours and complaints about the cost of living. He lit a cigar that he didn't want, to dull the edge of fantasy.

'We've undergone an interesting reversal of rôles since we first met, haven't we?' she went on lightly. 'I was then the headmistress of a grammar school, you were a detective sergeant. Now you're the head of Breckham Market CID, and I'm just the deputy head of a botched-up comprehensive.'

He stopped feeling sorry for himself. Jean Bloomfield's sense of personal failure was, with reason, far greater than his own. She was the one who deserved sympathy. 'I still don't know why you didn't get the appointment,' he said.

'Oh, it was only to be expected. I knew perfectly well that the education authority was too patriarchal to appoint a woman as head of the empire it was creating. I should have had more sense than to apply for the job. But I did, and it hurt to be rejected.'

'Yes,' said Quantrill slowly. One of her hands rested on the table a few inches from his own; now, if ever, was the moment to take it. He knew how much he wanted her. He was aware of a contraction and intensification of his vision, a shortening of his breath. 'It always hurts to be rejected,' he said, choosing his words with difficulty. 'I dislike applying for things—things I would very much value—for just that reason.'

Her eyes met his, and read the significance of his words. Patches of crimson began to appear on her cheeks and her neck. Her lips parted slightly.

The air about them seemed to have stilled and thickened. Quantrill felt that they were alone, enclosed in a capsule of privacy. He could see nothing but her eyes, her mouth.

He placed his cigar on the ashtray in slow motion, taking the exaggerated care of a man who had been drinking. He remembered her phrase; was this, he wondered, what it felt like to be high on happiness?

She spoke softly, breathily. 'Is that why you suddenly stopped coming to see me, four years ago?'

'You knew how I felt?'

'I guessed.'

'You didn't try to make it any easier for me, though.'

'How could I?'

He was suddenly bitter, thinking of the lost years. 'Because you were a headmistress, and I was only a sergeant?'

'No! Because you were married—'

'My wife had left me, remember?'

'But you were still the father of two of my pupils. And yes, I was their headmistress . . .' She shook her head regretfully. 'It really wouldn't have been possible, would it?'

Greatly daring, he put his hand over hers. 'But you did want it?'

Her hand was trembling again. 'Yes.'

His fingers closed on hers. His heart hammered loud in his ears. 'Well, then? Now that you're no longer in charge of my daughters—'

She shook her head again. 'Now it's *your* status that we have to consider. You've a good career ahead, and potential superintendents can't afford to indulge in extra-marital affairs.'

'To hell with my career!' he announced. He clasped her hand recklessly, delighting in the strong responsive pressure of her fingers; making the most of this moment because he knew that he didn't mean what he said.

She was right, of course. An affair was out of the question for him now: it would smash up his family and his career, both. 'We could be discreet,' he insisted, knowing perfectly well that in Breckham Market a discreet affair was impossible.

She smiled at him affectionately, relaxing her clasp. 'Holding hands in the Tudor Buttery at the Rights isn't the best way of exercising discretion,' she pointed out. 'To begin with, the waitress on the next table is the sister of one of my pupils. And the assistant manager's heading towards us, and it looks as though he knows you.'

The capsule that had been enclosing them dissolved. 'Blast!' said Quantrill despondently. He felt her hand slip unobtrusively out of his grasp.

'Excuse me, Chief Inspector.' The assistant manager, dark suited and silver tied, young and keen and professionally deferential, bent towards him. 'A gentleman would like to speak to you urgently, sir.'

Quantrill glanced towards the glass doors that led to the foyer. Sergeant Tait was hovering outside them, his eyes diplomatically averted.

''Scuse me,' Quantrill muttered. He left the table and strode to the doorway, conscious that Jean Bloomfield was watching him. 'Well?' he demanded belligerently.

Tait beckoned him away from the door. 'I've got the pathologist's report on Mary Gedge, sir.'

The chief inspector's emotions subsided as though he'd jumped into cold water. He came up gasping, but clearheaded: 'And?'

The sergeant began a catalogue: 'Cause of death, asphyxia due to drowning. No trace of alcohol or of drugs, no sexual interference at all, no external injury, no concussion. But—'

He paused, ostensibly for breath. Quantrill thought it was for effect. 'Get on with it.'

Tait contrived to sound casual, but there was triumph in his eyes. 'The only indication of injury, sir, is a cluster of small bruises in the deep tissues at the nape of the neck. According to the pathologist, they're consistent with considerable pressure applied by the thumb and fingers of someone's right hand.'

'You mean her head was held under water?'

'Yes sir. She was murdered.'

Chief Inspector Quantrill's face was impassive. 'Right. We'll start with house-to-house enquiries in Ashthorpe. Get the mobile information room over there, and have it parked outside the police house.'

'I've already asked for it to stand by, sir, and an enquiry team is being formed.'

'Good. You set up the Ashthorpe end, then. I'll be along in half an hour to do the briefing. And then I want the boy-friend—what's his name, Kenward—brought to the station for questioning.'

'Yes, sir. And the brother? He's got motive enough.'

'Jealousy? Agreed.'

The sergeant turned to go, but Quantrill called him back. 'Sergeant Tait!'

'Sir?'

There was no doubt that Tait found satisfaction in his work. His eyes had a controlled excitement; he was vibrant.

'Well done,' said Quantrill, straight-faced. 'You were the one who was suspicious about this death, and you were right.'

'Thank you, sir,' said Tait, without false modesty.

Quantrill surveyed him with distaste. 'All right, then, get on with it. Find out who murdered the poor girl. But stop looking so bloody *pleased* about it.'

# FIFTEEN

The drive with Jean Bloomfield to Ashthorpe was faster and far less pleasurable than Quantrill had fantasised. She sat beside him in silence, while he concentrated on what he was going to say at the briefing. It was not until they neared Ashthorpe and he slowed for the bridge that she said, 'Am I allowed to ask whether there's some new development concerning Mary's death?'

'Yes—we've had the report on the post-mortem,' he answered. He thought for a moment and then said, in a matter-of-fact voice, 'She did die by drowning.'

The ambiguous phrasing was deliberate. He didn't want to conceal the truth from Jean Bloomfield—she'd hear it soon enough in the village tomorrow—but he couldn't bring himself to spell it out to her now. She'd be shocked and upset. She'd need to be comforted.

He indulged in a fleeting recurrence of fantasy: Jean in tears, in his arms. They'd agreed that a prolonged affair would be impossible, but surely they were entitled to a few moments alone together?

Only not now. He couldn't spare the time, or the energy. And since it would be cruel to break the news of the girl's murder and then leave Jean alone at her gate, it would be better not to tell her any more than she needed to know.

'There'll have to be an inquest, of course,' he explained, 'and the coroner will want to know when and where Mary was last seen alive, so I must find out how she got back from Breckham last night. I'm sending some men to Ashthorpe to make house-to-house enquiries.'

He was tempted, for a moment, to promise that the enquiry team would not visit her. The least he could do, for the woman he loved, was to protect her from routine police enquiries. But what a giveaway of his emotions that would be! Quantrill remembered Tait's sharp nose and the mocking curve of his lip as they had stood together on the doorstep of Jean's house. Having renounced an affair with her, Quantrill had no intention of giving his sergeant any hostages.

'I'm afraid they'll have to come to you, as well,' he said. 'We need to cover everybody, just for the record.'

'Of course,' she said. 'There's nothing I can tell your men, but I realise that they have to do their job. Look, drop me here on the edge of the green. I'd have liked to ask you in for a drink, but I know you're too busy.'

He stopped the car on the main road, near the war memorial. The sky had cleared. Moonlight bleached the grass and softened the granite of the memorial cross. Before he had time to get out of his seat and help her, she had unclipped her seat belt and opened the door.

'Thank you for the lift,' she said. 'And for your company.'

He felt that she was slipping away from him. He wanted to seize her hand again, just for a moment, but she was already out of the car.

'Thank *you*,' he mumbled, quickly, inadequately. 'Another time, perhaps—the drink, I mean . . . ?'

'Why not? Good night.'

He watched her walk away from him, her long dark skirt brushing the moon-white grass. He was sweating; his hands were trembling almost as much as hers had trembled, though for a different reason. Love, he thought ruefully, played havoc with a detective chief inspector's powers of concentration.

She entered the house and closed the door without looking back. Quantrill heaved himself out of the car and took three long, deep breaths of night air. Then he sighed, wiped his forehead with one of the large white handkerchiefs that Molly always laundered so immaculately, put Jean Bloomfield from his mind and turned the whole of his attention to the investigation of murder.

Chief Inspector Quantrill kept the briefing short.

'According to the pathologist's report, death occurred some time between the hours of 5 am and 6 am. At this time of the year, of course, that means broad daylight. Apparently it was fine and sunny, so it's perfectly possible that she slept in her trailer and then went out for an early morning walk.

'At the moment, though, we've no evidence whether she slept in her trailer or not. She was last seen alive, wearing the clothes in which the body was found, at approximately eight forty-five last night in Breckham Market.

'We need to find out three things: how she got to Breckham from Ashthorpe; who she was with, or who she met, last night; and whether she was seen again in Ashthorpe before her death. Any additional information you can gather about a local boy-friend or admirer could be very valuable. Any questions?'

Quantrill left Sergeant Tait to allocate routes to the enquiry team and returned to Breckham Market. Dale Kenward had already been brought in for questioning. When the chief inspector entered the interview room, a uniformed constable stood up. Kenward, in an expensive suede jacket, remained slumped in his chair; but not, apparently, out of defiance. He looked shocked, absent from his body.

Quantrill sat down on the opposite side of the table. 'I'm Chief Inspector Quantrill. I'm enquiring into the death of Mary Gedge.'

The young man stirred, and looked up. He was handsome, with a heavy head of dark wavy hair, and blue eyes under straight brows; he had left his upper lip unshaven, and had a fine silky growth on it. Beneath the dark moustache his lips were full and red, sensual.

'You're Dale Kenward?'

'Yes.' His voice was strained, his eyes dull. 'I can't tell you anything about her death,' he added thickly. 'My mother says that you think she killed herself because of me, but it's not true, I swear it isn't.'

'And how do you know that?' asked Quantrill quietly. 'Were you there when she died?'

Kenward sat slowly upright. His eyes seemed to focus on the chief inspector for the first time. 'No!' he protested. His cheeks began to redden. 'No, of course I wasn't! I tell you I don't know anything about her death. It's just . . . incomprehensible.'

'Well, then.' Quantrill sat back, pulled open the drawer of the table and found a packet of cigarettes and a box of matches. He pushed them across to Kenward, who hesitated before lighting a cigarette with shaking hands and puffing at it inexpertly. He was right-handed.

'Let's talk about Mary's life instead,' said Quantrill kindly. 'You were friends?'

'Yes. Well, that is—until a few weeks ago.'

'And then you quarrelled? What about?'

He went sullen. 'I'd rather not say.'

'A lovers' quarrel, perhaps?'

Kenward looked up, his eyes hot with anger. 'We were *not* lovers. We were in love, yes, but not lovers. There *is* a difference, you know.'

Quantrill acknowledged it. 'You and Mary were in love until a few weeks ago, and then you quarrelled. Does that mean that you stopped loving her?'

Kenward stared down at his cigarette. 'No,' he said. The word was barely audible.

'You'd have liked to make up the quarrel?'

'Yes.'

'You tried to make up the quarrel?' The boy was silent. 'Come on,' said Quantrill. 'I need an answer. What did you do—ring her? Call at her house? Write to her?'

'Wrote,' Kenward muttered.

'And did Mary reply?'

He shook his head.

Quantrill lit a cigar for himself. 'When did you last see Mary?' he asked conversationally.

Kenward stirred in his chair and puffed and shrugged. 'At the end of last term,' he said.

'Did you see her yesterday?'

'No! I told you, I haven't seen her since the end of last term.'

'What were you doing last night?' Kenward's hand stiffened in the act of tapping his cigarette over the ashtray. 'When, last night?' he temporised.

Quantrill sat forward in his chair. The constable turned over a page of his notebook and held his pen poised. 'Last night,' said Quantrill distinctly, 'between eight forty-five and six o'clock this morning.'

Kenward screwed his cigarette into the ashtray, shredding a good inch of tobacco. 'I was bird-watching,' he said defiantly. 'In Lillington woods.'

'Alone?'

The boy tugged at his moustache. 'With my friend Colin Andrews,' he said.

Quantrill made no comment. He stared hard at Kenward, who moistened his lips and looked away. Presently the chief inspector said, 'You wanted to marry Mary Gedge, I believe?'

Kenward's blue eyes darkened with misery, but his voice was still defiant: 'Is there anything wrong with that?'

'A bit premature, perhaps?' Quantrill suggested. 'As you've said, you weren't lovers. There wasn't the—the usual reason for a hasty marriage.'

Kenward looked at him with disdain. 'I didn't want a hasty marriage. I wanted to marry Mary because I loved her—but I don't suppose you'd understand that.'

'Oh yes, I understand it. You loved Mary so much that you wanted to be with her all the time. I know exactly how you felt. It's only natural.' Quantrill got up from his chair and stood looking down at the boy. 'But I don't see that marriage would have achieved that, do you? Your mother told me that you're going to Manchester university. Mary was going to Cambridge. Were you intending to give up Manchester to be with her? Or did you expect her to give up Cambridge to be with you?'

Kenward shrugged. 'We couldn't have got married right away,' he admitted. 'But we could have been engaged.'

'For three years! Is that what you wanted Mary to do, to promise that she'd marry you in three years' time? No wonder she fell out with you! Everyone tells me that she was looking forward to Cambridge because she wanted to spread her wings a bit, meet new people, make new friends. Of course she didn't want to be tied to a local boy-friend. An attractive girl like Mary would have had no difficulty—'

Quantrill stopped speaking. He looked down at Dale Kenward's bowed head. 'That was it, then, was it?' he continued softly. 'You wanted to get engaged because you were worried about the competition—you were afraid that she'd fall in love with another man?'

Kenward lifted his head. Tears had begun to gather on his thick dark eyelashes. 'How could I trust her to choose the right friends?' he gulped. 'You know what it's like at Cambridge—far more men than women. I was afraid it would go to her head. She was so lovely, and so *unaware*. She'd have been picked up by some older man, she'd have been used and then just pushed aside. I couldn't bear the thought of it. So I decided that if we were engaged, it would keep the others away.'

The chief inspector nodded slowly. He looked hard at the desperate, immature face, trying to gauge what extremity Dale Kenward's love for Mary Gedge might have driven him to. 'But Mary wouldn't agree to marry you . . .' he said. 'I can understand how you must have felt. So what happened last night, Dale? You and Mary met, and discussed it? And you decided that if you couldn't have her, no one else would? Is that what happened?'

Dale Kenward looked up, frowning. He wiped his eyes with the back of his hand. 'I don't know what you're talking about,' he said.

The chief inspector loomed over him. 'I think you do,' he said heavily. 'Let's stop pretending. Dale. Where were you last night?'

'Bird watching.' But he said it without much conviction.

'And who with?'

'Colin Andrews.'

'Don't lie to me, boy. You told your mother that you were going out with Colin, but we've checked. He was with another friend until ten thirty, when he went home to bed. So where were you last night?'

Kenward pulled agitatedly at the hairs of his moustache. 'All right, I wasn't bird watching. But I wasn't with Mary—I didn't see her.'

Quantrill stared at him with hard green eyes. 'Did you kill Mary Gedge?' he asked.

Kenward's jaw dropped. '*Kill* her? For God's sake—what are you telling me? You mean she was—?'

'Murdered,' Quantrill confirmed. 'The girl you wanted to marry, the girl who didn't want to marry you, was deliberately held under water until she drowned. So I'll repeat my question: did you kill Mary Gedge?'

Dale Kenward's face had paled to a dirty grey. His mouth opened and closed again. He began to rise, put out his hand blindly towards the table for support, missed it and collapsed in a heap of dark hair and brown suede at the chief inspector's feet.

# SIXTEEN

Quantrill went out into the corridor. A fair-haired, uniformed, early-thirtyish policewoman was approaching briskly, and she gave a conspiratorial grin as she saw him.

'I was just coming to have a word, sir. *Councillor* Kenward's at the desk, and rather anxious to speak to you.'

Quantrill pulled a lugubrious face. 'That's all we need . . . His son's just fainted in there.'

The policewoman raised an elegantly shaped pair of eyebrows. She had a solid chin but attractive brown eyes, and she knew how to make the most of them. 'From guilt?' she asked.

'I wish I knew. Can you get him a glass of water, Patsy? We don't want Councillor Kenward accusing us of police brutality—oh Lord, too late!'

A short square sandy man was steaming angrily down the corridor, while the desk sergeant hovered and gestured ineffectually in his wake. 'Inspector Quantrill,' the man boomed, 'I demand to see my boy.'

Quantrill blocked the passage. 'Chief Inspector now, sir,' he said pleasantly. 'Your son is helping us with our enquiries.'

Councillor Kenward inflated the hand-stitched lapels of his checked suit. His cheeks were a strong mottled red, and his breath smelled of whisky; if the man became too obnoxious, Quantrill reflected, he could always have him followed and done for driving with excess alcohol in his blood.

Kenward senior snorted his contempt. 'You haven't any right to bring the boy here behind my back,' he asserted.

'Your son is eighteen years of age, sir,' Quantrill pointed out, 'and he came here voluntarily.'

'And he's going voluntarily an' all.' He raised his volume. 'Dale! Where are you?'

A groan came from the interview room. Quantrill beat Councillor Kenward to the door by a nose, but was too late to prevent him from seeing a large constable thrusting Dale's head between his knees.

For a few moments the small room was in an uproar. The councillor jumped and bellowed with rage, demanding his solicitor, invoking the chief constable and the *Daily Mirror,* threatening instant dismissals from the police force. Wpc Patsy Hopkins, returning with a glass of water, exercised her eyebrows at Quantrill; she found the DCI considerably more attractive and aggreeable than his uniformed counterpart.

'Who does he think he is,' she murmured, as Councillor Kenward stamped on the floor in his fury, 'Rumpelstiltskin?'

Quantrill, who had been brought up on Grimms' fairy tales, gave her an appreciative grin. She blushed, and went to deal more charitably than usual with the small group of women referred to scathingly by Breckham Market people as 'the overswill', who invariably celebrated the end of their factory working week and gave themselves the courage to face the quietness of the rural weekend of getting drunk.

The chief inspector waited diplomatically until the councillor was exhausted and his son had come round. 'I just fainted, Dad,' the boy mumbled through lips that were still white, 'it's all right, I just fainted.'

Councillor Kenward sat on the other chair, mopping his face with an ostentatious silk handkerchief. 'And what did they do to make you faint?' he growled.

'I told him that his friend Mary Gedge had been murdered,' intervened Quantrill.

The boy's father looked astounded. 'Murdered—the girl Gedge?'

'Yes sir. That's the subject of our enquiry.'

Councillor Kenward looked in horror from the chief inspector to his son. 'He didn't do it,' he said flatly. 'He didn't do it.' He glared at Dale, his reddened watery eyes suddenly bulging: '*Did* you do it? Because by God if you did—'

He was out of his chair and had seized his son by the suede lapels before Quantrill could stop him. Dale turned his head aside, but made no attempt to break his father's grip. 'Oh, for heaven's sake . . .' he said weakly, 'of *course* I didn't. I *loved* her—can't any of you get that into your thick heads?'

His father released him abruptly and shook a stubby, sandy-haired finger in the boy's face. 'Now, less of that,' he said. 'Less of your lip. Come on, you're coming home.'

Dale Kenward turned to Quantrill. His face was still pale, and he had begun to shiver. 'How did it happen?' he whispered. 'Please tell me, I've got to know.'

Quantrill looked at him impassively. 'I told you,' he said. 'She was held under water until she drowned.'

Dale Kenward swallowed. 'She wasn't—I mean . . .'

'No,' said Quantrill.

He could swear that the look of relief on young Kenward's face was genuine. 'But you still haven't told me,' he added sternly, 'what you were doing last night. Your son,' he informed Councillor Kenward, 'lied to me. He said at first that he was bird-watching with a friend all night. Now he's admitted that it's not true. So where were you, Dale? Who were you with?'

The boy lifted his head proudly. The colour had begun to return to his face. 'I can't tell you,' he said. 'I was doing nothing illegal, but I can't tell you what it was. I swear, though, that I wasn't with Mary and that I know nothing about her death.'

His father stared at him, simmering; Quantrill stared at him, rubbing his chin. There were tears in the boy's eyes but his look was stubborn, unwavering.

'All right,' said the chief inspector eventually. He turned away. 'All right, go on home.'

'You've finished with him?' Councillor Kenward demanded.

'For the moment. I shall probably want to see him again.'

'Then you'll see my solicitor an' all. *And* I shall be ringing the chief constable about this in the morning, don't you worry!'

'All that worries me, sir,' retorted Quantrill, 'is finding the killer of Mary Gedge. Now if you'll wait by the desk for a moment, I'll send a car to take you both home.'

'I don't want your car,' Kenward snapped. 'I've got the Merc.'

Quantrill smiled at him politely. 'I wouldn't advise you to drive it, sir, not in your condition . . . Excuse me, please, I have a lot to do.'

Sergeant Tait joined the chief inspector in his office. 'The first of the house-to-house reports, sir. Nothing really significant, though one of them is interesting.' He riffled through the papers he had brought. 'A Mrs. Daphne Bullock, of Back Street—I rather think that she's the woman who came barging into the shop when we were talking to Mr. Gedge this morning. She told Pc Bedford that she went into the shop yesterday evening just after six: Mary was serving Mr. Miller, the teacher. They were laughing about something, and Mrs. Bullock heard him ask Mary if she'd like a lift into Breckham this morning. She refused.'

'Hmm. Do you know if she gave any reason—said what she intended to do instead?'

'I asked Bedford the same question, and he'd already put it to Mrs. Bullock. A bright boy, that. But unfortunately Mary hadn't given a reason for refusing the lift. Just thanked Miller, and said that she didn't think she would.' ·

'I see . . . Well, if Mrs. Daphne Bullock *is* the faggot we met this morning, I'm not surprised that Mary didn't want to discuss any arrangements in her hearing. Miller knew the girl pretty well, obviously, and liked her . . . but with all her private correspondence destroyed, it's going to be a devil of a job pinning down her friends and finding out what her plans were.'

'I did try Mary's other Breckham friends earlier this evening,' said Tait, 'but none of them saw her yesterday. So Denning, the headmaster, is still the last person who saw her alive.'

'Yes, but that was at least eight hours before her death, and six miles from where the body was found. No one else in Ashthorpe saw her yesterday?'

'Half a dozen people saw her in the shop, but no one after about six thirty. Have you seen the boyfriend yet, sir?'

'About half an hour ago.' Quantrill took a cigar from his tin, looked at it, tasted the staleness of his mouth, and put it back. 'He's denied it, of course. Mind, he admitted that he still loved Mary, that he was out all last night, that he wasn't bird-watching and that he wasn't with his friend Colin.'

Tait sat up, astonished. 'Well—great! What more do you want?'

Quantrill shrugged. 'I felt that he was genuine. I'm sure he wasn't putting on an act. Whatever he was up to last night, I'm prepared to believe—at the moment—that it wasn't connected with Mary's death. And I had no reason at all to hold him.'

For his part, Tait had no reason at all to encourage the chief inspector to wrap up the case unaided. 'The path report doesn't give us much to go on, I agree,' he said. 'By attacking her from behind, her assailant made it impossible for her to mark him. All she had under her finger nails was gravel and shreds of river weed.'

Quantrill looked again at the report. 'She'd have put up quite a struggle,' he said. 'The damage to her finger nails bears that out. The murderer would have had a job to hold her head under water—he'd have been soaked in the process. That means he would have returned home sodden and muddy, and possibly trailing river weed. I think I'll send a Wpc round for a cosy chat with Dale Kenward's mother in the morning, to check.'

'I doubt whether Derek Gedge's womenfolk would even see him in the morning, let alone notice his condition,' said Tait. 'They probably aren't up before he goes to work. He was being taken into an interview room just as I came in, by the way. Do you mind if I have a go at him, sir?'

The chief inspector looked at Tait's sharp features. 'As long as you're not over-influenced by the man's job,' he said firmly. 'All right, so Derek Gedge is hardened to killing. It's his trade now. But remember, his sister wasn't butchered. She must have been killed quite . . . well, it's a stupid thing to say, knowing how she would have struggled, but quite mercifully when you think what happens to most girls who are murdered . . . Come on, then, I'll sit in with you. I'd like to hear what young Gedge has to say for himself.'

The chief inspector preceded Tait through the door, and the sergeant scowled at his broad back. Was the old man never going to learn to delegate?

Derek Gedge, in reasonably clean jeans and a PVC jacket that gave a poor imitation of leather, was sprawled on a chair in the interview room. He looked better than he had looked in the morning. The unhealthy pallor had gone from his face, but his eyes were heavy. He glanced up as the detectives entered the room, and made no attempt to hide his dislike when he saw Sergeant Tait.

Quantrill sat unobtrusively at the back of the room. Tait stood at the table, opposite Derek Gedge. 'Detective Sergeant Tait,' he announced crisply. 'We met this morning.'

Gedge tipped his chair back. 'So?'

'At the time,' said Tait, 'Chief Inspector Quantrill and I were making enquiries into the circumstances of your sister Mary's death.' He sat down. 'We are now investigating her murder.'

The front legs of Gedge's chair returned to the floor with a crash. He was jolted, literally. 'Oh my God,' he said softly, 'oh no . . .' His fair skin reddened to the roots of his blond hair. 'But it doesn't make sense . . . why should anyone want to kill *Mary*—?'

Tait sat back, arms folded. 'With girls,' he said, 'the reason's usually obvious. A stranger attempts rape, the girl struggles, the man loses his head and hits her, or chokes her to stop her from screaming. But as far as Mary is concerned, the pathologist rules out any sexual motive.'

'Glad to hear it,' muttered Gedge. He looked up at Tait. 'But what other motive could there possibly be for killing Mary?'

The sergeant unfolded his arms and leaned across the table. 'Well . . . there's jealousy,' he said softly. 'Plain, old-fashioned jealousy . . .'

For a few seconds the two young men stared at each other from a distance of a couple of feet. Derek Gedge's high colour had been fading, but it returned in a swoop of scarlet. He looked away.

'I don't know what you're getting at,' he said.

'Yes you do. You were all set for Cambridge, eighteen months ago, weren't you? All set for a bright career. Now look at you: married to a slovenly piece, living in a pig-sty, working in a stinking chicken factory, saddled with a kid that's probably another man's—'

Derek Gedge jumped to his feet, clenching his fists.

'Sit down!' Tait snarled.

Gedge sat.

'And as if that wasn't bad enough,' Tait needled on, 'your young sister Mary goes and gets a place at Cambridge. Well, no wonder you were jealous.'

'I wasn't jealous!' Gedge muttered. 'Mary was welcome to Cambridge—I didn't want it any more.'

'No?' Tait pursed his lips. 'Well, that's understandable, really. After all, you were only going to Selwyn, weren't you? I mean,' he taunted, 'who ever heard of Selwyn? It's hardly the

128

sort of college you'd mention in the same breath as King's, where Mary was going, is it?'

'Selwyn's a perfectly good college. No, it hasn't got the same reputation that King's used to have, and that's no bad thing either! Selwyn's a decent, straight college—I was proud to be going there.'

'You were? And yet you've just tried to tell me that you didn't want it any more. Oh, come on, stop fooling yourself, because you don't fool me. You were jealous of Mary, jealous as hell!'

Derek Gedge shook his head wearily and slumped back in his chair. 'I wasn't,' he mumbled. He looked up. 'Well, all right, I was, a bit; but if you think that means that I'd do anything to harm Mary, you must be out of your mind.'

Sergeant Tait tried to recall the dead girl's features. She and her brother must have looked very much alike. Would he have done anything to harm Mary? Tait couldn't be sure.

'What were you doing at nine o'clock yesterday evening?' he asked.

'Same as usual—working in the garden.'

Tait gave an abrupt laugh of contempt. 'The garden at Jubilee Crescent? That rubbish dump!'

'It's not a rubbish dump,' said Gedge indignantly. 'At least, not round the back. I grow vegetables there, to help with the food bills. I stayed out there yesterday evening as long as it was light, earthing up my potatoes. Some of the neighbours saw me, you can ask them.'

'I shall. What did you do then?'

'Went in and had my supper, watched a late film on television, went to bed.'

'Did you sleep well?'

'What?'

'You heard what I asked. Did you sleep well?'

Gedge shifted in his chair. 'Not really. They will fry everything. I had a stomach upset.'

'So you got up? What time?'

'Some time in the early hours—three-ish, I think, it was just beginning to get light.'

'And did you go out of the house?'

'No.'

Chief Inspector Quantrill, who had been listening quietly, suddenly interrupted. 'Hold hard—there's no sewer in Ashthorpe yet, and I know for a fact that those council houses haven't been modernised. If you went to the lavatory, you must have gone outside.'

Gedge shrugged impatiently. 'All right, then, I went out to the backyard! And I took a breath of air while I was at it, but I didn't leave the garden. I went back indoors after about ten minutes.'

'To bed?' Quantrill asked.

'No, the kid was howling. I stayed downstairs, made myself a cup of tea, read a bit.'

'How long for?' asked Tait.

'Until it was time to get up anyway. We start work at half-seven, so I'm usually up an hour before. I took my wife and her mother a cup of tea just before I got my bike out to go to work.'

Sergeant Tait told Gedge to stand up. 'Are those the clothes you put on first thing this morning?'

'To kill chickens in!' retorted Gedge sourly. 'No, I wore my filthy old working jeans.'

'I see. And did you happen to get your filthy old working jeans wet this morning?'

'No.'

'If I ask to see them, you'll have no objection to showing them to me?'

'Any time. You'll find them soaking in a bucket of detergent in the middle of the kitchen floor. That's what I do with my working jeans every Friday night—that way, there's a chance that one of the women will get them washed and dried by Monday morning.'

Both policemen stared hard at Gedge. He examined his finger nails.

'Did any of the neighbours see you in Jubilee Crescent this morning?' asked Tait eventually. 'Is there anyone who can vouch for your whereabouts between three and six o'clock?'

'I don't suppose so. Why?'

'Because that's about the time when Mary was killed.'

The blood left Gedge's face. He turned to Quantrill. 'But I don't know anything about it!' he protested.

'I'm the one who's asking the questions,' snapped Tait. 'Look at me: did you see your sister Mary at any time between nine o'clock last night and six this morning?'

'No, I swear I didn't.'

Sergeant Tait's jaws were stiff with anger. 'I can't see why you let him go, sir, not at this time of night. I wanted to try another approach. We could perfectly well have held him until tomorrow morning without charging him.'

'We haven't a shred of evidence against him,' Chief Inspector Quantrill growled, 'any more than we have against Dale Kenward.'

'I don't know why you let him go either,' complained Tait. 'I wanted to have a go at him.'

'I daresay you did. But in my judgement, we had no good ground for holding either of them—if you want to bring them in again, you'd better find some good stickable evidence first.'

Tait glowered.

Quantrill's eyes were beginning to feel boiled. He rubbed his hands over his face, and then looked at his watch. It was well after midnight, an uncongenial time to argue about hunches.

'It's been a long day, Harry,' he said. 'What we both need is some sleep. Stand your men down until daylight, and then I want two of them to check the regular early morning traffic crossing Ashthorpe bridge, while the rest comb the meadow. When they've covered the meadow once we'll split them, some to finish the house-to-house and some to sift through the bonfire where Mary Gedge's mother destroyed her letters and things. We're working blind until we can get some information about Mary's personal life, and that's what I want you to concentrate on. She must have kept at least an engagement diary, and that wouldn't burn easily. See what you can find.'

All very well for the old man, Tait thought; he hadn't seen the size of the bonfire. 'Yes, sir,' he said reluctantly. 'I suppose we've ruled out a random murder?' he asked.

'You mean some passing nutter who happened to see a girl gathering flowers, and took it into his head to drown her? No, there'd have been an assault of some kind. This murder was done without any more violence than was necessary. I'm sure that it must have been someone who knew her well. So you concentrate on the Ashthorpe end in the morning, and I'll see what I can find out in Breckham. We still haven't traced her movements after eight forty-five last night.'

'If you're seeing Denning again, sir, I'd like to come too. I've been hoping,' said Tait, 'to have a go at him.'

'You've already demonstrated your interviewing technique,' said Quantrill dryly. 'You do as you're told, and get that bonfire sifted. It's evidence we want now, not amateur theatricals.'

# SEVENTEEN

The chief inspector was back in Ashthorpe soon after seven in the morning, physically refreshed by a few hours' sleep but depressed after a row with his wife.

He had explained his lateness by telling her briefly about the girl's murder, but had thought it prudent not to mention that Mary Gedge had been at the grammar school; Molly would have been agog, clucking with the sympathetic horror appropriate to the mother of grammar school daughters, but eager for details to put in her weekly letter to Jennifer and Alison, whether they wanted to read them or not.

Knowing nothing about the victim, or the manner of her death, Molly had taken it upon herself to assume that Mary Gedge's morals must have been questionable. Girls these days, she said virtuously, often asked for everything they got. And Quantrill was so incensed on Mary's behalf that he had reminded his wife sharply of her own youth, and of a summer evening they had spent together, soon after they first met, on the banks of the Ouse. Some girls, he pointed out, don't attract violence, if only because they don't say No.

It was unforgivable, of course. She should have slapped his face; she should have done that nearly a quarter of a century ago, when he first laid hands on her beside the Ouse. But Molly had always chosen softer weapons. Now, as then, she cried.

# DEATH IN THE MORNING

It was a bad start to the morning.

The meadow had been combed, and nothing useful had been found. There were very few regular early morning road users, and none of them had seen a car parked by the bridge the previous day. The house-to-house enquiries had been completed, and in the mobile information room the reports were being collated.

Everyone in Ashthorpe knew Mary Gedge.

No one in Ashthorpe had seen her since six thirty on the evening before she was killed.

'I reckon somebody's lying,' said Pc Godbold, who was red-eyed from lack of sleep.

'But who, Charlie?' said Quantrill. 'Look, we've got to narrow this down. Make up a list of the boys of her own age, will you? The ones she would have been at the village school with, the ones she knew best. One of them was probably a childhood sweetheart—perhaps he's been hankering after her ever since.'

'A long shot, sir,' said Godbold doubtfully.

Quantrill recalled his own village sweetheart. Shirley, that had been her name, Shirley Howes. He'd hardly given her a thought, after he left school; but then, poor Shirley hadn't had much going for her, except a generous supply of sweets, a docile nature and white rather than navy blue knickers. There was a fair chance that Mary Gedge had inspired a much more lasting affection.

The chief inspector shrugged. 'Try it. We've got nothing to lose.'

Sergeant Tait was nowhere to be seen, but he had followed Quantrill's instructions. Four policemen, shirtsleeved in the morning sunshine, were sifting with glum patience through a great mound of partially burned packaging material in the orchard at the back of Manchester House.

Quantrill watched them for a few minutes. They had stopped grumbling as he approached, and now, in the quietness of the orchard, he could hear above his head a noise like a miniature racing circuit as the pure white blossom of a cherry tree was assaulted by a thousand drunken bees.

'You know what you're looking for?' he asked. 'Any luck?'

'Yes sir.' 'No sir.'

Quantrill waded through lush grass to Mary Gedge's trailer and unlocked the door. He was not hopeful that the dead girl's mother might have overlooked anything, but he searched every cupboard again, and took the bunks apart. Not a scrap of paper had been left in the trailer, apart from the calendar that hung from the knob of the locker.

And then he remembered that his wife kept no engagement diary, but used her kitchen calendar instead. Molly had big, sprawling handwriting; her calendar was so overscored and scribbled on that it was difficult, from a distance, to see the dates. But as he knew from her notebooks, Mary Gedge's handwriting was tiny. He snatched down the calendar, and carried it to the window.

Yes, she had pencilled on it. Against several dates were capital letters, presumably the initials of names; and sometimes there were times, as of meetings.

The April page had gone. Torn off by Mary herself, before she left the trailer for the last time before her death? Or deliberately destroyed by her mother in an attempt to conceal all evidence of Mary's plans for April 30th, the last evening of her life?

Chief Superintendent Mancroft, head of the county CID, had been furious when Quantrill, telephoning to report the murder, had told him of Mrs. Gedge's destructive foray. The chief super was coming to see her this morning, and it promised to be a sticky interview. Rather him than me, thought Quantrill.

He peered in the dim light of the old-fashioned trailer at the May page of the calendar. He looked for a consistent pattern, a recurrence of the same initial; there were several Ts, but they were all lower case and accompanied by a time—games of tennis, perhaps. Otherwise there were one or two Ls—conceivably for Liz—and an M18 which could possibly be a reminder of the eighteenth birthday of a school friend run to earth by Tait the previous evening, a Breckham girl who went by the nickname of Miggy.

The pencilled letter against May 1st was different from all the others. It was a capital D.

Very helpful: D for Dale; D for Derek; come to that, D for Denning.

\* \* \*

'*Murdered,* Chief Inspector? But it was an accident, surely—she fell in the river and drowned.'

'No, sir. That is, she might have fallen in, but her head was held forcibly under water.'

'I can't believe it . . .' Denning subsided into his big executive chair. His agitated fingers scrabbled among his whiskers. 'Who would have done such a thing?'

'We're investigating that at the moment, sir. That's why I've come to see you.'

Denning bounced to his feet, placing his hands flat on his desk as he leaned over it to emphasise his words. 'As I told you yesterday, Chief Inspector, at the time of her unfortunate death Mary had no connection with me or with my school. I can't help you in any way.'

Quantrill stared back at him. 'I think you can, sir. Our information at the moment is that you were the last person to see Mary Gedge alive.'

Denning straightened, slowly. For the first time all his movements stilled, except for those of his eyes.

'Would you like to add anything to what you told me yesterday?' Quantill asked.

'No.' Denning dropped back into his chair and began to swivel it from side to side. What could be seen of his face, among the whiskers, had turned pale, but he seemed to have recovered his natural buoyancy. 'Mary called here last night, that is true. But as I told you, it was simply to return a book. She left at about a quarter to nine.'

'And you watched her go? From the window, or the door?'

Denning put the tips of his fingers together and looked at the chief inspector with disapproval. 'From the door of course. It's a matter of courtesy, don't you think?'

'Quite. It was still daylight at that time?'

'Dusk, to be accurate.'

'Did Mary meet anyone? Did she speak to anyone?'

'No, she just walked away down the road.'

'To the left or to the right?'

'To the right.'

'And did anyone see her. Was anyone passing the house at the time, either on foot or by car?'

'I don't remember. Probably—it was a warm evening, there must have been people about. I didn't happen to notice.'

'I see. Then if I were you, Mr. Denning, I'd make a point of trying to remember. If Mary left here, we need to know where she went.'

The whiskers bristled. 'If! You have my word for it, Chief Inspector. And besides, my wife—'

'We met Mrs. Denning yesterday. I'm sure you remember that. She told us that she'd been staying overnight with a friend. She saw Mary come, but she was in a hurry—she didn't stay long enough to see her go.'

One of Denning's pudgy little hands shot out to the tooled leather address pad, the other to the telephone. 'I intend to ring my solicitor. You insinuations are intolerable.'

'Less so than murder,' pointed out Quantrill.

Sergeant Tait had decided to have another go, alone, at Derek Gedge. Like a terrier, once he got his teeth into something, Tait was inclined to hang on.

At number seven Jubilee Crescent the bedroom curtains were still drawn. From behind one of them came sounds that could only emanate from the practised lungs of dark-eyed Jason. Tait picked his way round to the long narrow strip of back garden and found Derek Gedge at the far end, spending his Saturday morning earthing up row after row of potential fried potatoes.

Gedge looked up as the sergeant approached, resting for a moment with his hands on the handle of his spade. 'You again?'

'Full marks for perception.'

Gedge shrugged and bent to his work. Tait prowled round, looking at the well-tilled earth from which onions were beginning to hoist delicate green spears, and carrots their feathers.

'Do it all yourself?' he asked. Tait was no gardener.

'Keeps me out of mischief.'

'So you say.' Tait folded his arms and stood watching. 'Came out here yesterday morning, did you? A lovely morning, and you had plenty of time to fit in an hour's digging before breakfast.'

Gedge went on working. 'No,' he said, 'I didn't.'

'Why not? Too busy elsewhere? Out for a walk, perhaps, down by the river?'

Gedge straightened his back, scowling. 'I had gut-ache,' he said. 'Good grief, man, I was in no condition to go any farther than the bog, just outside the back door. After that I drank tea and read and rested, getting ready to do a bloody hard day's work.'

'A well-chosen adjective,' said Tait. He leaned with conscious elegance, one ankle crossed over the other, against the door of the ramshackle garden shed. 'Are you using it literally, or figuratively?'

'Both,' said Gedge shortly.

'I can imagine. I can't think of a bloodier job. And I sympathise, honestly. Let's face it, you've got yourself in one hell of a mess, haven't you? I mean, anyone can have a go at a tough job on a temporary basis. I did all sorts of manual jobs during vacations, working on building sites, clearing a derelict canal. But I knew that it wouldn't last more than a month or so, and I didn't mind. But you're stuck with it, aren't you? Stuck with the chicken factory, and your wife and your mother-in-law and somebody else's kid . . . you've had a raw deal, haven't you?'

Derek Gedge turned the earth slowly, methodically, keeping his head down. Tait watched him, and spoke softly. 'Oh, yes—I can imagine the kind of pressure that must have been building up inside you during these past months. And then, Mary's getting a place at Cambridge must have put the lid on. You had to find an outlet, didn't you? You had to give vent to all your frustration and anger. You couldn't bear the thought of Mary's happiness, and so you put an end to it. That was it, wasn't it? Well, wasn't it?'

Gedge stood still, his head lowered. Then, suddenly, he whirled, spade in hand, eyes glinting. 'You bastard!' he said through clenched teeth. 'You smug bastard!'

He raised the spade. Tait, who had tensed himself, waiting for a reaction, saw the metal flash above his head. He flung himself to the ground in a rolling dive, protecting his head in his arms.

Slowly, Gedge lowered the spade. He laughed bitterly. 'Oh no,' he said, 'no, you're not getting me that way. You've been determined to pin Mary's death on me, haven't you, even before you were sure it was murder. But you've got no evidence against me—you can't have any, because I haven't seen or spoken to my sister this week, let alone done anything to harm her. But if I'd hit you just now, if I'd attacked a police officer in the execution of his duty, you could have had me for assault, couldn't you? And then who'd believe that I wasn't a violent man?' He turned away, throwing the spade down. 'You're a bastard, Tait, just like I said.'

Sergeant Tait got up, and began brushing the filth off his lightweight fawn trousers. 'You have to be, in my job,' he said.

'But do you have to get so much enjoyment out of it?'

Tait took a steady breath. For a moment he had really been afraid that Gedge meant to smash him down with the spade, and his knees were taking time to strengthen. 'Look,' he said. 'Eighty per cent of murders are done by a close relative, did you know that? That's why we take a good hard look at the family first. All right, so you say you didn't kill your sister— then presumably you want us to find out who did?'

Gedge nodded.

'But you want me to be *polite* about it? To say to suspects, "Excuse me, but do you by any chance happen to know anything about Mary Gedge's death? No? Right, I'll take your word for it, sorry to have troubled you, good-day." Is that how you want me to deal with the bastard who killed your beautiful, talented sister?'

The two young men stood glaring at each other for a moment. Then Tait pulled off his jacket, and began to brush it down; Derek Gedge fetched a rake from the shed and tried to repair the damage that Tait's fall had done to his bed of onions. Above them in the branches of a solitary apple tree, two bullfinches began to peck at the pink and white blossom, dropping it onto the vegetable patch.

Derek Gedge looked up at them, dropped his rake and clapped his hands. 'Whoosh!' he shouted, and the birds took off in a sudden explosion of leaf and twig and blossom.

He looked at Sergeant Tait. 'Show you something,' he offered, a little sheepishly. He went into the jumbled shed, beckoned Tait to follow him, lifted some old sacking and drew a polythene lunch box from a hiding place.

He opened it. Inside was a savings bank book. He flicked through the pages, showing Tait the small but regular cash deposits made weekly in Breckham Market; the sum amounted to nearly four hundred pounds, before interest.

'It may not seem much to you,' he said defensively, 'but it's all honestly earned. I've worked every hour I could, round at that disgusting factory, and this is what I've saved after I've paid my way. This is my outlet—my let-out, rather. Five hundred's my target, and then I'm off.'

Tait crouched beside him on the floor of trodden earth, smelling the wet rot in the crumbling planks of the shed. 'To take up your place at Selwyn?' he asked. 'Five hundred won't last you more than a couple of terms, man.'

Derek Gedge laughed. 'It's not for *me*! You've got me all wrong, you know. After what I've been through, I'm not a keen young student any more. I don't want to go to Cambridge and settle down to a routine of lectures and lab work and supervisions. I'm sick of routine. I want to be free. I want to get away from here, to travel. I've learned how to work with my hands and that's what I'm going to do, where and when I can find a job—and without a wife and a mother-in-law and somebody else's kid round my neck.'

'So what's the money for?'

'For them! Not that they're destitute, the old woman's got her widow's pension and Julie could get a job, but with me bringing in a good wage they're both been too bloody idle to think of working. They'll manage well enough without me. It's just that I feel . . . oh, they've given me a home of sorts, and the kid's not a bad little begger when he's clean and quiet. I might even miss him.'

He put the bank book back into its hiding place, and followed Tait out into the sunlight. Female voices could be heard from the back of the house, raised in shrill altercation; a smell of frying onions drifted down to them on the sunlit May air.

'Breakfast,' said Derek Gedge lugubriously. He picked up his spade and rake and propped them against the wall of the shed. 'You know, neither of them has ever had any prospect of getting her hands on as much as five hundred pounds, outside a pools win. I'm really looking forward to handing it over and telling them that I'm off. They'll be so excited, so full of arguments about whether to have a fitted carpet or a colour telly, that they won't even notice that I've gone.'

He walked with Sergeant Tait up the garden and round the side of the house to the junkyard in the front.

Tait chose his words carefully. 'If I don't have to see you again,' he said—he grinned, a little self-consciously; 'without prejudice, as they say—the best of luck.'

'Thanks,' said Derek Gedge. 'Mind you don't fall over Jason's pram on the way out.'

# EIGHTEEN

If Mary Gedge had left Denning's house, as he said, on foot and alone, Quantrill reasoned that someone must have seen her go. On a pleasant May evening there would certainly have been people about. The chief inspector put a house-to-house team to work in Mere Road; if that drew a blank, he could always try a public appeal.

Chief Superintendent Mancroft was coming from Yarchester for a ten o'clock briefing, before going on to Ashthorpe in an attempt to sort out Mrs. Gedge. Quantrill looked at his watch and decided that he had time to walk to his office before ten, thinking about the briefing as he went. He left the enquiry team, skirted the Mere, crossed the Dunnock by an echoing iron footbridge, took the path through the grounds of a derelict watermill which was in process of conversion to an expense-account restaurant, and emerged on asphalt at the foot of Water Lane. The lane led up past the shuttered cinema, now opened once weekly for Bingo, to the market place.

He was passing the main post office, preoccupied, when he felt bony fingers on his arm.

'Twice in one week, eh, Mr. Quantrill? Don't usually see you so often, these days.'

He squinted into the sunlight. 'Oh—hallo, Marje, you're about early.'

His would-be informant tucked a strand of her own greying hair back under her blonde wig, and gestured with her other thumb at the post office. 'Just been to cash me Giro cheque, haven't I? Friday, that's the day I'm supposed to have it, but do them snotty social security people care? Does the post office care? "Oh" they say'—she put on an affected voice—'"if it doesn't come Friday, you'll get it Saturday." And what am I supposed to do for money on Friday, eh?'

Chief Inspector Quantrill removed her hand from his sleeve, for the second time; like one of the mechanical grabs in the fairground amusement machines of his boyhood, it kept coming back to the same place. 'Yes, well,' he said pleasantly. 'Now you'll only have to make it last six days instead of seven.' He moved smartly away, and then stopped dead as an idea came to him. He turned back. 'Marje!'

Her seamed face brightened. 'Yes, Mr. Quantrill?'

'What *do* you do for money when you're short?'

She bridled. 'Well . . .'

He looked at his watch. There wasn't much time, but this might be important. 'Come and have a cup of coffee,' he said.

He took her by the arm and pushed her through the Saturday morning shoppers towards the market coffee tavern. She tottered in front of him, excited and protesting, on her platform-sole shoes: 'Ooh, Mr. Quantrill!'

The coffee tavern was reputed to have been in the same hands for sixty years. Outside, it was distinguished from the other commercial properties fronting the market place by its sober brown paintwork and its original sash windows, the white lettering on them announcing C FFLL, OT BOVR L and RE RESHM NTS. Inside, to Quantrill's certain knowledge, it had not been redecorated for the last twelve of its sixty years, and the rooms had been dingy when he first saw them.

Incomers to Breckham Market turned their noses up in distaste, or their mouths down in amusement, at the continuing existence of the tavern; but its many regular patrons—farmers, market traders and local business and professional men—knew that it served the best hot drinks and homemade snacks in the whole county.

Quantrill pointed his companion to an empty corner table. 'Tea or coffee?'

'Oh, coffee, thanks ever so much, Mr. Quantrill. It's more filling somehow—I didn't have time for any breakfast.'

He gave the order to the girl behind the counter. While she was filling the cups from a copper urn, an old woman shuffled in from a back room in carpet slippers and a clean cotton pinafore. She was carrying a wire rack of sausages, each one shawled in shortcrust pastry, succulent, hot from the oven.

She smiled with all her false teeth when she saw the chief inspector. ''Morning, Mr. Quantrill.'

''Morning, Mrs. Greenacre. My word, that's a terrible temptation to set in front of a man of my weight . . . thanks, Janet, and I'll have two of your grannie's famous pigs in the blanket, please.'

He carried the tray to the table. Marje's eyes widened. 'Ooh, Mr. Quantrill, you're a real gentleman, I've always said so.'

'No you haven't, and I'm not.' He snatched the plate out of her reach. 'I'm in a hurry, so we talk first and you can eat afterwards, right?'

She nodded cautiously, looking at him over her cup with apprehension. 'What do you want to know?'

'Whether you were back on your old beat on Mere Road last Thursday evening?'

She spluttered into her coffee. 'Mr. Quantrill!'

'Oh, come on, Marje, never mind *why* you were there. This is important. I'm asking you for information, and if you can give it to me it'll be worth your while. Now then: were you about in Mere Road last Thursday evening, between eight and nine?'

'Well . . . I went out for a walk, yes. Nothing wrong with that. I often do, Thursdays, can't afford to go to a pub. So if it's a nice evening, I go for a walk; it's nice, down by the Mere.' She adjusted her wig, licked her second finger and smoothed it over her plucked eyebrows. 'And of course, if a gentleman should happen to stop his car and ask me the way, I tell him. And if he's gentlemanly enough to invite me for a spin in his car, well . . .'

Quantrill was amused. 'He did, did he?'

She scowled. 'No, he didn't, the rotten so-and-so!' She gave a defeated shrug. 'Can't blame him, I suppose. Took one look at me mug, and drove off.'

'But it was a real compliment of your figure, Marje,' he consoled her. He drank some coffee. Chief Superintendent Mancroft could wait. 'All right, you were down by the Mere on Thursday; we won't worry about what you were doing. What I want to know is whether you saw a girl of about eighteen there.'

'Thursday . . . I don't suppose you've got a fag on you, Mr. Quantrill?'

Quantrill strode impatiently to the counter, bought a packet of ten and slapped them down on the table. 'Come on, Marje: a girl about five foot four, slim build, shoulder length fair hair and a long dress.'

She searched her bag for matches, absent-mindedly taking a cigarette from a packet of her own before slipping Quantrill's offering into the bag. 'Ankle-length dress, do you mean?' She lit the cigarette. 'Oh yes, I saw her a couple of times. Pretty kid she was, wandering along, in no hurry. Matter of fact, I got a bit riled—you know, thought she must be an amateur, trying to push her way in. But then I thought she couldn't be, because she was carrying a book. It's not a very convenient thing to carry, is it?'

'I don't suppose it is, in your job. Right, then: where was the girl coming from, when you first saw her?'

'Round from the far side of the Mere, as though she'd walked down from the town. She was carrying this book, and she walked on down Mere Road. I couldn't see where she went, there's this row of trees in the way. And then I saw her coming back again about a quarter of an hour later, without the book.'

'On her own?'

'Yes. Sauntering along, looking at her watch—waiting for somebody, I thought. And then this car came.'

'Where from?'

'From behind her, along Mere Road. That must have been who she was waiting for. She got straight in, then he drove off towards the main road.'

'He?'

'Ah, that I couldn't swear to. It was getting dusk, and I took it for granted it would be a man.' She took her cigarette out of her mouth in order to suck in some coffee. 'Here, Mr. Quantrill, why do you want to know?'

'You'll be able to read about it in the Press tomorrow. Come on, now, Marje, you're doing fine; just tell me about the car.'

She looked doleful. 'Oh, don't ask me, Mr. Quantrill! I take no interest in cars, it's just a matter of whether they're going to stop for me. I can't tell you anything about it, really I can't.'

'Try,' he urged. 'Think. Was it large or small, new or old? What colour was it?'

The lines on her face were concentrated in one cerebral effort, but her eyes remained blank.

'The number?' he persisted. 'Just part of it, then? The final letter?'

'I'm ever so sorry, Mr. Quantrill, I really am.' She leaned toward him. 'But I told you something helpful, didn't I? I gave you some info?'

'Oh yes. Yes, that's been a very useful chat, Marje.' He put his hand inside his jacket. 'Mind you, if you could think a bit harder and tell me something about that car, that would be *really* helpful. Will you try, and let me know the minute you think of anything?'

She nodded. Her bagged eyes were watching his hand, waiting for it to emerge with his wallet; her lips were parted expectantly showing crooked, decaying teeth. Quantrill was sorry for her. She had indeed been helpful, in establishing the fact that Mary Gedge had left Denning's house. It wasn't Marje's fault that the car that had later driven from Mere Road to pick Mary up could conceivably have been Denning's own.

But the fact was that he'd kept the chief super waiting for nothing. Besides, Quantrill had a strong objection to wasting public money. He hardened his heart, and pushed his wallet back.

'Ah, but you don't need anything at the moment,' he said jovially. 'You've just collected your social security, after all! Tell you what, Marje, you come and see me next Thursday, when you're short, instead of wasting your time down by the Mere.'

Her face sagged. She looked nearer sixty than fifty. 'Oh! Mr. Quantrill . . . !'

He pushed the plate of sausage rolls towards her. 'Eat your breakfast,' he advised, 'before it gets cold.'

Sergeant Tait looked at the plastic sack half-filled with charred rubbish that had been collected from the bonfire. Without expert investigation, it might well prove to be irrelevant. Forensic was going to love this.

'Shall I phone this list through to the chief inspector?' asked Pc Godbold. 'It's the names he wanted of the Ashthorpe boys of Mary's own age—he thought that one of them might have been her sweetheart when they were children.'

'Any idea if one of them *was* her sweetheart?'

Godbold shook his head sceptically. 'Anyway, that sort of thing doesn't mean anything when they're little. She's certainly never had a boy-friend in the village, not since she's been grown up.'

Tait took the list. There were six names. 'Were they all interviewed in the house-to-house?'

'Not necessarily the boys themselves. But all the houses were covered, except for Richard Weston's. That's the garage. There was no one at home when enquiries were made. Young Dickie should be there now, though, I know the garage is open.'

Tait went to the garage. It had a nineteen-thirties appearance, with a stepped facade of weather-stained concrete, but the pumps were squat and modern and the workshop area had obviously been considerably enlarged. A tall fair-haired eighteen-year-old in filthy overalls was working on a car engine and keeping an eye on the forecourt.

'Richard Weston? I'm Detective Sergeant Tait, county CID.'

The boy lifted his head. He was so fair-skinned that his cheeks had the appearance of a permanent blush. His eyes were heavy, and his mouth was set in a droop.

'Yes?' he said dully.

'I'm enquiring into the death of Mary Gedge.'

'Oh, yes.' Weston bent his head again. His hands kept at work, unscrewing and tightening the same nut on the carburetor.

'Mary was a friend of yours?'

The boy hesitated. 'Sort of.'

'What does that mean?'

'Well, we knew each other. We grew up together.'

'Did you go out together?'

There was a toot from a car in the forecourt. Weston hurried out to the pumps, wiping his hands on an oil-browned rag.

Sergeant Tait followed him and stood watching. The boy kept his head down while he was serving, speaking as little as possible. He was personable, discounting the occupational dirt on his overalls, but his appearance was marred by his hands.

They seemed disproportionately large for his slim body: ugly, roughened and reddened by weather and work, permanently grimed at the knuckles and finger-joints and round the nails.

Weston returned to the Chrysler he was working on. 'What do you want, then?' he muttered.

'To ask when you last saw Mary Gedge.'

It was impossible to tell whether the boy reddened, but his jaw tightened suddenly. 'Thursday,' he muttered. 'When I went to the shop.'

'What time was that?'

'Oh—just before half-past six. I locked the pumps a bit early because I was single-handed. When I went to the shop, Mary was serving.'

'And you talked to her? What about?'

'I don't remember. Nothing special.'

'I see. Well then, what did you do after that?'

The boy straightened, and for the first time looked Tait in the eye. 'Came back home, had a wash, got my supper. Ate it.'

'Do you live alone?'

''Course not. Mum and Dad have gone away, though, to Halifax for a wedding.'

'And after you'd had your supper?'

Weston ducked back under the bonnet of the car. 'Went to Breckham. Went to the main Leyland dealer for some spares.'

'What time did you leave here?'

'About eight, I suppose.'

'A bit late in the evening to go getting spares.'

'They stay open until nine. Anyway, they know us, and I'd rung to say I couldn't get away any earlier.'

'You'd *arranged* to go into Breckham Market that evening, then?'

Weston made a non-committal noise. Exasperated, Tait grabbed him by the collar of his overalls, hauled him out from under the bonnet and pushed him upright against the side of the car.

'I'm not playing games, sonny,' he warned, disregarding the fact that Weston was several inches taller. 'This is an official enquiry, and I want to hear your answers. I asked whether you'd made an arrangement to go into Breckham Market on Thursday evening?'

'Yes.'

146

'Did you take Mary Gedge with you?'

The boy's forehead was almost as red as his cheeks. 'No,' he mumbled.

'That's odd, then, isn't it? Because Mary was seen in Breckham about half-past eight. She hasn't a car, so someone must have given her a lift. Was it you?'

Weston shook his head.

'Speak up!'

'No,' said the boy hoarsely.

'You're lying, aren't you? You're trying to cover something up! What did you do to Mary?'

'Nothing!' His face was bleak with misery. 'I didn't touch her. All right, I gave her a lift into Breckham and back, but that was all.'

'And back? You brought her back? What time?'

'Oh—I picked her up in Mere Road about nine. She'd wanted to take back a book that the school headmaster had lent her. She did that while I collected the spares. We got back into the village about half-past nine, I suppose.'

'It doesn't take half an hour to drive from Breckham Market to Ashthorpe.'

'I used the back way, same as I did going. I came back by Fair Green and Lillington, and then round through Dunham and up the Heygate.'

It meant nothing to Tait. 'Where's the Heygate?' he demanded.

'Why, here.' The boy pointed through the window of the workshop to the narrow road that joined the main village street just between the school and the garage; the quiet road that Tait and the chief inspector had walked along the previous day, the road that led along the back of the Gedges' orchard, close to Mary's trailer.

'Oh yes . . .' Tait looked hard at the boy. 'And why did you choose to come that way?'

Richard Weston stood with his back pressed against the car, exactly where Tait had put him, his big hands dangling by his sides, his face wretched. 'Because it took longer,' he blurted out. 'Because I wanted to be with her as long as possible.'

'Did you go into Mary's trailer?'

'No, of course not. I just dropped her there, by the little gate.'

'And then what?'

'I came home.'

'But you saw her again later? You arranged to meet her later on, either that night or early next morning?'

'No! I told you, I left her at her gate. Then I came home and went to bed.'

'And can you prove that? Was anyone here when you came home?'

'Well, no . . . I told you, Mum and Dad are away.'

'Look at me!' Tait commanded. 'Do you know anything about the death of Mary Gedge?'

Tears filled the boy's eyes. He dashed them away with the back of one big ugly hand. 'No! Of course I don't, it was an accident.'

Tait shook his head, slowly. 'No it wasn't, it was murder. And it looks as though you were the last person to see her alive. So lock up your pumps, Dickie-boy, you're coming with me to the station.'

# NINETEEN

The interview between Chief Superintendent Mancroft and Mrs. Gedge had gone as Quantrill had predicted. She had accepted the news that her daughter had been murdered with a steely resignation, informing the policemen that God moves in a mysterious way. And on the subject of the bonfire, she reiterated that nothing she had destroyed had been of any conceivable interest to the police.

The chief superintendent was unable to disprove her statement. Finding, as Quantrill had found, that it was impossible adequately to combine reproof with compassion, he had retreated to investigate a more brutal murder in Yarchester, leaving the chief inspector in charge again.

Quantrill left his hat in his car and walked in sunlight from

# DEATH IN THE MORNING

Manchester House towards the village green, glad to have an opportunity to think quietly about the case. The almost total absence of evidence was its most frustrating aspect. Tait had reported having seen the marks of car tyres in a patch of roadside mud by the bridge; Quantrill himself had seen a bunch of wild flowers, gathered at about the same time as those that had floated round Mary's body, lying on the steps of the war memorial; and there was the pencilled D on Mary's calendar against the first of May. But there was no proof that any one of these facts was in any way connected with the girl's murder.

There was no proof of anything, except that she had died at the hand—literally at the hand—of a right-handed person. And all the suspect Ds were right-handed.

Quantrill paused at the memorial. Now that he knew that it was murder, he saw less significance in the bunch of buttercups. The flowers were still there, their petals fallen and faded, the leaves shrivelled. There was no litter on the steps this morning, but the maltreated wreath of British Legion poppies was lying facedown on the grass some yards away. Quantrill consciously picked it up and replaced it on the steps.

He had tried not to think of Jean Bloomfield all morning, but he saw her as soon as she emerged from her yellow front door. He stood quite still, watching her from under his eyebrows, holding his breath, assuming that she was going to get her car out or walk to another part of the village. Instead, she walked towards him.

He went across the grass to meet her. She was wearing pale green trousers, a long-sleeved cream shirt, a darker green scarf knotted at her throat. From a distance, apart from an understandable stiffness in her walk, she looked as though she had recovered from her weariness of the previous day; but at close quarters, the smudges of sleeplessness round her eyes were deeper and darker, the lines on her face more obvious. But still she looked beautiful. Quantrill felt uncouth, adolescent, unworthy; and somehow he would have to break the news to her that Mary Gedge had been murdered.

'Good morning!' Her voice had an artificial lightness, at odds with the heavy eyes. 'It's very good of you to keep our green tidy—as you see, we're not strong on civic pride in Ashthorpe. But I'm afraid you'll find it a full-time job.'

'I'm beginning to realise that.' He tried to match her light-

149

ness, surreptitiously wiping his palms on the seat of his second-best trousers.

She walked on past him, and shook her head over the litter surrounding the public bench. 'When I came to live here, I tried hard to keep the green tidy. I used to trundle out with broom and barrow every Saturday morning. Now—' she shrugged. 'Now, I've admitted defeat. I've given up trying.' She looked at him, attempting a smile. 'So it's very good of the head of Breckham Market CID to make up for our shortcomings. I watched you out here yesterday evening, clearing the litter off the war memorial.'

So she *had* seen him, though he'd looked in vain for her. 'Oh, I like a place to be tidy,' he said off-handedly. He sought for a tactful way to introduce the name of the murdered girl: 'I believe that the Gedge on the memorial is Mary's great uncle.'

'Yes—she told me about him after she'd seen some of those harrowing television documentaries about the First World War. Apparently he was just eighteen when he was killed.'

Quantrill hesitated. No, he couldn't tell her out here on the village green that Mary too, at eighteen, had been killed. It would be too public. Easier to tell her the news indoors; easier to offer her solace. He asked if she could spare a few moments to talk about the girl.

'Of course. As a matter of fact, I came out to ask if you'd like to have coffee. Oh, before we go in, I might as well finish the public-spirited work you began.'

She went to the memorial, gathered up the dead flowers from the step and carried them along the road to the litter bin. Quantrill watched her, regretting that she made a habit of wearing either trousers or long skirts. Such a waste, with legs like hers; but at least she looked good in trousers, unlike most women of her age.

A middle-aged woman who should have known better than to wear trousers was making a portly approach on a bicycle with large wheels. There was no other traffic on the road at that moment, and as the women passed each other Quantrill saw them nod in cool acknowledgement, and heard the greeting they exchanged.

'Good morning, Daphne. Lovely day.'

''Morning, Jean. That it is.'

The cyclist came on, giving Quantrill a stare as she passed.

He knew her instantly: the one who had tried to barge into Mr. Gedge's shop while he and Tait were there yesterday afternoon, the one who had overheard a conversation in the shop the previous evening between Mary Gedge and Miller. Mrs. Daphne Bullock, of Back Lane, Ashthorpe, who fed her husband on bacon and tinned rice pudding . . . How the devil, thought Quantrill sourly, did she come to know Jean Bloomfield well enough to call her by her first name, while he had never yet found the courage to do so?

The women were of the same generation, it was true; both in their forties, although Mrs. Bullock was certainly the senior. But that alone wouldn't put them on first name terms—unless of course they had grown up together. And Jean had referred to herself as a Suffolk village child.

Quantrill joined her as she walked back towards her house. 'I didn't realise that you came from Ashthorpe,' he said.

She looked surprised. 'How did you come to know that?'

'Oh, a policeman's nosey guess, I'm afraid. I heard that woman call you Jean, but you were obviously acquaintances rather than friends, so I thought that perhaps you knew each other as children.'

'Yes, we did. My family lived here for about three years during the nineteen forties. Daphne was one of the big girls at the school—I can remember her as an alarmingly well-developed thirteen-year-old, while I was an undersized eight. I was terrified of her.'

He grinned. 'I'm not surprised, after the earful I heard her give Mr. Gedge yesterday. Did you know him when you were a child too?'

'Yes—he used to serve in the shop until he went into the army. But I doubt if he remembers me, and he's certainly far too shy and polite to call me anything other than Mrs. Bloomfield. Most of the other people I knew as a child have moved away, or died. It's a very different village, now.'

They reached Coburg House. Jean Bloomfield led the way down the hall towards the smell of freshly made coffee. The kitchen was a comfortable room of the kind that Quantrill liked, with modern pine furniture, pots of plants, and a cat asleep on a cushion on an old Windsor armchair. Molly liked her kitchen to be streamlined, hygienic; she discouraged sitting about in it, most of all by the cat.

Jean poured coffee from the percolator, which had been glugging quietly to itself as they came in. He looked away from what she was doing, disturbed by the fact that her hands were shaking as much as they had been the previous day. Then, he had attributed it to tiredness and shock. Now it began to seem like a permanent manifestation of stress.

'I like your house,' he said quickly. 'Have you lived here long?'

'About eighteen months. When I first went to Breckham I lived in a modern flat, just by the river. It was very pleasant, and convenient for school, but when I heard that this house was up for sale I couldn't resist buying it. Do you know, it was my great childhood ambition to live either here or next door. My father was a farm worker. We used to live in one of the slummy old Ashthorpe yards—where the post-war council houses are now—and my mother came here to do the charring. I thought of these houses as mansions.' She sat on the bench by the table. 'Do sit down. Move the cat, if you'd prefer the armchair.'

The cat, a Cyprus, was curled tight. A segment of yellow eye, luminous in the dark-striped fur, indicated that it was aware of the intrusion and did not wish to be disturbed. Quantrill sat down elsewhere.

'And you enjoy living here?' he asked. 'Has it risen to your expectations?'

Her eyes were dark with disillusion. 'Does anything, ever? Oh, I certainly enjoyed redecorating and furnishing the house, and I had great hopes of being happy here. To be back in Ashthorpe seemed like a homecoming. The years we spent here when I was a child were the best we had. For once my father got on with the farmer he worked for, and there was plenty of overtime so money was easier. We had three happy years. Then my eldest brother was killed in 1945, and it broke the family up: my mother refused to believe that he was dead, my father started drinking again and lost his job, and Mother finally took me to live with her sister. Things were never the same after that. But I've always thought nostalgically of the Ashthorpe years, and I suppose I imagined that I could recapture some of that happiness by coming back.'

'It doesn't do, to go back,' observed Quantrill, who had never had reason to try.

'So I realise. At the time, though, it seemed a good idea. I'd been so distressed by my husband's death that for years I couldn't settle anywhere. But he was a Suffolk man—Bloomfield's as old a Suffolk name as Quantrill, isn't it?—and we'd talked about returning one day to East Anglia. I was delighted to be appointed head of Breckham girls' grammar school, and then to find this house for sale. I really thought that life might begin again. Instead, it all seems to be falling apart.'

She turned away to find a cigarette, and lit it before Quantrill could produce his lighter.

'But you've still got the house,' he argued, 'whatever happens to the job.'

She shook her head slowly, speaking with her back to him as she went to open the window. 'The house hasn't been a success,' she said. 'This has always been a family home, you see. It's bigger than it looks—and what do I want with four bedrooms and two attics? I feel lost in it. I've hated living here alone.'

Her shoulders were downcurved. It occurred to Quantrill, for the first time, that a woman in a position of authority and responsibility, who lives alone in a small community where social life is geared to families or couples, must almost inevitably feel lonely.

But loneliness is not exclusive to women. And you can be just as lonely, he knew, inside marriage as out of it. Lonelier, sometimes.

He put his coffee mug on the table and stood up, calculating the distance between them. Three strides, and he could put his hands on her shoulders. Three strides, and they could both begin to put an end to loneliness.

And to his marriage. And to his job.

To hers too, probably. Small communities demand high moral standards, especially from those they isolate socially.

She moved away from the window, and Quantrill sat down abruptly. She returned to the bench. The cat raised its head an inch, opened both eyes sufficiently to survey her vacant lap, and took a considered decision to stay where it was.

'You wanted to talk about Mary?' she said.

Quantrill jerked his mind back to his job. 'I'm afraid I have some distressing news—' he began.

She spoke as gently as if she were comforting him. 'I know.

It's all right, I do know. Mike Miller rang me this morning. He'd heard it on the local radio programme—the police suspect foul play, he said.'

Solace was not, after all, going to be required. There would be no excuse now for taking her in his arms. He'd let the opportunity go for good, and he didn't know whether to be glad or sorry.

'It does look like murder, I'm afraid,' he said. 'The pathologist found that she'd been deliberately drowned. But—as you thought—there was no trace of drink or drugs, and she hadn't been assaulted in any way. As murders go, it wasn't a violent one. She'd have died quite quickly, I imagine.'

Jean Bloomfield carried his empty mug to the coffee percolator. 'It was done by a stranger, presumably? I mean, everyone who knew Mary liked her—she hadn't an enemy in the world.'

'We're still making enquiries,' said Quantrill, professionally evasive. 'One of our handicaps is that we don't seem to know a great deal about the girl's private life, which is why I wanted to talk to you. Tell me, did you know that Dale Kenward wanted to marry her?'

'To *marry*?' She stared at him, amazed. 'Well, well . . . I had no idea, but come to think of it I'm not surprised. Dale Kenward is an extremely nice young man. If he was in love—and he *was*, that was obvious—then I'm sure he'd think in terms of marriage. Have you met him?'

'Yes,' said Quantrill.

She heard officialdom in his voice. 'Oh, no,' she said, appalled. 'Surely you don't imagine that Dale would have killed her? He's not one of your suspects, is he?'

'He's been helping us with our enquiries,' Quantrill agreed.

She ground her cigarette into the ashtray. 'Then I'm sure you're wrong,' she protested vehemently. 'I'm sorry, I realise I oughtn't to interfere, but I do know Dale. I get very little chance of sixth-form teaching now, there's always some middle school crisis when I'm timetabled for a senior class, but I did teach both Dale and Mary on several occasions last term and the term before. He genuinely loved Mary. The fact that he wanted to marry her is surely proof of that. Their love affair was touchingly serious. So many of them at that age are simply experimenting with sex—they think they've invented it, and they have to make sure that it works. But with Dale and Mary it was different, and I think you're wrong to imagine that he would harm her in any way.'

Quantrill accepted her reproof philosophically. 'But I've heard from several sources that they had quarrelled,' he said. 'I understand that although he wanted to become engaged, Mary didn't.'

Jean Bloomfield reached for another cigarette. 'Yes, well—I can believe it. Mary loved Dale, anyone could see that; but she wasn't actually *in* love with him, as he was with her.' She got up and walked restlessly to the window. 'Being in love,' she explained, 'is exclusive. Loving isn't, and Mary had a great capacity for affection. She loved her family and she loved her friends. If she was *in* love at all, it was with the idea of going to Cambridge—so it's understandable that she didn't want to become engaged.'

'That's what I told young Kenward. But he explained that he wanted to protect her from older men. He described her as being "unaware". Would you agree with that?'

She returned to the table and took her own mug to the percolator, although it was still half full of coffee. 'Yes,' she said after a moment's thought. 'I know exactly what he meant, and I think that he was right to be afraid for Mary. You never saw her alive, I suppose?'

'She was very attractive, I believe,' said Quantrill.

'Yes. But it was a particular kind of attractiveness that some blonde girls have—a kind of radiant innocence. I don't mean the innocence of ignorance, but of simplicity—guilelessness. Yes, Dale was right: Mary was tremendously unaware. She trusted people indiscriminately. When she finally fell in love, she would have given herself totally, without reserve—and, I'm afraid, almost inevitably to the wrong man. Mary was a born victim.'

'A *born* victim?'

'Yes. Have you ever seen any of the old Marilyn Monroe films on television? She had a different personality, of course, but she radiated this same kind of virgin innocence that Mary Gedge had. Unfortunately, it's an aura that attracts the kind of man who—consciously or not—enjoys corrupting the innocent. Poor Marilyn Monroe was destroyed in early middle age. And obviously Dale could see the danger for Mary.'

Quantrill floundered. 'Wait a minute! Are you trying to tell me that someone—another man—was trying to corrupt Mary?'

'Oh no!' She spoke urgently, impatiently, trying to make him understand. 'Don't you see, that's the whole point. Mary had always lived a very quiet life, and so far she was completely unscathed. But she'd have been preyed on as soon as she set foot in Cambridge, there isn't much doubt about that. She was looking forward to it so happily and innocently, imagining that it was all going to be wonderful, but heaven knows what would have been in store for her in the way of disillusion and heartbreak. No wonder Dale was worried for her, poor boy. But that doesn't for one moment mean—'

The telephone rang. She went to the hall to answer it and was back almost immediately, looking half-amused, half-embarrassed.

'It's for you, Douglas. Sergeant Tait.'

# TWENTY

'**H**ow the devil did Tait know I was here?' grumbled Quantrill when he returned from the telephone. He had tried to bark at the sergeant, but had been so much elated that Jean Bloomfield had at last called him Douglas that he had failed to put up a convincing performance.

She stubbed out her cigarette. 'Oh, he was very discreet,' she said lightly. 'Had-I-by-any-chance-happened-to-see-you-passing . . . ? And in the circumstances, I didn't think you'd want me to deny it. He's called you away, I imagine?'

'Yes, but he can wait. The chance to stand back and think about a case while someone else does the legwork is one of the perks of being a chief inspector, and I intend to make the most of it. What were you saying about Dale Kenward?'

'That I'm certain that he wouldn't have killed Mary. He loved her, and he recognised and respected her innocence.

# DEATH IN THE MORNING

That boy deserves to be given a medal for his restraint, not to be questioned about her death.'

'And you don't think she knew any other—older—men?'

'Not to my knowledge. If you're thinking of the school staff, I don't believe that any of them knew her socially.' She got up and emptied her cold coffee into the sink. 'Anyway, why does it have to be someone who knew Mary? Isn't it often a stranger who sees a girl alone and kills her?'

'Too often—but not in this case, there was too little violence for that,' Quantrill explained. 'But tell me, would other people—besides Dale Kenward and yourself, I mean—have thought of Mary as a potential victim?'

Jean Bloomfield toyed with her packet of cigarettes, obviously trying to resist the temptation to take another. 'High-flyers are always vulnerable,' she said slowly. 'Anyone who teaches knows that. In the nature of things, high-flyers are bound to peak early. Sometimes they go on from university to a brilliant career, and then falter in middle age. Sometimes they're in their element at university, but fail to find a satisfactory career. And sometimes they reach their peak at eighteen. There are always a few who never live up to their early promise when they reach university, for one reason or another: they find the work completely different, they're homesick, they make the wrong friends, they become emotionally disturbed.'

'And you think that would have happened to Mary Gedge?'

'I think it was a possibility, particularly in view of her innocence. But I doubt if any of us had consciously formulated the idea of her as a victim—I didn't, until Liz Whilton mentioned Ophelia.'

'But that was because of the flowers and the long dress, wasn't it?'

'Yes, superficially. But Ophelia was a victim too. She was a beautiful innocent who fell in love with the wrong man and positively invited him to humiliate and destroy her.'

Quantrill's eyebrows jumped. 'Did she? And what you're suggesting is that Mary Gedge hadn't yet met her particular Hamlet?'

Jean Bloomfield took a deep breath, and spoke with slow deliberation. 'I'm sure she hadn't. Mary was very lucky. She died without ever meeting disappointment or unhappiness, let along being destroyed by it.'

Quantrill nodded, appreciating the point she had made. And then, suddenly, his practicality reasserted itself: 'She met a violent end at the age of eighteen,' he pointed out bluntly, getting to his feet. 'There's no luck in that.'

Jean Bloomfield blinked as though he had snapped his fingers in her face. 'But—but you said that her death wasn't violent,' she protested.

The chief inspector looked at his watch and moved into the hall. 'I was talking about degrees of violence,' he said. 'However murder is done, the taking away of someone else's life is still an act of violence, isn't it?'

She followed him and stood fiddling with her wedding ring. 'I see what you mean, of course.' She looked up, and he could see nothing but desolation in her eyes. 'The fact is, I suppose, that someone whose husband was killed in the way mine was, has a different understanding of violent death. You see, when two aircraft meet head-on at a combined speed approaching a thousand miles an hour, there isn't much left of the pilots.'

Chief Inspector Quantrill was anxious to go, but Douglas Quantrill took his hand from the worn brass doorknob. 'They couldn't have known anything about the crash,' he said gently.

'That's true. But . . . can you imagine what it's like to know that the body of the man you love has been blown to fragments? The most they ever found was a flying glove, in a field half a mile away. It had part of a thumb in it, but they couldn't tell whose.'

There was nothing that Quantrill could say. He found that he was holding her hand, and he gripped it to try to stop it trembling while she spoke.

'The really terrible thing was the charade of the military funeral. I expect you did your national service, so you know about their funerals.'

Quantrill didn't. There hadn't been much call for military funerals at the training camp where he'd been stationed. The body of the boy he'd known who had committed suicide had been sent home for burial. He said nothing, but pressed her hand.

'I've never been able to talk about this to anyone else,' she said. Her eyes were remote, her voice quick, unemotional. 'As you know, in the RAF they have this inflexible rule about putting bodies in coffins immediately, and screwing them down. I knew why they did this. Philip had a friend who was killed flying, and he told me then. But the other pilot's wife didn't know, she didn't realise—she was only nineteen, they'd been married just three months, and she wanted to take a last look at her husband. And of course no one had the heart to tell her that there wasn't a body, that the coffins contained just sandbags and a few fragments of unidentifiable flesh. But still the RAF went through this grotesque ceremonial of a full military funeral, with best caps lying on the coffins, the station band playing, the flag at half-mast, a firing party, and a bugler sounding the last post over the sandbags as they were lowered into the graves . . .' She released her hand, and looked at him. 'That's violent death, Douglas,' she said. 'In comparison with that—'

He put his hands on her trembling shoulders, and felt a moment's surprise at their muscularity, until he remembered that she was a tennis player. 'Yes,' he agreed gently.

She gave a shaky half-smile. 'You can see why I took so long to get over my husband's death,' she said. 'People were very kind, of course, but none of them really understood. I've always remembered a letter from a senior officer we knew. He quoted to me what Lord Edward Cecil said, when he heard that his only son had fallen in battle in the First World War: "It is a splendid thing to leave life so clean and bright as that." It would have been a wonderfully comforting epitaph, if only I'd known as little as the other pilot's wife; if only Philip had left life whole, if he hadn't been blown apart . . .'

She made an effort to compose herself. 'But the Gedges would find it a suitable epitaph for Mary, don't you think? I must tell them—later, of course, when they've buried her and come to terms with their grief.'

Quantrill remembered his duty. He pressed her shoulders, trying to convey his love and reassurance. 'I must go,' he said. 'I'm sorry to leave you, but I must. I'll see you again, though. Goodbye, Jean.'

She said nothing, but tried to smile. He bent his head and kissed her gently on the cheek. It tasted salt.

Sergeant Tait, with Weston's statement in his hands, was waiting impatiently for the chief inspector's return. Quantrill read through the document and drummed his fingers loudly on his desk.

'And I suppose,' he said, heavily sarcastic, 'that the boy's right-handed, and that he's known as Dick?'

'Yes; but Dickie, according to Pc Godbold, sir.'

Quantrill snorted. All he needed to complicate the case was another right-handed man who fancied Mary Gedge, whose name began with a D, and who had no alibi at all for the early hours of the first of May.

The policemen went to the interview room. Weston stirred uneasily in his chair as they went in, as though offering to get to his feet. Quantrill sat at the table opposite the boy, and looked him over.

Weston lowered long eyelashes. His big grimy hands were awkwardly laced together on the table in front of him, and he stared at them fixedly.

'Have you had a cup of tea?' Quantrill asked.

The boy looked up, surprised. 'Yes, thanks,' he mumbled.

'Right. So you're an old friend of Mary Gedge?'

'Well . . . not really a friend. We just knew each other.'

'But well enough for you to offer her a lift to Breckham, and for her to accept?'

'She hadn't any transport. She was glad of a lift sometimes.'

'Sometimes? How often was that?'

'About once a week, in the school holidays.'

'Once a *week*—and yet you weren't really a friend?' Quantrill raised his heavy eyebrows. 'I'd say you must have known Mary pretty well.'

The boy shrugged. 'We'd always known each other,' he muttered, 'ever since we were kids. We didn't go *out* together—I provided her with transport, that's all.'

'And what did you get out of it?' asked Tait from the doorway.

The boy looked up at him. 'Being with her,' he said simply.

'Were you in love with Mary?' asked Quantrill.

'Yes.'

The chief inspector stared at him silently for a few minutes. Then he said, 'We've been talking to Mary's family and school friends, Dickie, and the strange thing is that no one has mentioned your name. You were in love with Mary, you often gave her lifts to Breckham, but no one seems to know that you were one of her friends. How do you account for that?'

The boy cracked a big raw knuckle. 'That was the way I wanted it to be,' he said. 'I didn't want anyone to know. That was why I always picked her up and dropped her on the Heygate, by her trailer.'

'Why on earth didn't you want anyone to know?' demanded Tait. 'I'd have thought you'd be proud for everyone to know that you were one of Mary's friends.'

Weston gave him a bleak look. 'You wouldn't understand,' he said.

'But I would,' said Quantrill. 'It's village life,' he explained to Tait. 'Once a boy and girl are known to be friendly, the gossip starts. The couple are teased and tormented, and this puts pressures on the relationship. They're either hustled into marriage, or pushed apart. So the longer you can keep it secret, the better chance you have of making up your own minds about whether or not it's real love. That's it, isn't it, Dickie?'

Weston nodded half-heartedly. 'Yes—except that I'd made up my mind months ago. Years. Only I knew that Mary didn't love me, so it was hopeless.'

'How did you know that she didn't love you? Did you ask her?'

'No!' Weston pushed his thick fair hair out of his eyes with a dirty paw. 'Of course I didn't! If I'd said anything about love, I'd have frightened her off. She thought of me just as an acquaintance, and that was better than nothing, so I kept it that way.'

'How can you be sure you'd have frightened her off?' asked Quantrill.

Slowly, reluctantly, the boy spread out his hands on the table.

'Take a look,' he said.

They were not, Quantrill acknowledged, the kind of hands that he'd like any boy-friend of Alison or Jennifer to have; but then, he was reluctant to think of any man's hand on either of his daughters. As for the ingrained dirt on Weston's, well, that was honestly acquired. Quantrills had always worked with their hands, until he had broken the hitherto inescapable family tradition by joining the force.

'They're hard-working hands,' he said kindly.

Weston looked at them mournfully. 'They're hideous,' he said. 'Do you think I don't know that? How could I ever touch a girl like Mary with hands like these?'

Quantrill looked up. 'Did you touch her?' he asked. 'Did you try to touch her?'

'No! No of course I didn't! That would have finished me with her, wouldn't it?'

The chief inspector leaned his arms across the table. 'Someone finished Mary,' he said quietly. 'Someone, for some reason, put one of his hands on the back of Mary's neck and held her head under water.'

Tears began to gather in the boy's eyes. 'But it wasn't me! How could it have been me, when I loved her?'

Quantrill caught at Weston's right wrist, turning it so that the hand pointed upward—rough, red and black, thick-fingered. 'How do you know your hands are hideous, Dickie?' he asked softly. 'Did Mary tell you so? Did she shudder over your hands? Did she—*laugh* at you because of them?'

'What do you think, Harry?' asked Quantrill.

'I think he's a strong possibility, sir, despite his denials.'

'I agree. It would certainly fit in with what young Kenward said about Mary—she was "unaware", he said, and Mrs. Bloomfield confirmed it. Mary was fond of her friends, and she trusted them. She probably had no idea that Weston was in love with her, and it must have been slow torture to him to be with her.'

'He had the opportunity, too,' said Tait. 'Perhaps he took her to his own home, since his parents were out. Or perhaps he dropped her by her trailer, as he said; perhaps she'd told him she intended to get up early to gather flowers and so he took her down to the river next morning.'

Quantrill rubbed his jaw. 'I can't apply for a warrant,' he said, 'we haven't enough to go on. But take the boy back home, and ask him to show you the clothes he was wearing yesterday morning. And take a man with you to search his car—you never know what might turn up, a dead buttercup or a bit of river weed . . . Only we mustn't let ourselves be misled by the appearance of Weston's hands, any more than by the violence of Derek Gedge's job.'

'Ah, I saw Gedge again this morning, sir,' said Tait, 'and I'm inclined to think that he really does know nothing about his sister's death.'

Quantrill shrugged. 'You were the one who was so keen to

pin it on him. Frankly, I'm beginning to think that it might have been an older man. I had a very interesting conversation with Mrs. Bloomfield. She thinks that Mary was the type of innocent girl who unconsciously invites corruption—a born victim, that was how she described the girl. I think I'll have another talk with Denning. Perhaps Mary mentioned to *him* that she was going to gather flowers; he could perfectly well have driven over early on Friday morning.'

Tait frowned thoughtfully. 'Interesting theory, about the born victim . . . Why Denning rather than Miller, though, sir? I'd say that Miller knew the girl a good deal better than Denning did—he taught Drama, and she loved acting. *And* he was heard to offer Mary a lift on the evening before her death.'

'Not Miller,' said Quantrill decisively. 'Mrs. Bloomfield referred to him as Mike, and it's the men whose names begin with D that we're interested in: if not one of the youngsters, Derek or Dale or Dickie, then conceivably Denning.' He suddenly remembered that the sergeant did not know about Mary Gedge's calendar. 'Look, Harry,' he said, spreading it out on the desk. 'The first solid bit of information we've come across so far. Her writing's so tiny that it's easy to miss, but that's definitely a capital D in the square for the first of May.'

Tait bent over the calendar, then picked it up and carried it to the window. He glanced across at Quantrill. 'Eyesight getting a bit unreliable, sir?' he asked kindly.

Quantrill scowled, and joined him. 'Why—?'

Tait pointed. 'Not just D, sir. "Dusty".'

It was small and faint, but unmistakable. 'Terrible light, in that trailer,' Quantrill grumbled. 'Well . . . Dusty . . .' He snapped his fingers. 'Didn't Mr. Gedge say that Dusty was one of Mary's friends? Did you make a note?'

'Of course.' Tait found the page in his book. 'Yes, that's it: Sally and Liz and Miggy are all girl-friends; Dale we know; Dusty we don't . . . yet.'

'It doesn't necessarily signify the murderer,' Quantrill pointed out cautiously. 'Still, it's the first real lead we've got, Harry—'

The chief inspector looked surprised. He had no intention of addressing the sergeant by his first name, until he had made up his mind whether to like him.

'I used it as a nickname,' he said coldly.

'I haven't a nickname,' said Tait, who had no intention of being saddled with one at the whim of a chief inspector.

'Oh, well, if you feel like that about it . . .' Quantrill was huffed; if the man was going to be so toffee-nosed, their relationship could stay on a strictly formal basis. 'All Taits are nicknamed Harry—that was what a Tait I knew in the RAF told me. He said that it was on account of a famous old music hall comedian.'

'Really, sir?'

'Yes, really.' Quantrill found his sergeant's supercilious look immeasurably irritating. 'Surely you've been around long enough to know that some surnames have traditional nicknames: we've got Larry Lamb and Chalky White stationed here in Breckham, for a start. And then, Tuckers are called Tommy, and Carpenters are called Chips, and Millers—'

Tait was instantly alert. 'Yes, sir?' he asked with gratifying attentiveness. 'What are Millers called?'

A wide, unamused grin spread across Quantrill's face. 'Millers,' he said, 'are called Dusty . . .'

He rang his home number. Peter answered.

'Hi, Dad. Hey, have you changed your mind about letting me have a portable telly?'

'Not a hope. Tell you what, though, we might go fishing at Southwold at the weekend—it's my day off on Sunday.'

'It's the weekend now. You mean we'll go fishing tomorrow?'

'Oh—oh well, I'm likely to be a bit tied up tomorrow. But next time I have a day off at the weekend, that's what we'll do.'

Peter gave a cynical laugh. 'I've heard that one before . . .'

Quantrill gave his son a hurried, elaborately casual reason for wondering whether the staff at Peter's school had nicknames. The boy co-operated cheerfully enough.

'Well yes, there's Fred—that's Mr. Wright, I don't know why he's called Fred because that isn't his name, but he is. Mr. Parrot is Polly, Mr. Bell's Ding-dong, Mr. Miller's Dusty, Mr. Brown's Kojak—guess why—Mr. . . .'

Quantrill let his son ramble past the significant name before interrupting him. 'Right, thanks very much, Peter. See you.'

He put down the receiver. 'See you'—small chance of that. Police work ruined family life, and it was no use pretending it didn't. Heaven knew when he'd see Peter next; a fine thing, when the only communication a man had with his son was by telephone.

But even as he was grumbling to himself, Chief Inspector Quantrill was on his way to the door. 'You check out Weston,' he told Sergeant Tait. 'I'm going to see Dusty Miller.'

# TWENTY-ONE

At the Old Bakery, Miller sat on the scuffed Habitat settee, in a rough-dried cotton shirt and youthfully flared trousers, and denied everything that the chief inspector put to him.

'No, I did *not* make an arrangement to see Mary Gedge yesterday.'

'My information is, Mr. Miller, that when you went to the shop on Thursday night, you asked Mary if she would like a lift into Breckham the following day, yesterday.'

Miller jumped up, knocking a crumpled copy of *The Guardian* to the floor. 'You can't bloody *breathe* in this village without being overheard,' he said bitterly. 'And did your informant think fit to mention that Mary refused the lift I offered?'

'Yes, sir. But it occurred to me that she might not have wanted an acceptance to be overheard.'

'She said "No" and she nodded "Yes", you mean?' asked Miller. He jerked the ring from a can of beer, and the ensuing 'splltt' conveyed his derision. 'Well, she didn't. I offered a lift, simply by way of neighbourliness, because I knew that the girl hadn't any transport, and she refused. That's all there was to it.' He tipped back his red-gold head and swallowed some beer.

'I see.' Quantrill looked at the table, on which was the bachelor's meal that he had interrupted: a hunk of buttered brown bread, a pork pie and a jar of home-made chutney. The handwritten label was a reminder that Miller was not a bachelor, but a married man whose wife had left him. And Quantrill knew all about the needs of wifeless married men.

He suppressed his sympathy. 'Would you like to explain, then,' he asked sternly, 'how it is that on her calendar for yesterday, Friday the first of May, Mary had written the name Dusty?'

Miller sat down again abruptly. For the first time, he looked uneasy. 'Dusty . . . ?'

'Your nickname at the school, I believe?'

'How the devil—oh, I know! Quantrill. You've got a boy who used to be at the Alderman T, haven't you? Yes, all right, the kids there used to call me Dusty. But most of the girls at the comprehensive call me Mike—Mary certainly did. You can check with her friends.' He got up, cut himself a slice of pork pie, carried his plate back to the settee and began to eat with more defiance than appetite. 'If Mary put "Dusty" in her diary, it's nothing to do with me.'

Quantrill tried another tack. 'You had a party here on Thursday night?'

'I had a friend in for a drink.'

'There were several dirty glasses about on Friday morning.'

'I don't wash up very often.'

'Did Mary Gedge come here on Thursday night?'

'No.'

'Who was the friend who came for the drink, then?'

'I prefer not to say.'

Chief Inspector Quantrill pushed himself up from the uncomfortably low-slung armchair. 'Mr. Miller,' he said, 'I am engaged on a murder enquiry. You knew Mary Gedge. At the moment, you are living alone in this house. If there is anyone who can vouch for your whereabouts on Thursday night and up to six o'clock on Friday morning, I suggest that you would do well to tell me who it is.'

Miller sat back, defeated. He pushed irritably at *The Guardian* with the toe of his battered suede boot. After a long pause he said gloomily, in his beautifully modulated voice, 'It's a bugger, isn't it, to hold egalitarian beliefs and yet be lumbered with the instincts of a gentleman?'

'It must be,' said Quantrill. He waited.

And then, suddenly, he took fright. Supposing the woman that Miller was presumably trying to protect was Jean Bloom-

166

field? Supposing she had come home early from her holiday, and had spent the night with Miller? He couldn't bear the thought.

'Is she a married woman?' he asked urgently.

Miller accepted the cue gratefully. 'Yes. And I'm sufficiently fond of her not to want to smash up her marriage, however much I may want to get my own back on her husband. Come to that, I don't want to make it any more difficult than it already is for my wife and children to come back to me. So the last thing I want is publicity.'

Quantrill breathed again. 'If you had nothing to do with Mary Gedge's murder, the question of publicity doesn't arise. If you're telling me the truth, I can promise discretion. But I shall need corroboration before I can eliminate you—I need the lady's name.'

Miller sat with his face in his shapely hands and struggled with his bourgeois conscience. Then he stood up abruptly, scattering pie-crust crumbs. 'Of course! There's an independent witness—Dale Kenward, who used to be Mary Gedge's boy-friend. Do you know him?'

Quantrill's eyebrows lifted. 'A witness to what?'

Miller began to move about the room with eager, graceful strides. 'Look,' he explained. 'Dale and Mary quarrelled some weeks ago. Dale was sick as hell and—stupidly—he started to be jealous of me because I sometimes gave her lifts. I've had the impression that he's been keeping an eye on me during the holidays, and late on Thursday night I saw that new sports car of his parked just down the road.'

'When you were entertaining your visitor?'

'Yes. I suppose he thought that it might be Mary, and hung around trying to find out. My visitor had planned to leave discreetly early in the morning, but when she went out just before six to get her car from the garage, he was still sitting in his car in the same place. She had to dash back before he recognised her.'

'He would have recognised her, then?'

'Oh yes. We just hope that he didn't! But he certainly would have seen enough of her to realise that it wasn't Mary—wrong colouring, very dark rather than fair. He must have been satisfied, anyway, because he'd gone when I looked out an hour later.'

'That was when your visitor left?' asked Quantrill, who was beginning to think that he knew her identity.

'No, there was too much activity in the village by then. To make it properly respectable, she had to wait until mid-morning so that she could pretend she'd called for coffee. Well, actually—' he gave a reminiscent leer '—what with one thing and another, it was lunch-time before she left.'

Quantrill nodded, and went to the door. 'All right, then, Mr. Miller—I'm obliged to you for your information. Just tell me—off the record, of course—how do you get on with the headmaster of the comprehensive?'

Miller's widened eyes showed a grudging appreciation of the chief inspector's accuracy. Then he grinned. 'Alan Denning,' he said, 'is a fascist pig. It's all, "In my school I . . ." with him. And he even has the temerity to tell a teacher of my experience what is and is not a suitable form of dress to wear in front of the kids!'

He opened the door for the chief inspector. 'Can you think,' he asked 'of a better way to get even with Denning than having a torrid affair with his wife?'

Offhand, Quantrill couldn't.

Sergeant Tait was disappointed. Dickie Weston had artlessly offered his entire wardrobe and his car for inspection, and nothing of any significance had been found. What had looked like a strong lead had petered out.

There had to be some evidence somewhere, and Tait was determined to find it. He had instituted a second search of the river meadow, with no result, but the scraps from the bonfire were still being analysed. Forensic science ought to be able to come up with a lead of some kind.

Tait thought about the girl's body as he had first seen it, on the river bank. Pc Godbold had been right, of course, to pull her from the water and try resuscitation; at that stage, there had been no suggestion of foul play. But the removal of the body from the river had inevitably removed or distorted some possible evidence.

Tait thought hard about the body. Then, suddenly, he sprinted to his car and drove to the public mortuary.

It was a small, windowless Victorian building, tucked away behind a depressing shrubbery of laurel bushes in the grounds of the county hospital. Tait went to the attendant's office, and came out carrying a plastic bag containing Mary Gedge's clothing just as the pathologist came down the corridor to the white-tiled cubby-hole that served him as a wash-room.

'Oh—excuse me, sir,' Tait said.

Dr. Palgrave was a small, thin, harrassed man, wearing a plastic cover-all. He looked at Sergeant Tait with disfavour. 'You again? Not another body?'

'No, sir—still the same one.'

The pathologist snorted. 'Lucky you, Sergeant, to have so much time to spend on one case!' He stripped off the protective plastic, rolled up his sleeves and began to wash. Tait, standing in the doorway, was surprised by the condition of the cramped, ill-ventilated room. It looked like a particularly disreputable public lavatory, with cracked tiles, a chipped basin and a permanently damp cement floor; only the graffiti were missing. The police federation would have had something to say about it if it were police property—and Dr. Palgrave was a hospital consultant, a man of importance. Tait felt glad that he had not pursued a childhood ambition to be a doctor.

'Do you know,' the pathologist went on wearily, 'I've done three post-mortems since the one you're working on? And police work is just an extra, something I've been lumbered with on top of all my other responsibilities simply because there was no one else to do it. So don't, please, try to unload any of your problems on to me, because I've enough of my own. I identified the homicide you suspected, I gave you my report, and as far as I'm concerned that's it. The Mary Gedge case is entirely your responsibility now.'

The whites of Dr. Palgrave's eyes were dulled from lack of sleep, and in his sallow face had a greenish tinge. Tait knew when he was unwelcome, but he declined to retreat.

'I appreciate that, sir. I'm following a line of my own, and I didn't intend to trouble you, but since we've met I'd be very grateful if you would confirm something. Your report shows that the girl's head was held under water by the pressure of someone's right hand on her bare neck; now, if his right hand was on her neck, isn't it likely that his left hand would have been pressing down on her shoulder?'

The pathologist sighed, but he gave the question his full attention as he dried his hands. 'Yes,' he agreed, 'that's a reasonable assumption. From the position of the bruises on her neck, the assailant must have been on her left. Yes, he would almost certainly have borne down on her left shoulder or upper arm with his left hand.'

'That's what I thought,' said Tait eagerly. 'Our problem is, sir, that we have a number of suspects, but nothing to pin on any one of them. I know that there isn't yet a method of taking fingerprints from bare skin, but it *is* possible to take fingerprints from fabrics. That's why I've come for the girl's dress. I'm going to send it to the forensic lab for a radio-active sulphur dioxide test. We can then compare the prints with those of our suspects.'

Dr. Palgrave paused in his drying and peered open-mouthed at Tait. 'You've got a *number* of suspects and you're going to—? You mean you're going to ask the lab to run what is virtually an elimination test—?' He began to laugh, wheezing a little at first and then throwing back his head and bellowing with laughter so huge that the whole of his thin body was shaken.

Tait was offended. 'Sir?' he said, when he could make himself heard.

The pathologist tossed aside his towel and gave the policeman a friendly clap on the shoulder. 'Sergeant,' he chuckled, wiping his eyes with the back of his hand '—Tait, did you say? I must remember the name . . . Well, Sergeant Tait; fresh from police college, eh? And no doubt you've been having interesting lectures there, all about the marvels of forensic science?'

'Yes, sir.'

'I thought so. I agree with you, modern forensic science *is* wonderful. And when you've reached the stage in your investigations where you want to nail a particular suspect, the lab may well be able to come up with the proof you need. But to ask them to run an expensive and time-consuming test when you haven't carried out an obvious elimination procedure—oh, come now, Sergeant, you've let yourself be blinded by science. Try using your common sense, eh?'

Tait looked at him unhappily. 'Sir?'

Dr. Palgrave closed his eyes and spoke with patience. 'You saw in my report the fact that the girl had clawed up gravel. Her knees and toes were badly grazed, also by gravel. So she

170

must have been drowned in shallow water—am I right? Then tell me, what position would her assailant have had to assume in order to hold her under the water?'

Sergeant Tait frowned: 'He'd have had to bend right over . . . Or kneel. Yes, the water was only about eighteen inches deep, so he'd almost certainly have to kneel in order to keep his balance.' His face brightened as the solution clicked up on his mental display board: 'Of course! The murderer's knees will probably be as badly grazed as Mary's were!'

The pathologist grinned at him genially, refreshed by the encounter. 'That's what I think, Sergeant Tait. So don't bother the scientists yet—try one of the old-fashioned methods of detection instead. Get all your suspects to roll up their trouser legs.'

For the first time in years, Martin Tait felt a complete fool.

Chief Inspector Quantrill went from the Old Bakery to Manchester House. Mr. Gedge was in the locked shop, but no longer trying to work. He sat in his brown dust-coat on the customers' bentwood chair, staring sightlessly at his shelves.

Quantrill was gentle with him. 'We're trying to trace Mary's friends, you see. You mentioned some names, Mr. Gedge, and one of them was Dusty. Do you happen to know who that was?'

The shopkeeper made an effort to focus on Quantrill's face. 'Why, yes,' he said. His voice was high with stress. 'Yes, that would be Mrs. Bloomfield. The girls at the grammar school always called her that—something to do with a singer, I think. Yes, that's what Mary told me when Mrs. Bloomfield first went to that school. They called her Dusty because her name was like a singer's, Dusty Springfield.'

Quantrill was disappointed. So much for the new lead he'd hoped for.

'I see,' he said. 'Mary wrote the name Dusty on her calendar for the first of May, so I thought she must have arranged a meeting.'

'Very likely.' Mr. Gedge got up like a man of eighty and shuffled behind the counter to peer at a calendar of his own. 'That would have been the day Mrs. Bloomfield was due back from holiday,' he said dully. 'I made a note of it myself because she wanted me to keep some bread for her. I expect that Mary had arranged to play tennis with her, or something like that. They quite often did, in the holidays. Mrs. Bloomfield was always very good to Mary.'

'She tells me that she knew you when she was a child,' said Quantrill, hoping to take the man's thoughts from his daughter for a few moments.

'Why yes.' Mr. Gedge almost managed to smile. 'She was about ten years younger than me, but I was friendly with one of her brothers, so I do remember her. Jean Ransome, she was then. Bright as a button, you could see she'd get on in the world. But then, the whole family was clever—four children there were, with Jean the youngest. Her eldest brother, Roy, was killed while they were living here, just before the end of the war.'

'Mrs. Bloomfield mentioned him. In the army, was he?'

'RAF. He was a sergeant air gunner. Only a boy really, of course, he joined up straight from Breckham grammar school. Poor little Jean thought the world of him—really hero-worshipped him. It broke her heart when he was killed.' He looked up. 'I tell you what, Mr. Quantrill: you remember you asked me whether Mary had put a bunch of flowers on the war memorial? Well, she might have and she might not, I don't know. But it could have been Mrs. Bloomfield.'

'Is her brother's name on the memorial?'

'Yes. He was shot down over the North Sea. I remember we heard about it from a Breckham chap who was the navigator in the same Lancaster. They all bailed out and were rescued, except Roy. He got out but caught fire, parachute and all. Went down like a Roman candle going the wrong way, this navigator said. Terrible way to die, poor boy.'

Quantrill remembered what Jean Bloomfield had said about Mary Gedge's death: yes, in comparison with some, Mary's death had been clean and easy. She'd died whole, unspoiled, in the brightness of youth. It was a thought that would do nothing to lessen her father's grief now, at this moment. But as Jean had said, in time the girl's parents would find it a great consolation.

What was it Jean had said that somebody wrote to her after her husband's death? Something about it being a splendid thing to die so young and clean . . .

Jean knew all about grief, and the mastery of it. She'd been through so much herself that she would be the best possible person to console Mr. Gedge. Besides, she could use words so well, so much better than an uneducated copper.

Quantrill muttered an awkward goodbye, and drove back to Breckham Market remembering all the wise and comforting things Jean had said about dying young. And as he thought about what she had said, the frown between his eyes deepened.

He took the steps to the police station two at a time.

'Is young Bedford in?' he asked the desk sergeant. 'Then tell him to go straight round to the library, will you, and see if he can find me anything by or about an American writer who died young, Dorothy Parker.'

# TWENTY-TWO

'• • • so I persuaded them,' said Tait, 'that if they had nothing to hide there was no reason why they shouldn't roll up their trousers. I checked them all, Dale Kenward, Derek Gedge, Denning, Dickie Weston and Miller. Not a graze on any of them. But of course, the fact that none of them is marked is no proof that every one of them is innocent—'

He stopped talking, because it was obvious that the chief inspector wasn't listening. The old man sat slumped in his chair looking, Tait suddenly realised, like an old man—or at any rate a very much older man than he had been that morning.

Quantrill pushed aside a half-empty coffee cup and an untouched cheese sandwich. He picked up a library book. 'Know anything about Dorothy Parker?' he asked.

Tait was unwilling to admit complete ignorance of anything between hard covers. 'Rings a bell, sir.'

Quantrill opened the book at the introduction. He'd read it three times, and at each reading his depression had increased.

'Mrs. Bloomfield told me about her,' he said. 'Dorothy Parker was a brilliant young American writer between the wars, and one of her themes was the desirability of dying young.'

He looked up at Tait. It was, the sergeant saw, distress that had scored the aging lines so deeply on the chief inspector's face.

'I thought,' Quantrill went on, 'from what Mrs. Bloomfield said, that Dorothy Parker *did* die young. But she didn't. She just stopped being a fashionable and popular writer; she reached her peak early, and after that she went downhill. She was lonely and unhappy, and she drank too much. She tried suicide two or three times, but it was only half-meant; she clung on to life as long as it would have her and in the end she died alone in a hotel room, at seventy-three, of a heart attack.'

Dorothy Parker . . . ? The old man must be going off his head, thought Tait. Well: a vacancy in the division? A reshuffle? Quick promotion to acting inspector for a promising young sergeant? What the hell did Dorothy Parker have to do with anything, anyway?

'Really, sir?' he said politely.

The chief inspector sat hunched and brooding in his chair. 'When we first saw Mrs. Bloomfield yesterday,' he said presently, 'when she was wearing a tennis dress—did you notice her legs?'

Martin Tait was not interested in the legs of any woman much above thirty. 'No, sir. I was looking at Liz Whilton's.'

'Mrs. Bloomfield has very good legs,' said Quantrill, as if to himself, 'but I never saw them from the front. She deliberately hid them with her sweater. Since then, she's been wearing either trousers or a long skirt.' He looked at Tait. 'And now you've provided me with a reason why a woman with legs as good as hers might want to hide them.'

'*Mrs. Bloomfield!*' said Sergeant Tait incredulously.

Quantrill pushed himself heavily to his feet. 'I don't know. I can't be sure. But start checking, will you? Ask the Whilton girl if she noticed anything about Mrs. Bloomfield's knees while they were playing tennis. And get someone to ring Southampton and find out when Mrs. Bloomfield crossed the Channel on Thursday, and what time she landed. And tell Godbold to see if he can find out from her neighbour exactly what time she arrived home on Friday morning.'

# DEATH IN THE MORNING

Tait relinquished his fantasy promotion, and reached for the telephone.

Mrs. Bloomfield was out, but her under-occupied neighbour thought it likely that she would return early in the evening.

Chief Inspector Quantrill parked his car on the access road near her house, then fidgeted across to the war memorial and passed the time pulling sticky lolly wrappers off the granite. Among the names he revealed was that of Roy Ransome, Jean Bloomfield's admired brother, who had jumped from his aircraft and fallen, burning, several thousand feet into the sea.

No wonder she was haunted by a horror of violent death. But haunted to such an extent that she could believe that unnatural death was not, by definition, violent? Haunted out of reason?

He saw her car approach along the main road. If she were guilty, surely she would want to avoid him?

She slowed, stopped, got stiffly out, gave him a tired smile. Was he about to make some dreadful irretrievable blunder? His heart bumped unsteadily, his mouth was dry.

'Still trying to clean up, Douglas?'

'Just waiting to have a word with you.'

'You'd like some tea, I expect.'

It was not a pressing invitation; rather, Quantrill thought, trying to armour himself against her, a patronising assumption that a policeman must be always on the cadge for free refreshments.

'No, thank you.' Despite her obvious unease—the air of tension, the restless movement of her hands—she was still beautiful. Too beautiful and too desirable for him to be able to face her in her own home with the questions that he must ask.

'Was it you who put that bunch of buttercups on the memorial?' he demanded, nervousness making him abrupt.

For a second she looked startled. Then, 'Yes,' she agreed warily.

He took courage. 'I have to ask you,' he said, 'why you deliberately misled the police: why you said that you travelled overnight from France, when in fact you crossed the Channel on Thursday evening? Why you led us to believe that you got back to Ashthorpe in the middle of Friday morning, when you actually returned to your house very much earlier, just before six?'

175

She turned away impatiently. 'Do such details matter?'

'Yes, if you crossed Ashthorpe bridge early on Friday morning. Did you?'

Jean Bloomfield said nothing. She lowered her eyes, and closed her lips in a line that, unbecomingly, turned down at each corner. Quantrill's confidence increased, though he took no pleasure in the fact.

'Did you see Mary Gedge when you crossed Ashthorpe bridge? Did you see her gathering flowers, and stop to speak to her?'

She lifted her head. The lines on her face seemed deeper; her suntan had begun to look an unhealthy yellow. 'Have you any proof that I did?'

Quantrill chewed his lower lip. Confidence in his hunch was not the same thing as proof. 'Do you know anything about Mary Gedge's death?' he temporised.

Her eyes had narrowed, but she continued to look straight at him: 'What possible reason can you have for imagining that I do?'

He would have liked to deny his reasoning, to put his hands on her shoulders and reassure her, just as he had done that morning. He recalled the arousing warmth of her flesh through the thin shirt, and the muscularity that had taken him by surprise until he remembered that she was a tennis player.

For all her thinness, she had strength in that right arm. She could, physically, have been capable of killing Mary Gedge. He felt almost certain that she *had* killed the girl. But being almost certain was not enough.

'I think,' he said carefully, 'that you must have had some very good reason for misleading the police.' He looked down at her summery trouser suit. 'Just as you seem to have some very good reason for keeping your legs covered.'

Her suntan abruptly changed to a darker shade as the blood returned to her skin. Yesterday, or this morning, Quantrill would have attributed her blush to modesty; now it began to seem like an admission of guilt. 'It was a rough Channel crossing,' she insisted. 'I fell and grazed my legs on a companionway.'

'I've heard that's how you account for it. Is it just coincidence, then, that Mary Gedge's legs were grazed too, as she was struggling for her life?'

# DEATH IN THE MORNING

'I don't know what you're talking about.' She turned away.

'I think you do.' Quantrill took a deep breath and began to spell out his conclusions. 'Of course, I can't say exactly how it occurred, I can only guess—but I don't imagine that it was in any way premeditated. You happened to be driving home from your holiday, early on the morning of May the first. It was a beautiful morning, and as you crossed Ashthorpe bridge you saw Mary Gedge, on her own in the meadow in her romantic long dress, gathering buttercups. Naturally, you stopped and spoke to her.'

Jean Bloomfield stood quite still with her eyes lowered. Sunlight shone on her hair, unkindly emphasising the number of silver-grey strands that had infiltrated the ash-blonde.

'I expect you were depressed,' Quantrill went on. 'Your holiday was over, you were returning to a job you disliked and a house where you were lonely. But Mary was happy. Seeing her there, in a long dress with her hands full of flowers, made you think of Ophelia; and it reminded you that Ophelia was a victim. It must have made you wonder what life had in store for Mary. After all, even if she didn't fall in love with the wrong man and become corrupted and die an early death, she was bound sooner or later to lose that radiant happiness. You told me that yourself. Mary was a high-flyer, so she would reach her peak early—perhaps she'd even reached it already. And after that, there'd be nowhere to go but downhill.'

She shrugged. 'It happens, of course. Inevitably.'

He paused. Then, 'It happened to you, didn't it?' he asked softly. 'You were a high-flyer—you must have been, to work your way from a poor background to Oxford. You must have reached your peak during your marriage—and then your husband was killed, and your world was blown apart. But in those days, you must have been a trier. You picked yourself up, worked at your career, made a success of it and eventually became a headmistress. For a time, when you first bought your house in Ashthorpe, you even thought that you could be happy again.

'But it didn't last, did it? A man you dislike and despise had been made head of the comprehensive; you've been relegated to the middle school, where you're dealing for the first time with ordinary unacademic children, and you find you can't

177

cope. You feel a failure, and you've given up trying. You know you're on your way downhill.'

She had begun to breath more quickly. Her nostrils arched with disdain. 'We can't all be police officers, and start making a success of our careers in our mid-forties!'

'That's true. But people like me, the Pc Plods of this world—ordinary people—don't have the same problem as you high-flyers. We're not brilliant, so we have lower expectations. We don't climb high in our youth, so it hurts that much less if we fall. We don't have the same experience of either happiness or hurt. But you're bound to resent your present life all the more for remembering what you once were, and the happiness you once had.'

'You've taken to reading psychology?' she asked, tight-lipped. 'Thank you for that analysis.'

'There's nothing there that you didn't tell me yourself,' he pointed out. 'You also told me that you were glad—for your husband's sake—that he died young, before he became disillusioned. You're accustomed to the idea of high-flyers dying young; first your brother, then your husband. In fact, you *like* the idea of dying young, as long as death isn't violent. But—along with Dorothy Parker—you think of early death as something for other people, rather than for yourself. For Mary Gedge, say. There she was in that meadow, innocent and happy; and it came into your head that you could be the means of preserving her innocence and happiness for ever.'

Her face had paled again under her tan, but her head was high. 'You have no proof . . .'

'I've no proof of the way it happened, but I can guess. Perhaps Mary slipped or tripped, and fell in the river facedown. It wouldn't have done her any harm, she could have got up laughing. You must have gone in too, and perhaps you stretched out a hand to help her—your right hand. And then, suddenly, you took it upon yourself to give her what you thought would be a quick and painless death at the height of her happiness.'

'. . . and you know that you can never have any proof. This is nothing but crude speculation, and there is no reason why I should listen to it. Excuse me.' She began to walk quickly towards her house.

She could be right, too. It was by no means certain that forensic would discover anything on the dead girl's clothing that would identify her assailant. As long as Jean Bloomfield maintained her composure he could not be sure of obtaining sufficient proof ever to charge her with murder.

But he thought that he knew how her composure could be broken. It was a weapon he hesitated to use, the more so because he had loved her, but it was all he had left. He strode after her, and blocked her way.

'I want to tell you something,' he said urgently. 'Something that happened while I was doing my national service. I've never told anyone before, but I'd like you to hear it now.'

Surprise made her stop and listen. 'I wasn't an officer like your husband,' he went on quickly. 'I was just an erk, an airman, and it happened while I was square-bashing—doing my recruit training.

'There was a boy in my hut, in the next bed to me, called John Sweeting. Well, it was tough enough for all of us in that camp, but anyone with a name like Sweeting went through a special kind of hell. John was small and quiet and sensitive— and some of the drill instructors were real sadists. I used to hear him crying sometimes, after lights out, but I didn't know how to help him. I'd got problems of my own. And then, to cap it all, he had a letter from his girl-friend saying that she was going out with someone else. Not that I heard about the letter until afterwards. He didn't tell his troubles to anyone, poor devil.

'Then, in the middle of our course, we were allowed out one Saturday afternoon. We all went into Manchester. It was a cold, damp, foggy day at the beginning of December, and the shops were lit up for Christmas. Most of us stuck together, but John went off on his own. He spent his money on Christmas presents, but he also bought a coil of rope.'

Jean Bloomfield had been listening quietly, reluctant but intent. Now, she sidestepped: 'I don't think I want to hear any more.'

He caught at her sleeve. 'But I'm going to finish,' he said. 'This is something that has haunted me for years, and I'm going to tell you, just as you insisted on telling me how your husband was killed. Listen: that evening, we all went to the NAAFI, except John. He stayed by himself in the billet, and he wrapped up all his Christmas presents and wrote the labels— one for his girl-friend as well. He wrote a letter to his mother.

Then he changed into working overalls and PT shoes, and polished his uniform boots and buttons and badges. Then, he laid all his kit out on the bed as though there was going to be an inspection, and he put the Christmas presents and the letter on his bed too, and he took the rope and went out.

'I was on fire picquet later that evening. It was a hutted camp, with coke stoves in each hut, and there was always a danger of fire. We had to patrol round in twos, keeping our eyes open. It was quiet among the huts, with most of the boys either in the NAAFI or at the camp cinema; in fact it was a bit eerie, what with the quiet and the fog. And then, when we were walking past the water tower, I heard a bumping and a scraping and a kind of choking gurgle from above my head. I shone my torch, and saw something swaying from one of the iron girders.

'We both panicked, though I tried to pretend not to. We knew it must be someone hanging, though we didn't know who. I sent the other airman running off to fetch the orderly corporal, while I waited. Of course, I should have tried to cut the boy down, but I was only eighteen and I was frightened. I just waited for help to come, and prayed that the horrible noises above my head would stop.

'Then the orderly corporal came, with the station duty officer. The corporal had been afraid to come on his own, but the officer was an older man and he knew what to do. He swore at me for not even trying to cut the boy down, and he made me follow him up the iron ladder and hold the torch while he cut the rope. So I could see everything.

'I didn't know it was John, even then. There was no way of recognising him. He wasn't dead, you see, just slowly strangling to death. His knees were drawn up in the position of a foetus, and the weight of his body had stretched his neck. He had hooked his fingers under the noose, as though he had tried to loosen it, and there were livid scratches from his finger nails on his long white neck.

'The officer kept shouting and swearing at me to hold the torch steady so that he could see what he was doing, and I had to watch the boy's face jerking above me as the officer sawed at the rope. The face was dark and congested, except for the eyes which were rolled up and showed nothing but the whites. His

180

tongue was protruding. He was coughing and snorting, choking his lungs up through his nose—'

'*Stop it!*'

In the horror of total recall, he had almost forgotten Jean Bloomfield, and his purpose. Her face was distorted by distress, her hands were clapped to her ears.

'Stop it, I don't want to hear any more! Why did you have to tell me such a dreadful thing?'

Quantrill wiped his damp forehead with the back of his hand. 'I had to tell you,' he said, slowly and deliberately, 'because I know that you have a horror of violent death. Not of death itself—you're prepared to welcome that, as long as it's for other people—but of the violence with which it came to your brother and your husband. I think that you imagined that by holding Mary's head under water, you would be giving her a quick, clean, easy death.

'But it couldn't have happened like that. I don't know whether you and Mary had been discussing the idea of dying young—perhaps you had, perhaps you'd encouraged her in that romantic nonsense you told me about the desirability of dying at the height of your happiness. Perhaps she even believed it.

'But that doesn't mean that Mary Gedge seriously wanted to die! And even if she did, or thought she did, the instinct for self-preservation would have been too strong. Think of poor John Sweeting: no one could have wanted to die more than he did. No one could have prepared himself more thoroughly for death. And yet, when he swung himself off the girder of the water tower and found that death wasn't—as he must have imagined—instantaneous, he struggled instinctively to live. He gouged strips of skin from his neck with his finger nails in his efforts to loosen the noose.

'And it was the same with Mary, wasn't it? She was young and healthy and happy, she didn't want to die. She didn't simply lie in the water and go limp under your hand, she fought for her life. You were above and behind her, so all she managed to claw at was gravel and river weed. But she tore her finger and toe nails and lacerated her knees on the gravel in the struggle.

'Poor Mary's was no gentle death! I wonder what you

thought, when you realised that you couldn't kill her without using violence, and yet you'd gone too far to be able to stop? How did it feel, to be down there in the water with her, cutting your own knees on the gravel as you tried to hold her down? What did you think, as you forced her head under water while she kicked and clawed and thrashed in her struggle to live? How long did you have to hold her under? It must have seemed like an eternity. How long did it take her to die—three minutes, four—?'

'No! You're exaggerating, it wasn't like that, it didn't take so long!'

Quantrill's physical reaction was not quick enough. By the time his legs got the message to move, she had reached her car.

He guessed that she would head for the river; not the inadequate Dunnock but the Dodman, which runs west from Breckham Market, slow but moderately deep, towards the Ouse. Quantrill followed, radioing for support. She drove recklessly fast along a minor road, skidded her car to a halt, scrambled out and began to run along the river bank towards a footbridge that spanned one of the deeper reaches.

Quantrill abandoned his car behind hers and pounded after her, forcing himself far beyond a reasonable speed for a man of his age and bulk. He knew that he had to catch her before she reached the bridge. He disapproved of heroics; besides, he couldn't swim.

He tried to spurt. His arms and legs pumped into protesting rhythm, his chest swelled to bursting.

He reached out a hand toward her. She glanced over her shoulder, stubbed her toe against a tree root, and went sprawling on the grass of the river bank. She might have fallen into the water if she had not, instinctively, grabbed at a tuft of grass to save herself.

Quantrill collapsed beside her. There was a red haze in front of his eyes; his heart was thumping against his ribcage with the ferocity of a badly loaded spin dryer.

Jean Bloomfield turned her back on him and covered her face with her hands. 'Go away,' she said, her voice muffled. 'Leave me alone . . .'

He drew in enough knife-edged air to enable him to gasp out

an answer. 'You can't run away from yourself. You've got to learn to live with what you've done.'

'But I don't want to live! I want to die.'

It was an effort to find the right words, too much of an effort to speak them in more than an exhausted monotone: 'No you don't, you know you don't. You're not one of the born victims. You're too strong-minded, you've survived too much. You'll go on clinging to life, just like your friend Dorothy Parker, however unhappy it makes you.'

Her shoulders began to shake. She was crying silently, her head on her arms. Beside her, Quantrill lay flat on his back, spent.

Gradually, the mist began to clear from in front of his eyes. His heart-beat steadied, the pain in his chest began to lessen. His unacknowledged fear that the sudden exertion might have brought on a heart attack receded, to be replaced by an awareness of his surroundings and a pervasive melancholy.

He listened to the slow gurgle of the water and the hum of a dragon fly, smelled the dankness of the river weed, felt the rough grass of the bank under his hands. All his sensations had a surprising familiarity, as though somewhere, at some time, he had been through this before.

He closed his eyes, trying to conjure up the past.

Twenty-odd years ago . . . that was it, a turning point in his life. And now he could recall it vividly: another early summer evening, another river bank, another bout of exertion, another sense of energy drained; another girl who had turned from him and cried, another victory that had tasted of defeat.

'Have you arrested her, sir?'

'Not yet.' Quantrill stood in his office, staring out of the window. The sun, setting red in a thick evening haze, looked like nothing so much as a giant fluorescent lolly of the kind sucked by his son's favourite New York television detective. He turned back to Tait. 'She's with Patsy Hopkins, writing out a statement.'

'Was it jealousy? Of a middle-aged woman for a young one?'

The chief inspector was too weary to try to explain. 'A lot more complicated than that. But I've no doubt she'll put it clearly in her statement. She's good with words.'

Tait felt mystified, excluded. 'Sir, what about Joy Dawson? Do you think Mrs. B. killed her?'

'Joy Dawson?' Quantrill rounded on his sergeant, incensed. 'Of course not! Good God, what kind of person do you think Mrs. Bloomfield is?'

Tait was affronted. 'I beg your pardon, sir,' he said stiffly. 'But then, I haven't the advantage of being a personal friend of the murderer.'

As soon as he spoke the words, Tait knew the enormity of them. The old man was in a bad way, there was no doubt about that: shattered. It was indefensible to make capital out of it.

The sergeant stood to attention. 'Sir,' he said, genuinely contrite, 'I apologise. I shouldn't have said that.'

The flash of anger faded from Quantrill's eyes. He nodded dully. 'And I shouldn't have jumped on you,' he said. 'Of course you're right to bear Joy in mind, and to consider every possibility.'

He looked at the photograph of the missing girl that stood on his desk, and tried to shake off his depression. A newly promoted chief inspector had no business not to be positive; a good detective had to keep on trying.

'Not that we've any reason to believe that Joy is dead,' he said briskly. 'A good many girls run away from home, wanting to cut loose. It takes months, years even, for them to face up to going back, but some of them do. And did you hear about the girl who went missing from the other side of the county seven years ago, and was traced last January?

'There's an even chance that Joy has been one of the lucky ones, and is alive and well somewhere. Take a good look at her file on Monday, will you? I'd be glad of your opinion—you may well spot something that I've missed. Oh, and will you make the formal arrest in the Mary Gedge case?'

'Me, sir?' Sergenat Tait boggled at the prospect of being credited with the arrest of a murderer in his first week in the division. 'Oh, but that seems hardly fair—'

'I'd consider it a favour, Martin. I'd like to get away. It's my day off tomorrow, and I want to take my boy fishing—if nothing else turns up between now and then, of course. If it does, you'll know where to find me.'

Chief Inspector Quantrill brushed a few stray blades of grass from his suit, and went home to his wife.

## ABOUT THE AUTHOR

SHEILA RADLEY is a well-known British writer of romantic thrillers as well as mysteries. She holds a degree in history from the University of London. For nearly two decades, she has helped run a village store and post office in East Anglia, England. She is the author of DEATH IN THE MORNING, THE CHIEF INSPECTOR'S DAUGHTER, and FATE WORSE THAN DEATH, as well as the forthcoming WHO SAW HIM DIE?

# 50 YEARS OF GREAT AMERICAN MYSTERIES
## FROM BANTAM BOOKS
### Stuart Palmer

"Those who have not already made the acquaintance of Hildegarde Withers should make haste to do so, for she is one of the world's shrewdest and most amusing detectives."  —*New York Times*
May 6, 1934

☐ 25934-2  THE PUZZLE OF THE SILVER PERSIAN (1934) $2.95
☐ 26024-3  THE PUZZLE OF THE HAPPY HOOLIGAN
(1941)                                               $2.95
Featuring spinster detective Hildegarde Withers

---

### Craig Rice

"Why can't all murders be as funny as those concocted by Craig Rice?  —*New York Times*
☐ 26345-5  HAVING WONDERFUL CRIME           $2.95
"Miss Rice at her best, writing about her 3 favorite characters against a delirious New York background."
—*New Yorker*

☐ 26222-X  MY KINGDOM FOR A HEARSE          $2.95
"Pretty damn wonderful!"           —*New York Times*

---

### Barbara Paul

☐ 26234-3  RENEWABLE VIRGIN (1985)          $2.95
"The talk crackles, the characters are bouncy, and New York's media world is caught with all its vitality and vulgarity."            —*Washington Post Book World*
☐ 26225-4  KILL FEE (1985)                  $2.95
"A desperately treacherous game of cat-and-mouse whose well-wrought tension is heightened by a freakish twist that culminates in a particularly chilling conclusion." —*Booklist*

For your ordering convenience, use the handy coupon below: